Walker's Wedding

LORI COPELAND

HARVEST HOUSE PUBLISHERS

EUGENE, OREGON

Cover by Left Coast Design, Portland, Oregon

Cover photos © Plush Studios / Bill Reitzel / Blend Images / Getty Images; iStockphoto / lobaaaato; iStockphoto / tsmarkley; Kirk Geisler / Shutterstock; Author photo © The Picture People

Published in association with the Books & Such Literary Agency, 52 Mission Circle, Suite 122, PMB 170, Santa Rosa, CA 95409-5370, www.booksandsuch.biz.

WALKER'S WEDDING
Copyright © 2010 by Copeland, Inc.
Published by Harvest House Publishers
Eugene, Oregon 97402
www.harvesthousepublishers.com

Library of Congress Cataloging-in-Publication Data
Copeland, Lori.
  Walker's wedding / Lori Copeland.
    p. cm.—(Western sky series)
  ISBN 978-0-7369-2761-1 (pbk.)
  1. Marriage—Fiction. I. Copeland, Lori. Marrying Walker McKay. II. Title
PS3553.O6336W35 2010
813'.54—dc22

                    2009053459

Printed in the United States of America

10 11 12 13 14 15 16 17 18 / DP-NI / 10 9 8 7 6 5 4 3 2 1

Prologue

Wyoming Territory, April 1870

S.H., I need a wife about as much as I need a square-dancing bull."
Walker McKay released the steer he'd just branded and shoved his
dusty Stetson to the back of his head. What would he do with a wife?
He had it made: no interfering woman to tell him what to wear, when
to eat, or whom to eat with. His life was his own, and he had no intention of changing it.

A cowboy galloped in, roped a calf, and then dragged it toward the
branding fire. Drovers tackled a heifer and held it to the ground while
Walker applied the mark of the Spring Grass Ranch: a large S with a
lowercase g intertwined in the bottom. They had branded close to two
hundred head since dawn; it would be close to five hundred before the
work let up.

"Yer as hardheaded as a blind mule," S.H. complained. Sizemore
Horatio Gibson—"S.H." to friends—released the heifer, and the animal sprang to its feet bawling. Realizing she was free, she trotted off to
join the others. The grizzled old man met Walker's eyes. "How old will
you be on yer birthday? Twenty-nine?"

"Yes. Why?" But Walker knew why. S.H. was on him again about
an heir, or rather, the lack of one.

"Twenty-eight and nary an heir to carry on the McKay name. It's a shame. Yer pa would sit up in his grave and spit if he knew how you were avoiding the altar."

If Walker had a brother or sister, the pressure to marry and have a child would be off him and he would be free to concentrate on running the ranch. He scowled. He probably would have been a father by now if Trudy Richards hadn't walked out on him. Walker still saw red when he thought of how he'd spent two years convincing himself that he loved that woman enough to marry her. It had taken her less than a day to prove him a fool. He could still smell her rose-scented perfume even as he recalled the egg on his face as a neighbor informed him that Trudy had beat it out of town on horseback, running off with a fellow who sold hats—bowlers, no less; a drifter she'd met two weeks earlier at a town social.

Dust swirled around the milling cattle, who bawled when the ropes found their marks and hauled them in. Overhead, clouds drifted across a clear Wyoming sky. Only the unusually warm spring sun, stinging horseflies, and memories best forgotten marred an otherwise flawless day.

Walker laid the branding iron across a steer's rump. Disgrace was still a bitter pill to swallow. Never again would he allow a woman to make a fool of him. Not for S.H. or anybody else.

"You can't let one woman ruin your whole life," S.H. said, grabbing a steer and riding it to the ground. "You got to pray harder and ask that the good Lord will send the right woman. You got to produce an heir, son. Your pa worked hard for this land—nearly killed himself building Spring Grass. It was work that put yer mama in an early grave. You don't want to leave the ranch to strangers, do you?"

"I tried it Pa's way and your way, and it didn't work. I'm content with my life and I don't intend to change it—not now, and not any time soon."

He had plenty of time to worry about marriage and kids. Youngsters were okay, but in Walker McKay's book, women were good for just two things: cooking and childbearing, and not necessarily in that order. Other men might put up with being led around by their noses, but he sure as the dickens wouldn't do it. After Trudy's betrayal, it would be a cold day in July before he gave his heart to another female.

"Who's gonna inherit the McKay fortune if you die? You ever think about that?"

Why think about it? He figured he had a good fifty years to settle the matter before his number was up. He wasn't a gunslinger. He didn't pick fights and tempt death to his doorstep. He ran a ranch, lived a temperate lifestyle, and visited town only when supplies ran low. He enjoyed hunting, catching a trout or two, and reading seed catalogues. Hardly the kind of lifestyle that threatened an early grave. He hadn't even had a cold since the winter of '62.

Longevity ran in the McKay family. Grandpa McKay lived to be way up in his nineties; Great-grandpa, ninety-six. If Pa hadn't tangled with that bull last year, who knew? He might have lived to be a hundred. Maybe by the time Walker was forty, he'd give serious thought to death. Right now he had his hands full running the ranch. He was responsible—the ranch made a sizable profit each year, and he made sure that his thirty-five ranch hands were the first to help out when trouble hit the community. He went to church, took a bath regularly, combed his hair, and put on his clothes every morning all without a woman's help.

"Let me tell you, son. You don't put off what needs be done today. A man never knows how long he's got on this old earth."

A man S.H.'s age would naturally be worried about such things. "Can't we talk about this another time?"

"You ought to ask Willa Mae Lewis to the grange social Saturday night." S.H. paused, knocking the dust off his trousers. "Now, that woman is as pretty as a prize heifer and bakes a mean rhubarb pie. Got the hips to birth a cow."

"I have all the livestock I need, S.H."

"Rolene Berry?"

"Too immature."

"Ruthie Gaines. Now there's a fine-looking woman."

"Vain. She'd rather stay home and stare at herself in a mirror than attend a social."

"Heidi Watson."

"Spoiled. Get off my back, S.H. I don't want a wife."

A drover whistled loudly, ending the conversation. Walker stood and wiped sweat off his forehead. The whistle shrilled again and Walker turned, shading his eyes against the sun. A large bull, crazed with the need to escape the rope, twisted and bucked. Then, head bent and bellowing, the animal broke the cowboy's grip.

"Watch out!" S.H. bolted for the fence as the bull charged. Walker turned too quickly and lost his balance.

Staggering, he retained his footing, but not before images of an earlier scene raced through his mind. Frenzied cries, pounding hooves, and the spurt of bright red blood as the animal's horns sank into Pa's flesh.

"Walker!" S.H. shouted over the milling herd.

Other warnings sounded. "He's headed your way!"

"Give him room!"

Before he could respond, the bull struck. Walker let out a muffled yell. The impact propelled him backward and spun him around. Reeling, he struggled to stay afoot and catch his breath.

The animal whirled and then paused for an instant to snort and wag his head before charging again, eyes red with rage as he thundered in for a second strike.

Dropping to the ground, Walker curled into a tight ball, arms shielding his head. He gasped for breath, feeling a trickle of blood coursing down his chin.

This can't be happening! Not to me.

Three ranch hands charged the bull, shouting, waving their arms in an attempt to divert the animal's attention.

Horns caught Walker in the side and he felt muscles tear, then blinding pain. Confusion broke out as other wranglers raced to the rescue, trying to divert the bull as it spun and lunged again, catching Walker in the upper thigh and tossing him like a rag doll. S.H. bolted to the fence where his rifle rested, shouting something Walker couldn't make out.

The bull struck again from a new direction. Walker struggled to stay conscious, trying to ward off the assault. From somewhere past consciousness he heard S.H.'s voice prodding him to produce an heir.

The bull was going to kill him.

I'm twenty-eight years old. I have all the time in the world…

He burrowed his face in the dirt. His time was up, his number called. The realization was as certain as life itself had been only scant minutes ago.

Riders galloped in and managed to divert the animal's attention long enough for his men to pull Walker to safety.

Drifting in and out of consciousness on a sea of pain, Walker opened his eyes to see S.H. hunched over him, getting in the way as ranch hands tried to cut the clothing from his wounds. The old man folded his battered hat against his chest, and tears rolled down his cheeks.

"Come on, S.H.," Walker muttered. "It's just a couple of broken ribs…"

But he didn't need S.H. to tell him it was bad. He could feel blood oozing from his left side. Instead of S.H.'s voice, past conversations drifted through his mind.

I'll think about an heir someday. I have plenty of time.

S.H. knelt beside him, openly weeping. "I tried to warn you! Didn't you hear me?"

"I heard you…S.H.…couldn't get out of the way." Walker struggled to focus, barely able to comprehend or respond now. Men were working over him. The pain in his leg felt like a branding iron.

"Hang on, son, hang on," S.H. urged. "They've gone for the doc… don't die on me, boy…"

I'm twenty-eight…got all the time in the world…

Reaching for the old man's hand, Walker grasped it tightly. S.H. had been with Pa when he drew his last breath, had been with Spring Grass since Mitch felled the first tree. It was right that he would be here now.

"Saw the bull…couldn't…"

"Lie still, son." S.H. gripped his hand, and Walker felt the old man's trembling. "You can beat this."

"Take care of Spring Grass, S.H., and take care of Flo. She's a good woman…"

"None of that talk. You're not going to leave us, Walker. Hold on."

Walker closed his eyes, allowing the gathering darkness to suck him under.

S.H. bellowed, "Where's that doctor!" Sobbing, the old man sank back onto his knees.

I thought I had all the time in the world.

Chapter One

Boston, Massachusetts, June 1870

I'm dying. I'm dying, Wadsy."

"You ain't dyin', honey chile. Now hold still and let Wadsy put this cold cloth on your forehead. Lawsy me, you're hot as a poker." The old nanny squeezed water from a cold compress and laid it across Sarah's forehead. "Runnin' off in this cold rain, entertainin' the idea of marryin' some no-good riverboat worker. What were you thinkin', baby girl? Tyin' yourself to some man who'd end up breakin' your heart? Goodness, do you want your papa's dyspepsia to flare up again? He's gonna have a conniption fit when he hears what you been up to!"

Sarah lay on the bed, arms flung spread-eagle, staring at the ceiling. Hank was a bit unstable, and Papa would point that out, ranting about how she'd known the "scoundrel" less than a week, but the riverboat worker had promised to settle down and devote himself tirelessly to family life. He'd vowed he was weary of traveling from town to town, wasting his life on women and strong drink.

Unlike Papa, she didn't have to know someone a hundred years to judge his character.

"I was this close to marriage, Wadsy." She measured a minuscule distance with her thumb and forefinger. "I could have been a bride."

Wadsy groaned. "Praise the good Lord that he intervened. Law, girl, you're going to put this ol' woman in an early grave."

"This close," Sarah repeated. "Why did Abe have to come along when he did? Why couldn't that old mare have thrown a shoe any other time but today?"

"You're 'this close' to feelin' the strap of your daddy's belt to your backside, Sarah Elaine Livingston." Wadsy lifted the cloth off of Sarah's forehead and soaked it in a pan of cool water. "Good thing Abe came along when he did or you'd be in a fine how-de-do."

Curling up into a tight ball, Sarah released her misery in wailing sobs.

"Now, child," Wadsy soothed. "It ain't the end of the world."

"But it is!" Sarah cried. "All I have ever wanted was to marry and have children. Just look at me. I'm twenty-five and an *old maid*!"

Sarah wadded up her pillow and wept into it. Her muffled voice came through the crisply ironed pillowcase. "I'm going to die before I ever get to be a wife."

Every time she got close to the altar, someone interfered with her plans. When would she ever escape Papa's attempts to suffocate her dream? When would she finally have the husband she ached to care for or an infant to call her own?

Wadsy rescued the pillow, clucking her tongue and shaking out the creases. "Never seen such carrying-on. Sit up, honey chile. Your nose is gonna be all red and uglylike. You'll never find a husband if you have an ugly red nose."

Sarah bolted upright, pinning Wadsy with a cold stare. "I'm never going to find a husband no matter what my nose looks like. And who cares? No one, that's who!"

Old Abe could have helped today, but no. He had to come by the landing on his way to have the mare shod, spot her boarding the boat with Hank, and drag her off like an errant child. And the worst was yet to come. She still had to face Papa.

"We all care, baby girl. We just don't want you goin' off half-cocked and marryin' the wrong man." Settling her bulk on the side of the bed, Wadsy smoothed Sarah's fiery red tendrils from her forehead. The dark-skinned woman had practically raised Sarah from infancy; she was like a second mother. "I know how your heart aches for a husband. Lord knows you've clomped around this house with a curtain over that unruly hair, wearin' your mama's gowns, gettin' pretend married since you could toddle. Lawsy me, I've attended more weddin's during your childhood than I can count, but marriage is powerful serious, baby girl. The good Lord intends marriage vows to be spoken in earnest. You got to get it right or you'll live with the mistake the rest of your life. None of us want to see you go through that—cain't you understand?"

"Oh, Wadsy." Sarah sniffed and then blew her nose into her handkerchief. She knew she was spoiled and demanded her way, but how long could she stay under Papa's thumb? Marriage was sacred and shouldn't be entered into lightly, but the perfect man—the one Papa insisted on, simply didn't exist. Papa was rich beyond belief—he owned his own railroad, half of Boston, and hundreds and hundreds of acres of abundant cotton land—so he could purchase anything she wanted. Yet he was powerless to buy what she needed: a husband, someone to love and care for, someone who would love and care for her when Papa and Wadsy and Abraham passed on.

No amount of money in the world could assure that kind of happiness.

Over the years dozens of young men, mostly men who worked for Papa, had courted her. Something—usually Papa—always interfered with those promising relationships. No one was ever good enough for her in her father's eyes, though he insisted that she was being overly dramatic when she said so. Yet here she was, getting older by the minute and not a lick closer to a husband than she'd been the day Wadsy helped Dr. Mason bring her into the world.

"Come on, now." Wadsy lumbered to her feet, taking Sarah's arm and urging her up. The old nanny was three times Sarah's size, her fleshy bulk swaying with the motion. "Suppa's on the table, and there's no need to make your papa angrier than he already is."

Sarah dug her heels into the rug, refusing to be led to the slaughter. She knew that supper would be an emotional scene, with Papa vowing to send her off to Uncle Brice. She'd die before she'd live in Uncle Brice's stuffy old mausoleum. His humorless laugh sounded like a crow lodged in his snout.

Wadsy's eyes flashed with determination and she pulled, hauling her struggling charge across the Turkish carpet, out the door, and into the hallway. Sarah tried to get back into her room, but Wadsy blocked the door and called for Abe.

The towering black man quickly appeared at the bottom of the stairs, and Sarah's heart sank. She shrank against the wall, trying to avoid his gaze, but the white-haired servant pinned her with a stern look that she knew meant business. His low-pitched bass rumbled deep in his massive chest.

"Come on down now, missy. Suppa's gettin' cold."

"I'm sick, Abe. I have the sniffles and I feel flushed. Don't make me eat with Papa!"

"Ain't no use, Abraham. You're gonna have to come after her," Wadsy called. "She's in one of her moods."

Stiffening, Sarah fixed her body in a rigid stance, keeping an eye on Abe and a hand clenched on the banister as he slowly ascended the stairway.

"I'm too ill to eat."

"Makes no difference to me if you eat suppa or not, but your papa wants you at his table while he eats his."

Gently but firmly prying her hand from the rail, he swung her over his left shoulder and hauled her down the winding stairway. When the battling duo reached the foyer, Wadsy hurried to straighten Sarah's skirts, avoiding the flailing legs.

Crossing her arms, Sarah refused to let her captors intimidate her as Abe transported her into the dining room. They might force her to sit at Papa's table, but they would need a crowbar to make her eat. Or speak.

Lowell Livingston glanced up when Abe stepped into the dining room, carrying Sarah over his shoulder.

She made sure that settling her was no easy task. She kept her knees locked straight out and slid out of her chair twice before Abe could get her planted. Then the servant excused himself and left the dining room.

The mantel clock ticked away the seconds as Lowell fixed his daughter with a harsh stare down the long, silver-laden table.

"Exactly whom," he began in an even tone, "were you about to marry this time?"

Sarah pursed her lips, focusing on the gold-rimmed plate. "I don't care to discuss it. I'm dying."

"You're not dying. Wadsy says you have the sniffles and a fever from your reckless outing this afternoon. What were you thinking, daughter? Were you honestly going to run off with this man?"

"I was. And I'm thinking," she answered in a carefully modulated voice, "that I want to get married, Papa!"

Leaving his chair, Lowell paced the floor. Sarah recognized the stubborn set of his jaw and knew it meant trouble. She'd stretched his patience to the breaking point.

"A dockworker? A common stranger? Have you no shame?"

"You make him sound terrible. He's better than most of the other dockworkers. Name one man more suited for marriage."

"Joe Mancuso, train master. An up-and-coming young man making a real name for himself at the railroad."

"Mr. Mancuso doesn't want to get married."

Lowell snorted. "You can't know that! You spent one evening—one very short evening, if I recall—with him."

"I asked him."

Lowell paused, looking faint. "You *asked* him?"

"I asked him. He muttered something and excused himself. I knew what that meant."

"What about Richard Ponder? A splendid example of a young man going places. His parents are fine people. I spoke to them personally before I arranged the meeting. Twenty-six and already a station agent. Youngest man in the division to obtain such a position—" he paused to look at her. "You didn't ask *him* to marry you, did you?"

Sarah shook her head. "He volunteered the information. His *mother* doesn't want him getting married. Not now and, judging by his tone, not ever."

Papa slapped his forehead. "Great day in the morning!"

Sarah shrugged. He was clearly aghast at her candor, but how was a woman expected to know a man's potential if she didn't ask? If Papa could be nosy, why couldn't she? Papa's health was precarious. Three heart spells in two years reminded them both of his mortality. Wadsy and Abe were even older, and someday she was going to be completely alone. Alone. With no one to love her or for her to love. If she were married, losing Papa would still be devastating, but she could surround herself with her family and ease the pain.

She had seen the way Mama had looked at Papa during her illness— as if he owned her soul. He'd looked back at her exactly the same way, with so much love and need in his eyes it took Sarah's breath. That was what she wanted. Love so strong that even death couldn't snatch it away. If it was wrong to seek that kind of devotion, then she was guilty as charged. Wadsy said she shouldn't depend on others for happiness, but if she had her own home, babies to look after, and a husband to love, she could cope with the losses certain to enter her life sooner than later.

"Sit down, Papa. Remember your heart."

"Humph. You remember my heart."

The somber reminder calmed her. She did remember. She thought about it every day.

"I'm sorry, Papa. I love and respect you, and I don't mean to be such a bother. I wish you could understand."

Lowell sat down, allowing Will, their cook, to spoon thick slices of beef swimming in a rich brown broth onto his plate. Dr. Mason had advised him that he should eat more vegetables and fruit, and he said Lowell was going to die from eating so much rich food—but Lowell wouldn't hear of it. When the cook moved to serve Sarah, she waved his efforts aside. "I'm not hungry, Will."

"May I bring you some nice broth, Miss Livingston?"

"Nothing, thank you." She watched Papa lather thick butter onto a slice of warm bread as she waited for the inevitable. This time she'd gone too far. This time he would carry through with his threat to send her to Uncle Brice. She couldn't bear even the thought of a dreadful, hot Georgia summer full of long, boring days in Brice's company. Tears of self-pity and hollow remorse threatened to break loose, and she quickly averted her eyes. Clenching her fists, she waited for the storm to break.

"I'm at the end of my rope, Sarah."

"I know, Papa. I'm sorry."

"Today's little escapade has convinced me that you will be better off with your Uncle Brice."

"Papa, no!" A tear coursed down her flushed cheek and hung on the tip of her quivering chin.

Slamming his fist down on the table, Lowell glared at her. "Daughter, yes! I can't watch you every waking moment, and you have proved to be too much for Wadsy and Abe to handle. Wadsy will pack your bags and Abe will take you to the train Saturday morning. A year in Savannah will help to refine you and make you see the error of your ways before you drive us all into an early grave."

"A whole year? Papa!" Her thoughts turned from self-pity to anger. "I won't go!"

She'd run away. She'd run so far this time that Papa would never find her. The times she'd been forced to endure living under Brice Livingston's roof were intolerable. He was ill-tempered and would keep her confined if she did the least little thing to rile him. Brice wouldn't let a man near her for the whole year. Why, last summer he'd locked her in her room every night! Papa couldn't just ship her down South and consider the problem solved.

Brice had survived three loveless marriages, all ending in bitterness, and he had nothing but contempt for the bond she held so dear. He would strip her of her spirit and do everything within his power to color her outlook on life, love, and, most certainly, marriage.

Staring at her empty plate, she vowed softly, "I won't go to Uncle Brice."

"You have no choice." Picking up his fork, Lowell speared a piece of beef, fixing her with a hard look. "End of discussion."

Chapter Two

"A h don't like it. Ah don't like it one little bit." Old Abe set the brake Friday morning, and then he climbed down from the buggy and turned to help Sarah. Boston still slept beneath a heavy blanket of darkness. A dog barked in the distance, the only sound in the predawn stillness.

"I'll name my first son after you," Sarah promised. If it weren't for Abe's help, she couldn't have slipped out of the house unnoticed or reached the train station in time to escape town before anyone awoke.

"The only reason I agreed to bring you here is 'cause I can't bear to see you shipped off to your Uncle Brice. That man's the devil if I ever seen one. He don't believe in the good Lord, and I don't want baby girl subjected to Lucifer hisself. No, sir. Ain't none of my doings, but I can't bear to see you go to that man one more time."

"Oh, Abe. You understand. I'm sorry I was so ugly to you before supper last night."

"That's all right, Miss Livingston. I knows what you was facin', I wouldn't let a cur live with Brice Livingston—don't know why your Papa can't see the mean in dat man. The good Lord knows you got no business traipsin' round the country by yourself, but I reckon if you're not old enough by now to look after your needs, Wadsy's done a poor job of raisin' you."

Leaning forward on her tiptoes, Sarah kissed the servant's shaving soap-scented cheek. "Wadsy would hang us both out to dry if anyone suggested that she'd failed in her duties."

Abe chuckled. "That she would, young'un. She'll not hear it from me." He lifted a bag from the buggy and set it down on the ground, his eyes assessing the empty terminal. "I'd carry this inside, but if anyone was to notice—"

"You've done enough, Abe. I won't jeopardize your place with Papa by asking you to see me inside." Giving him a brief hug, she whispered, "I'll write and let you know where I am."

"Yes'm, you do that. We're going to be powerful worried until we hear that you're safe."

"Take good care of my papa."

"I will. You take care of yourself, young'un."

Sarah watched him return to the buggy. He drove away without looking back.

Picking up the valise, she entered the station. A mellow light bathed the deserted waiting room. Ordinarily she wouldn't have to purchase a ticket. Papa owned the railroad and the Livingston family traveled free, but the sleepy-eyed man behind the ticket counter wouldn't recognize her today. She'd carefully dressed in Abe's grandson's clothing, pulling a hat low over her face. Other travelers would assume she was a teenage boy traveling alone, exactly as she intended.

"One way to New York," she said, trying to make her voice gruff and manly. The ticket agent didn't look up. She laid the bills on the counter, smiling. Moments later, ticket in hand, she sat down to await the arrival of the five forty southbound. Julie Steinberg had a small apartment above her father's Jewish delicatessen. She and Julie had been roommates in boarding school and still corresponded regularly. Sarah was sure Julie would let her stay with her until she could get her bearings. Papa would look for her there first, no doubt, but Julie would divert his efforts and lead the Pinkerton detectives on a merry chase.

Sarah knew that her educational skills were above most other young women's; finding suitable employment shouldn't be a problem. As soon as she had a job, she would bury herself so deep in New York City that it would take Papa's men months to find her. By then she hoped to be married and settled.

The door opened and a young woman, followed by an older couple, caught her attention. The girl was crying, trying to sop up the stream of tears coursing down her cheeks with a soaked hankie. The older man set his jaw, ignoring the waterworks.

"You'll be thanking us in a few years. Love ain't got a thing to do with happiness, girl."

The young woman shook her head, murmuring a rebuke and then crying harder.

Realizing she was witnessing a private matter, Sarah looked away and concentrated on the double wooden doors that led to the train platform. In a matter of hours she would be independent—free from Papa's tyranny. The older couple shuffled past her, practically dragging the girl behind them.

"Dry your eyes, Lucy. Your father is right. You'll come to understand that we only have your best interests at heart."

The girl shrugged off her mother's hand. "How can you and Pa be so mean? I love Rodney!"

Sarah watched the struggle from the corner of her eye, reminding herself that she shouldn't be so nosy. She had enough trouble with her own papa.

The coarse-looking man took off his hat and ran his hands through his graying hair. "You'll do what we say, girl. You're not too big to take a switch to yet."

"It's my life! And you ain't fair!"

The sound of a train whistle interrupted the heated discussion. The five forty was arriving. Retrieving her bag, Sarah made her way out the doors and watched as the big black locomotive pulled into the station, steam bellowing from its coal stacks.

The young girl followed, sobbing as she continued to argue against her parents' intention to get her on the train. Their angry voices followed Sarah as she climbed aboard and took a seat in coach. She closed her eyes and breathed deeply. The voices of the girl and her parents were only murmurs that faded as the train pulled out of the station.

Once daylight had broken across the horizon, Sarah watched the passing scenery, her heart thumping with the rhythm of the tracks. When her watch hands reached close to seven, her stomach reminded her that she hadn't eaten since breakfast the day before. Getting out of her seat, she walked to the dining car, struggling to keep her balance as the train moved over rough tracks.

Her eyes searched the confined space, lighting on the young woman who still sobbed into her hankie. Her red nose and swollen eyes assured Sarah that the crisis—whatever it was—still bloomed. Her heart dropped when she saw there was only one empty seat, and it was across from Lucy. Sighing, she walked over to Lucy's table and said, "Mind if I sit with you?"

The girl refused to meet Sarah's eyes. "I ain't very good company."

Sarah slid into the seat and unfolded a napkin. "That's all right. I'm too hungry to be much company either." The girl finally glanced up, frowning at Sarah's appearance.

Of course. She would think a boy was sitting opposite her. Sarah was still wearing Blue Boy's clothes.

Removing her cap, she released the pins from her hair and a cloud of brushed red spilled over her shoulders. "It's too complicated to explain why I'm dressed this way, but I am a woman. You don't have to worry."

The girl didn't reply but instead focused her gaze on the passing scenery. When breakfast was served, she pushed the plate away. Sarah ate with gusto, feeling like a bird finally free of its cage.

Sniffing, the young woman turned without warning. "My name is Lucy Mallory. Actually, it's Sarah Lucille Mallory, but ain't no one called me that ever."

Sarah reached for a hot roll. "Small world. My name is Sarah Elaine Livingston, and unless someone's angry with me they just call me Sarah. I noticed you've been crying. Is there anything I can do to help?"

"You can marry Walker McKay."

Sarah blinked, dropping the roll she was about to butter. "Pardon?"

"Marry Walker McKay. I'm being shipped off to be a mail-order bride. My father is *making* me marry some old dirty rancher so I can produce an heir." Her head hit the table with a dull thud as she resumed weeping. The force of the vibration tipped the butter from the knife to the tablecloth.

Sarah's mind churned. Marry? She leaned closer to the sobbing girl. "Have you seen this Walker McKay? Is he…beastly looking?" She could tolerate unattractiveness as long as a man was clean about his personage. She could even tolerate an older man as long as he was kind. But beastly—ugly and having mean tendencies? It would be like marrying Uncle Brice.

"I haven't seen the man. All I know is what Pa told me. He was hurt real bad by a bull or something, and now he's decided he needs an heir to his fortune." Lucy bawled harder.

A desperate man looking for matrimony. Gravely injured—he'd have health issues, but at least he was alive. "Why doesn't he marry someone he already knows?"

Shaking her head, the girl wiped her nose. "I don't know nothin' about him, and I ain't got no say in the matter. Pa set this up. Answered some ol' ad in a newspaper. I just know I don't want to marry Mr. McKay so Ma and Pa can save the farm—" She paused, her face flushing a bright crimson. "I jest cain't marry him," she corrected.

Sarah absently bit into the unbuttered roll. "Awful circumstances, indeed. What are you going to do?"

"I don't know. I ain't got a choice, I tell you."

"Maybe you do." Sarah chewed, mulling the situation. "You really love this Rodney?"

The girl wilted with grief. "Like a pork chop at dinner! He was gettin' ready to ask Pa for my hand in marriage. We were both bumfoozled when Pa told me he'd offered me to this Mr. McKay to be a mail-order bride."

Mr. McKay is expecting a bride. I need a husband. Sarah calmly bit into her roll and swallowed. "I'll do it."

Wadsy's voice echoed through her mind. *Baby girl! Marriage is a sacred act!*

And Sarah agreed. She would marry this Walker McKay and spend the rest of her life devoted to this man. Many marriages were arranged and turned out just fine. She paused. "Did your father say how old this McKay man is?"

"Pa ain't said, but I don't think he's ancient."

"Do you think he could still sire a child?"

Lucy shrugged. "I suppose. All he wants is an heir."

"Okay, then I'll do it."

The girl sat up straighter. "But how—"

"This is what we'll do. You'll get off at the next stop, hire someone to take you to Rodney, and then it will be up to you and him to go far away for a while to give me sufficient time to marry Mr. McKay. Then you can tell your ma and pa what you've done."

The girls eyes rounded.

"It won't be easy. Are you sure you love Rodney enough to do this?"

"I love him, all right. I'd save the farm for Ma and Pa ifn' I could but—"

"How much do they owe?"

"Five hunnert dollars."

Sarah smiled. "I'll give you the money to pay off your parents' farm." *Granted, it is sort of like buying a husband, but...*

"You have that kind of money?"

Sarah nodded. "I do. Do we have a deal?"

"You'd also have to lend me enough to hire someone to take me to Rodney. I only have fifty cents." Lucy slid to the front of her chair, her desperate brown eyes searching Sarah's. "I have a wedding dress. It's small but you can have it if you kin wear it." She looked Sarah up and down. "It's nothing fancy, but it would look bad if you didn't show up with one."

"I'll wear it."

Lucy stared at Sarah as if sizing up her seriousness. "McKay paid Pa a hunnert dollars for me to come."

Sarah smiled, ignoring the strange lurch in her stomach. "He'll have his bride."

Breaking into a grin, Lucy nodded. "Done."

Leaning across the table, Sarah shook hands and sealed the bargain. "I'll go to my seat, get the money, and be back in a few minutes."

"I'll be here."

Chapter Three

Wadsy glanced at the foyer clock, frowning. Sarah was usually the first one at the breakfast table, cheeks aglow, eager to start a new day. It was well past sunup, and the girl was still in her room. "Is baby girl gonna stay abed all day?"

"You can't run after her every time she has one of her temper tantrums," Lowell muttered from his place at the head of the table. Lifting his newspaper, he shook it out. "Let her be. She'll be down when she's ready."

Wadsy cleared away the untouched meal and then busied herself in the kitchen until Will's resulting scowl sent her off to the parlor. Keeping an eye on the stairway, she dusted, pretending not to listen for the girl's soft footsteps. By late afternoon the temptation to comfort her charge won out. Armed with some of Will's fresh-baked biscuits and hot tea, she crept up the back stairs to Sarah's bedroom door, careful not to let Mr. Livingston hear her.

She rapped softly. "Honey, open up now. Ain't no use starvin' to death over havin' to go to Brice's. It won't be that bad, you'll see."

Sarah's door remained closed.

Baby girl was determined to make a body suffer. Wadsy balanced the tray on her hip, rattling the door handle.

"C'mon, Sarah, open the door. Your mammy wansta talk to you. I got tea." She cracked the door open to peek inside. The room was dark, the curtains drawn. "Lawsy me, you gonna grow to the mattress, honey chile. Get on out of the bed. Why, it's almost suppa time." Nudging the door open, she set the tray down on the floor and slid it through the narrow opening. "I'll leave it on the floor and you can eat when you're ready."

Silence met her efforts.

Straightening, Wadsy rose slowly and peeked around the half-open door. Finally entering, she shuffled to the window and pushed the drapes aside, tying them to the walls with braided gold fasteners. The window was open. *Surely that child hasn't climbed out again!*

"Sarah?" She turned around and found the bed empty. "You hidin' from your mammy?"

A faint breeze fluffed the bottoms of the heavy satin drapes, throwing a flicker of light across the untouched bed. A quick search of the room revealed nothing but absences. The silver brush was missing, as were Laverne Livingston's antique ivory brooch, the wooden money box Sarah kept her personal funds in, and the calico dress Wadsy had sewn for Sarah to wear when she wanted to help weed the garden. The hook where the frock usually hung was conspicuously empty. *Baby girl wouldn't leave and take that ol' rag with her, would she?* Wadsy moved to the closet, where Sarah's fine garments hung. *Taffetas, silks—if baby girl has left, why is that calico gone and the others still here?*

Wadsy made a full sweep of the room. Also missing was the monogrammed travel bag that Sarah's father had bought her when she traveled with him to the opening ceremony for the first California railway station on the line. Land, that child's excitement before the trip was contagious. She'd laid her best dresses in the trunk at the foot of her bed.

"Imagine," the girl had said with a sigh as she twirled around, a green silk evening gown clutched to her chest, flaming hair in wild disarray. "Just imagine all the prospects! Handsome young cowboys with spurs and guns. Dangerous men on fast horses." Pausing, Sarah had carefully laid the dress with the others. "I know he's there, Wadsy. He has to be. I couldn't bear coming home without having met my future husband."

"California ain't Boston, doll. Menfolk out there ain't seen a woman in years. Dirty, nasty men ain't gonna touch my baby girl."

"Oh, Wadsy, I'll never get married if the man has to meet your and Papa's standards. I think it'll be wildly exciting out West!"

But, as always, Sarah had returned unbetrothed.

Wadsy picked up the untouched tray, worried now. Mr. Livingston was gonna be powerful upset when he learned that Sarah was missing. She dreaded telling him that his daughter's bed wasn't slept in the night before, partly because of the news itself and partly because she knew she would be reprimanded for taking tea to the pouting girl.

"Baby girl, you're gonna get your mammy in a mess of trouble," she muttered, closing the door behind her. "A whole mess of trouble."

Chapter Four

Lowell started at Wadsy's knock, his leather chair squeaking. "What is it?" he asked, swiveling to face her. The nanny came in, carrying a tray of biscuits and tea. "Has Sarah come out of her room yet?"

"No, sir, she ain't."

"Ah…tea. Thank you, Wadsy, but I'm busy." He turned back to the mound of papers littering the desktop.

She set the tray on the polished desk and wrung her hands in her apron. "I know you ain't gonna like this, but…she's gone."

Lowell kept writing. "Who's gone?"

"I know I wasn't suppos'ta go up, but I did, and the window was open and the bed ain't been slept in all night."

Sighing, Lowell looked up. Sarah's rebellion was hardly newsworthy. The chit sorely tested his patience, but he refused to give in to this recent show of defiance. He shuffled a stack of papers for a moment and then irritably shoved them aside. There were days when he would give his railroad to have Laverne back to deal with their only child.

"Where is she this time, Wadsy? Should I send Abe over to her cousin Eleanor's to see if she's hiding out there?"

"I don't know, sir. Do ya think she'da left for good? She was powerful upset."

"Certainly not. She's just out of sorts." He ran a finger along the inside of his heavily starched collar. "I can't buy her a proper husband, so

26

I can't make her happy. She has to settle down and have patience until the right man comes along."

He glanced at the nanny, who had been staring at the tray since she'd set it on the table.

"Give her until evening. If she doesn't come home by then, we'll start looking." He reached for a pencil. "Take the tray when you leave. I'm not hungry."

"Sir…you didn't touch your breakfast this morning. A body got to eat…"

"Run along, Wadsy. We both have work to do."

Picking up the tray, the old woman shuffled toward the doorway. Before she could leave, Lowell spun the chair back to face her.

"I've tried, Wadsy. The good Lord knows I've tried." His face crumpled, bravado slipping. "What more can I do?"

"You're a good papa, sir. Baby girl will be home in time for suppa—don't you fret none."

"Yes, you're right. She'll come home when she realizes no one loves her like family."

"Yes, sir. No one loves her more than us…she know that."

❖

Fit to be tied, Lowell paced the study floor. "Two days! My daughter has been missing for two days!" He looked as though he'd aged a good ten years in those two days.

"'Member your heart, sir." Abe poured sassafras tea, wiping away a drip with a snow-white cloth before returning the pot to the silver tray.

"Heart, my foot." Lowell drew on his stogie and puffs of blue smoke hazed the room. "She'll be the death of me yet."

Abe fanned cigar smoke away from his nostrils. "Yes, sir."

Pausing before the window, Lowell watched the falling rain, his shoulders slumped with weariness. "Where is she, Abe? If anything has happened to her, I'll never forgive myself."

Setting a steaming cup on the desk, Abe said quietly, "You know the child's tendency to worry a soul to death afore she decides to come home, Mr. Livingston. She'll be back when she's ready and not a minute sooner. There no use frettin' yourself sick."

"But two days. Two days and not a word. Are you certain you've checked with all of her friends? Is she with that giggly Liddy Snow? I wouldn't put it past those girls to try and pull the wool over my eyes. It wouldn't be the first time."

Abe fussed with the cream pitcher and sugar bowl. "Done checked with her, the Montgomery girl, sir, and everybody else Sarah knows. Ain't no one seen her in the past few days, but I feel in my bones she just fine, sir. Try to drink a little of this tea. Gettin' wore out ain't gonna help nothin.'"

Lowell drew on the cigar, waving Abe's efforts aside. He couldn't eat or drink with Sarah running around the countryside doing who knew what. Had she followed that German fellow she'd talked about the week before? He searched for a name but came up empty handed. Or had she gone off with that dockworker again? After a while the candidates blurred together, a seemingly endless stream of handsome young swains who hadn't given a thought to marriage, only to what they could get from Sarah's innocence.

"The spring cotillion…Wadsy's been sewing her dress for months. If she misses that cotillion…"

"No, she surely won't miss the cotillion, sir. But if she do, that just means she ain't got all her meanness out yet."

"If she's not back in time for that ball next week, Abe, I'm calling in Pinkerton and his detectives."

Abe glanced away. "Yes, sir. You did that the last time."

"And they found her, didn't they? Had to go all the way to Philly to do it, but, by gum, they found her, selling flowers on a street corner like a regular hoyden. Her mama would sit up in her grave and shout if she knew that."

"Yes, sir. Miss Laverne shorely would."

Smoke boiled around the portly figure. "Never saw the like— You said the dockworker she was about to run off with hadn't seen her?"

"Dat's what he say, Mr. Livingston, sir. Say he hasn't laid an eye on her since the mornin' afore she disappeared."

"And you believe him?"

"Yes, sir. He tell me he had no idea she was your daughter or else he wouldn't have touched her with a ten-foot pole."

"Touched her!"

"No sir, he did not touch her, he say that fore sure. Jest meant he wouldn't have had fanciful thoughts about her."

Turning away from the window, Lowell snubbed out his cigar. "You're right. All this worrying and not eating is making me sick. Have Will fry me up a couple of fatback sandwiches, and I'll have some of those creamed potatoes too."

"But the doctor done said—"

"Don't remind me of the doctor! I know what the doctor says. He wants me to starve to death, that's what he wants. Go on, now, Abe, and tell Will to not be stingy with the butter on those sandwiches."

"Yes, sir. Slather on the butter. Be buildin' a pine box tomorrow," the old servant grumbled, turning around to leave.

When the door had closed, Lowell reached for a picture that sat on his desk. He felt the tension ease from his face. "Ah, Laverne, what am I going to do? We've sired an outlaw. I do my best, but Sarah's stubborn streak would put yours to shame. It doesn't matter what I do or say or buy for her. Our daughter is intent on ruining her life."

Memories flooded him as he traced the outline of the ornate silver frame, softly chuckling to himself. Sarah and her mama were two peas in a pod. Laverne had the same red hair, fiery spirit, and ornery zest for life. Many a time Lowell had thrown his young, sassy wife over his shoulder and carried her around the house, singing "Amazing Grace" at the top of his lungs until her temper cooled. They would have a good laugh, and then she'd look at him with Sarah's wide, trusting eyes and all would be well. One time Laverne had sat up three nights in a row nursing a sickly newborn kitten—she wouldn't hear of giving up on the runt of the litter. No one had been more surprised than Lowell when the weak little animal made it. Laverne had named the kitten

Pertinacity before exhaustion overtook her and she collapsed in Lowell's arms. He'd carried her and the cat to bed, where they had both slept twenty-four hours through.

Yes, Laverne had spunk. That was what he'd loved about her.

Much as he hated to admit it, Sarah came by hers naturally.

"Ah, Laverne," he whispered. "I miss you, ol' gal." Absently placing a two-fingered kiss on the frame, he strode to the double doors and opened them.

"Abe! I'm not waiting a minute longer! Get me those Pinkerton detectives. That girl's gone too far this time!"

Chapter Five

Gusty wind greeted Sarah as she stepped from the train at Tall Timbers station. It snatched a lock of red hair from its clip and sent it flying above her head. She tried unsuccessfully to rein it in while holding her skirts. Her gaze skimmed the bustling town.

The knot in her stomach painfully tightened. She couldn't do this. Last night she realized that she couldn't pretend to marry a man—take vows before God and live in sin. She couldn't perpetrate the fraud. But…she was here, and Walker McKay was expecting a bride.

The platform teemed with activity—mothers and fathers greeting returning children; sweethearts embracing, caught up in the moment of blissful reunion, unashamed of their public displays of affection. Families bumped against cattle ranchers and farmhands apparently waiting for supply shipments.

Stepping from the bottom stair onto the ground, she searched the milling crowd, her heart fluttering like a trapped sparrow. Her eyes swept the area for Walker McKay. Lucy couldn't provide a physical description of the man beyond the possibility of disfigurement from his recent accident. Sarah's eyes leapt from face to face, trying to match the features she'd formed in her mind—frail, perhaps in a wheelchair. She would just have to tell the truth about her identity and hope that he understood. Her cheeks warmed. What reasonable man would approve of such a silly act?

A man wearing a gun in a holster slung low and heavy from his belt made his way through the crowd, his eyes searching the platform. His cragged features were ringed in dust, his clothes spattered with—Sarah recoiled—was that horse dung? When his gaze locked on her, he offered a tobacco-stained grin.

Her worst fears were realized. Lucy's husband-to-be was grizzled *and* not the most handsome man around.

He paused a foot away. He was four inches shorter than she, and as he removed his hat she saw that he was as old as Papa. She closed her eyes. Backing out might be easier than she thought. Lucy had lied. The wench had needed someone to marry this shriveled old pipsqueak so she wouldn't have to.

Sarah checked her temper, reminding herself that she had made the choice to switch places. She'd admit what she'd done and be on her way.

"Miss Lucy Mallory?" The tender excitement in his voice softened his countenance but did nothing to ease Sarah's disappointment. "Is that you, girl?"

"Actually…the agency made a mistake. My name is Sarah Livingston. I'm not Lucy Mallory."

There. That was easy enough. With the safety of the train and a return trip no more than five quick steps behind her, she didn't have to admit to anything. But as the days spent traveling to Wyoming territory would certainly have given the detectives ample time to have located Julie's apartment, traveling to New York now would mean almost certain return to Papa. It didn't take a crystal ball for her to know that he would banish her to Uncle Brice's forever. She took a long look at her future and repeated, "Sara Elaine Livingston. I'm not the woman you sent for."

"Names don't matter." The old man's smile spread across his worn face, deepening the etched lines. "Yer finally here. And yer even purtier than I'd pictured." He appeared barely able to contain himself as he replaced his hat and reached for her bag. "This way, ma'am."

It took every ounce of resolve for Sarah to drag her feet across the station, past young, handsome men greeting their wives, past young children on the platform who were engrossed with a dead coyote near the tracks. What would her children look like? Rosy images of a perfect home life with a handsome husband and strong, beautiful children whipped off with the hot wind. How Papa and Wadsy would laugh. Even Abe would tease her about this one, but a bargain was binding.

She berated herself for her foolishness. If she started being picky now, she might as well reconcile herself to being an old maid. He was most likely a very kind soul. Her dream, however bittersweet, was about to be realized and all she could see were flaws—a few missing teeth and some battle scars. A lot more years than she'd anticipated. She studied the man, her heart sinking.

With newfound resolve, she caught up to him as he tried to maneuver himself and her bag into a buggy. She was just gathering up the nerve to ask him how long the ride to his ranch was when a particularly strong gust snatched his hat and sent it skittering into the crowd. Without thinking, Sarah lifted her skirts and ran to catch it, following it as it skipped along.

The hat bounced merrily in front of her, and she quickened her pace to catch up with it. The felt hat paused momentarily as if to tease her and then bounced on. A break in the wind lent her hope and she made an ungraceful lunge, propelling herself forward at the very moment a set of dusty boots appeared on the opposite side of the hat. Unable to break her fall, she lurched forward into the waiting arms of a man who caught her with surprising grace and easiness.

Her face flaming with embarrassment, Sarah mustered her composure and lifted her gaze to meet two of the clearest blue eyes she had ever seen. Her gasping breath caught in her throat, and for a moment she forgot to breathe. Arms—gloriously strong and stout as oak posts—casually lifted her to her feet and then reached down to recover the hat. Her eyes were held captive by his long, denim-clad legs, slim hips, and broad shoulders. This was the man she'd hoped who would meet her at the train, sweep her into his arms, and marry her.

His eyes discreetly skimmed the length of her gown down and back up before he extended the hat. "This must be yours?"

"It's not mine." She was amazed at how a brief jog across the station could make her feel so giddy. "It's his hat," she said, handing it to the older man, who had caught up with her and was trying to adjust the unruly felt hat back to the shape of his head. "Mr. McKay's."

Both men paused, and for a moment she was confused as they glanced at each other and winked. Was there a joke she was missing?

The handsome stranger smiled. "You must be Miss Mallory," he said in a deep, rich baritone.

"Miss Livingston. The agency made a mistake. Please call me Sarah. And you are?"

"Walker McKay. This is my foreman, S.H. Gibson."

She swallowed. "*You're* Walker McKay?" Her recent thought of backing out collapsed. This incredible man was young and brawny, with strong features and a commanding presence, and apparently in perfect health. Before leaving the train, Lucy had said something about Mr. McKay being a Christian. If this man standing before her was truly all he seemed to be, the mere thought of taking vows with him left her a little breathless. God had abundantly answered her prayers.

S.H. stepped up. "Sorry about the confusion, Miss Mallory."

"Livingston." She lowered her tone for fear Mr. McKay might have reservations about the name change. *Livingston,* she mouthed.

The man bowed, sweeping his hat from his head. "I shoulda introduced myself. S.H. at yer service."

When she glanced back at Mr. McKay, she noticed that his electric blue eyes were focused on her, but he made no comment.

If this man was Walker McKay, that changed everything. She shook off her shock and reached for his hand, breaking into a wide smile.

"Relieved...I mean, pleased to meet you, Mr. McKay." She drew a long breath and released it.

He had no idea *how* pleased.

S.H. courteously extended an arm. "Shall we go?"

Sarah glanced at Walker McKay, her grin widening. "By all means, Mr. Gibson." She sent one last glance at the handsome rancher who was handling her bag. "By all means."

Chapter Six

Walker informed her that they would waste no time with court-ing; the wedding would occur as soon as possible. The switch in names didn't appear to bother him, but truthfully he didn't appear overly interested in her, period. There was an impatience about his re-quest to marry right away that puzzled her, as if he thought she might bolt and return to Boston, but leaving Spring Grass was the last thing on her mind. The ranch itself was enormous—thousands of acres of pas-tures, smooth hills, and gently rolling valleys. The homestead consisted of the main house; a smaller log home for the foreman and his wife, Flo; a shed; a bunkhouse for the ranch hands; a large barn for horses, hay, and equipment, and several smaller cattle and horse pens. The house it-self was grand: a large colonial with seven bedrooms—obviously a house built to be filled with children. The only part of the ranch that wasn't perfectly kept was a flower garden behind the den that stood in disar-ray. Sarah hadn't asked Walker about it, and S.H. and Flo hadn't men-tioned it.

S.H. insisted that Sarah stay with him and Flo until the wedding. So far, Flo had been invaluable to Sarah, who, for all her zest and desire to be married, knew next to nothing about weddings beyond what she'd read in books. Flo volunteered to orchestrate the whole affair. Now they sat in Flo's tidy kitchen discussing the guest list for the ceremony

only days away. The list was large—all Walker's friends. Sarah was determined they would be hers too in a short time.

Flo shook her head. "Poor Sadie Miller. She'll bawl for days when
she finds out Walker chose a mail-order bride over her." Walker's white-
haired housekeeper couldn't contain a chuckle. "Of course, I'd have to
say every man in the county would make the same choice." She wrote
Sadie's name on a growing list of families from the surrounding area.

Sarah picked up the sheet of paper, scanning the column of names.
"Who's Katie Brown? Is she single?"

"Katie? She's single and a nice enough girl, I suppose. Walker's
known her since the two of them were knee-high to a grasshopper, but
I think he considers Katie a friend—more like a sister than a wife."

Sarah sighed. It seemed to her that Walker could have had his pick
of women, yet he'd chosen a woman he'd never seen. "There has to be
at least one woman in the whole territory of Wyoming he doesn't have
sisterly feelings for." She couldn't understand how any woman with
an ounce of sense could let a man like Walker McKay get away. Her
face flushed and her knees turned to jelly whenever she saw him striding from the house to the barn with long, assured steps, or when she
sneaked a peek at him riding out to the fields in the morning. Her excitement was tinged with worry too, considering that apparently he
wanted nothing more than a woman to bear his child. Since arriving,
she had done and said everything she could to reassure him that she
was delighted to be at Spring Grass, even going out of her way to show
him she was thrilled to be his bride. Yet she felt his hesitancy—almost
as if he wanted to avoid any mention of permanency. Maybe he didn't
want to fall in love, but in time that would change. She'd be such a doting wife that he couldn't fail to fall in love with her.

"You're gettin' a fine man," Flo said, breaking into Sarah's thoughts.

"But he could have chosen any single woman—"

"He had his pick and he picked you." Getting up from her chair, Flo
refilled Sarah's lemonade, her red, roughened hands proof of her work-
load.

Sara sighed. He hadn't exactly picked her. "Has he been married before?" It wouldn't matter if he had been, but…

"No, you'll be the first Mrs. Walker McKay. Might be best if I told you about Trudy, though, so you won't go asking him and getting him all riled up. She done a terrible thing to him. He's real touchy now and has a bitter streak towards women. And if you break that man's heart—"

Ah. Another woman had hurt him. A knot rose in Sarah's throat at the thought of a hitch in her plans. She would see that he forgot her quickly. "I won't break his heart. I will be a good wife. What happened?"

"They was engaged a couple of years back. She ran off with a hat salesman just before the wedding. It was real humiliatin' for Walker." Flo picked up the wedding list, her eyes scanning the columns. "She ran off with a man who sold bowlers, so I wouldn't mention hats to Walker, if I were you." She tossed the list aside. "Needless to say, we were all shocked. She hurt him real good."

Sarah couldn't help wondering how anyone could be so cold. Walker was ten times better than any man she'd tried to marry in Boston. It would take fifty Joe Mancusos, from what she'd seen, to make one Walker McKay. Desert this man—this handsome, wonderful man— for a hat salesman? Trudy's actions were inconceivable.

"I'd also best warn you to not go anywhere near that weed patch behind the house. That was Trudy's garden, the place where the wedding was to take place. Walker ain't allowed anyone near it since the day she left."

"I was wondering about that. What a shame to let such beauty go to waste." She paused. "Why would Walker be considering marriage now?"

"He had a brush with death, and the accident got him to thinking. He ain't gonna be young forever, and there's no heir to Spring Grass. He needs a son or daughter. Simple as that." She glanced over. "Sorry—"

"No, that's quite all right. I understand my responsibility." Sarah might want love and bliss, but it was understandable that Walker wasn't ready for that. In time, though, she was sure he would grow to adore her.

Flo sat back down at the table, smiling. "Speakin' of beauty, what about you, young'un? You haven't said much about yourself. Seems a girl as pretty as you are could have her pick of any red-blooded young man. What made you decide to be a mail-order bride?"

The weight of Sarah's ruse was heavy on her heart. From the moment she'd arrived, it had been on the tip of her tongue to tell Walker about the switch of brides on the train. She had given her real name, and he certainly hadn't seemed to care. But would he care if he knew that she had lied about the agency mix-up and that in truth she and his intended bride had met and decided to change their circumstances to suit themselves? And poor Papa was most likely beside himself with worry. She would have to send word soon on where she was, but first she would marry. She was so close to realizing her dream. In a few days, she would finally be a bride, and then she would immediately send word to Papa of her whereabouts. She was comfortable with Flo, but not enough to confide her secret. Better to wait until after the wedding, when the marriage was a done deal.

"I've never wanted anything but to be a dutiful wife and mother, to raise children and keep a home for a loving man." She paused, deciding to keep as close to the truth as possible. "But when the opportunity to marry now rather than later arose, I seized it." A bead of sweat trickled down the back of Sarah's neck and into the collar of her blouse. The heat in the kitchen had grown insufferable. "The men in Boston are so intent on their work or the rail system."

She bit her lip. The train yard was almost too much information. What if Flo linked her to the railroad and thus to Lowell Livingston? Sarah glanced up from her hands to see Flo staring at her as S.H. breezed in through the back door and removed his hat. "Are you all right, dear? You look flushed."

"It's hot in here. May I have another glass of lemonade?"

"You set where you are, Mama. I'll pour the pretty lady another glass of lemonade. It's warming up," S.H. said, picking up Sarah's empty glass for a refill.

Flo's cheeks pinked when S.H. planted a kiss on her forehead as he

passed by on the way to the sink. The love between the two had been
evident from the first day Sarah met them. They had spent nearly all
their married life in the log cabin at Spring Grass, and they were obviously as enraptured with each other as they had been when they first
came to work for Mitch Walker years ago. It was exactly the kind of relationship Sarah wanted with her future husband.

How long would it be before she could trust the couple enough to
let them, and Walker, in on her secret? They couldn't send her away.
They just couldn't. She had already come to love the long days at Spring
Grass and the cold nights on the prairie. Lying in her soft featherbed,
she listened to the lowing cattle and stared out the window at the bright
stars that twinkled high overhead. She loved the clear blue skies and
the courteous cowhands, who were careful to take their hats off as she
approached to say hello. Most of all, she found she was already falling
deeply in love with Walker McKay, although she barely knew him.

S.H. set a full glass in front of Sarah and she smiled. She sipped the
lemonade and then said, "Thank you, S.H. With all this planning and
the wedding only days away, I haven't had time to catch my breath."

The old man grinned. "Don't worry, miss. Flo and me'll take care
of everything. We're just so dern tickled to have you, we cain't sleep for
thinking about the weddin'."

"You've both been wonderful," she said, softly stifling a yawn.
"Maybe I'll lie down for a while. I'm suddenly very sleepy."

"You go right ahead, young'un." Flo got up from the table, swatting
S.H. away from the apple pie that was cooling on the windowsill. "I
think I'll go out and see if Potster needs any help at the bunkhouse."

"Potster can feed the men without your help," S.H. complained
good naturedly. "Too many cooks in the kitchen spoil the taters."

As they gently argued over the feeding of the ranch hands, Sarah excused herself from the table and went into the back room.

Shaking her head, Flo watched the girl leave. "What do you think of her, S.H.?"

"I think she's exactly what Walker needs. Once he slows down and pays her a little attention, I think he'll agree."

Frowning, Flo picked up Sarah's glass and carried it to the sink. "You don't think there's something odd about a young woman who's that pretty and well mannered wanting to be a mail-order bride?"

"Now, Flo," S.H. teased, tweaking her under her chin. "There you go thinking about Trudy again. Miss Livingston wouldn't do that to Walker. Maybe you should be lying down for a while to get those crazy ideas outta your head." He stole another brief kiss. "He'll take care of himself. Stop yer frettin'."

When he left, Flo sat down at the table and stared at Sarah's closed bedroom door. What was it that had her on edge? The girl seemed warm and honest. Her manners were faultless, her tone that of a woman of higher education and refinement. She should be happy that such a find had practically fallen into Walker's lap. Her eyes traveled back to the guest list.

So what about Sarah Livingston had her on edge?

Chapter Seven

Late that afternoon, Walker watched S.H. from the corner of his eye. They had been stringing fence for hours, and he could tell that the old man was dying to ask what Walker thought of his new bride-to-be.

What did he think of her? She was pleasing to the eye, no doubt about that, but that concession hadn't softened his feelings regarding women. Walker refused to say anything about Sarah or the wedding. S.H. should know he was too much like his pa and not about to talk about things he didn't find necessary to discuss.

S.H. took off his hat and wiped sweat off his forehead.

Bearing down on the posthole digger, Walker twisted the rusty iron through the topsoil and into the hard-packed ground below. The muscles in his arms quivered with the strain. He grimaced when he knew S.H. wasn't watching, his still-tender ribs screaming for relief. He wasn't going to let up on his duties, get soft, and lie around the house like an invalid. He'd rather mend the fence now than spend hours this winter slogging through drifts of snow searching for lost cattle.

He let up on the digger, drawing a deep breath. S.H. was staring at him again. The two men's eyes met—one pair brown, older, more experienced; the other, sky blue, clear, and stubbornly unrelenting.

Walker leaned on the tool, buying a few moments of rest. "You're staring at me. Is there something on your mind?"

S.H. threw the hat back on his head and bent over to pick up the post. "Just wondering about the weddin' an' all. You ain't said a thing about Sarah since she got here."

"She'll do." Walker lifted his hat and ran a hand through his sweat-soaked hair.

"What about the weddin'? Her'n Flo have been working hard puttin' it t'gether. Ain't you gonna help?"

"I plan on doing my part."

"Sarah's a fine woman, looks to me like—"

"Never had a neighbor refuse to show up for a barbecue yet."

S.H. glanced up, looking confused. "You mean for a weddin'?"

"I said for a barbecue." The digger met its mark and Walker pulled it up, depositing the last of the dirt in a pile to the side of the new hole.

"What are you talkin' about? You don't mean you—"

"I mean I'm telling everyone I'm having a barbecue. It's early in the year but the weather's holding good. I'm not making a fool of myself in front of the whole town again." Walker motioned for S.H. to bring the post over, and the two men centered it and drove it into the hole, packing the soil back in on it. "If the bride shows up, I'm in fine shape. If she doesn't, the town will never be the wiser. They'll have a good meal and go home."

"If that don't beat all, Walker! Sarah's a sweet little gal. She's not gonna disappoint you. You gotta give her a chance."

"I gave the last one a chance, S.H., and look where it left me."

S.H. took his hands off the post and turned to face Walker. "Does Flo know about this?"

"She does, and she doesn't like it either. Don't see where she has much say in the matter, though. I refuse to be humiliated again."

S.H. straightened and frowned at Walker.

"When are you going to get Trudy out o' yer head? And what makes you think that Sarah's gonna let you turn her weddin' day into some kind of country hoedown? I've been on this good earth long enough to know that no woman wants her weddin' turned into a barbecue."

Walker shrugged. His mind was made up. S.H. stared at him in disbelief. "Son, yer askin' for a heap of trouble. You know that, don't you?"

Walker refused to reply as he tightened the line around the post. He simply moved himself and the equipment down the line.

Chapter Eight

Two days later Sarah ran her hand across the large four-poster with its dark, masculine-looking spread. In a few hours she would be sharing it with Walker McKay. Her heart thrummed against her rib cage as Flo stuck the last few hairpins in place. Finally, it had come. Today was her wedding day. The day she'd dreamed about from the moment she was old enough to whisper the words "I do." Sadness momentarily washed over her. She'd always thought Papa would walk her down the aisle, that Wadsy would look on, beaming. Will would cook for days, and… No matter. She would write tomorrow and inform Papa of the wedding. No doubt he would bring Wadsy and Abe to visit. And soon, she hoped, he would adore his grandchildren. Dote on them. She was doing the right thing.

After sliding another pin into place, Flo loosened a few strands of hair. "There. That softens your face."

Sarah caught a glimpse of herself in the long mirror. Her eyes shone with barely contained impatience as she prepared to take vows that would forever bind her to a man she hardly knew. She was marrying a complete stranger, yet she felt as if she'd known him forever. He barely glanced at her each morning, despite her efforts to converse. That didn't prevent her from loving the way one lock of unruly hair fell across his forehead at the oddest times.

Stepping back to inspect her handiwork, Flo beamed. "You're about the prettiest thing I ever laid eyes on."

"Thank you, Flo. Will Walker think so?" Sarah hadn't seen her husband-to-be all day, and only briefly the day before. Flo said Walker and S.H. were busy mending fence. Sarah had awakened this morning to the sound of shouting voices outside her window as the last of the sawhorse tables were erected in the yard and tablecloths and decorations were arranged. The day was mild. Five hours later, here she was, preparing for the nuptials while S.H. was busy a few doors away getting Walker ready for the big event.

Bending closer to the mirror, she asked, "Are you sure I look all right?" Lucy's gown was simple, yet it fit as if it had been made for her.

"You'll be the prettiest bride this county's ever seen. Any man would be proud to have you as his wife. You're so much prettier than—" Flo broke off, color dotting her cheeks.

Sarah turned to look at her. "Than who?"

"Than Ettie Mae Simpson's daughter. That's a plain girl. Even a fancy weddin' dress couldn't help her."

Sarah had hoped the answer would be "prettier than Trudy." Outside the help continued setting up for the reception following the ceremony. Walker insisted that he would take care of that part, and Sarah hadn't argued. She hadn't argued when he said he wanted to take care of the invitations. This was his town and his people. She took hope he was thoughtful enough to want to arrange the festivities of their wedding. "It's going to be a beautiful ceremony," she said softly.

"Hold still," Flo complained around a mouthful of pins.

Sarah spun around. "Do you think his friends will like me?" Other than the ranch hands, and S.H. and Flo, she hadn't met anyone in his life.

Walker's extensive guest list proved that he was popular among the families who lived in the area. Until today he had been one of the state's most eligible bachelors. The flurry of arriving guests downstairs caught her attention. She glanced at the clock, surprised that people would be arriving nearly an hour before the wedding was scheduled to begin. She finished dressing to the sound of friendly voices as men, women, and children entered the house and were greeted by ranch hands and servants.

A bubble of panic erupted in Sarah's stomach. She really was about to marry a complete stranger. Had she lost her mind? Flo brought the wedding dress, and then both women lifted it high over Sarah's head, careful not to disturb her hair. Sarah's uncertainty faded as Flo fastened the long line of buttons up the back of the dress. Hooking the last fastener, the housekeeper paused for a moment and both women admired Sarah's reflection.

"Simply beautiful."

"Every bride is beautiful on her wedding day."

Flo snorted. "Ettie Mae's daughter won't be."

Downstairs, the voices grew louder as guests continued to arrive. Above the din, Sarah heard a door open down the hall where S.H. was helping Walker into his wedding attire.

"Flo?" S.H.'s loud voice cut through the noise. Flo rolled her eyes and stepped over to open the door.

"What?" she yelled back.

Sarah grinned at the exchange.

"She still here? Walker says he's not puttin' this blame coat on till he's sure she's—" Flo slammed the door shut before S.H. finished his inquiry.

Sarah stared at Flo questioningly.

"It may not be Walker, honey. It could be S.H.'s misplaced sense of humor. You know how he likes to tease. Don't fret your pretty head none." Flo rearranged a stray hairpin, securing it more tightly. A moment later Sarah got up. She wasn't sure what that exchange had been about, but she wouldn't let it ruin the day. Putting on a pair of slippers, she sighed. What was she worried about? In less than an hour she would be Mrs. Walker McKay and her worries would be over.

Flo took her by the shoulders when she straightened. "Be patient with him, young'un. Walker is a good man, but you've got to bear in mind that he *is* a man, and sometimes he's going to be stubborn and occasionally he'll seem blind." Her knowing eyes filled with wisdom. "Things might not always be the way you want at first. There'll be days when you wonder how you ever got into this mess, but you'll have to remember that Walker's been a bachelor a long time and been real hurt by a woman, and that's still stuck in his craw. Things'll work out, but you're gonna need the patience of Job."

"I'm used to hardheaded men. Papa is as stubborn as ragweed," Sarah said. *Oh, Papa, I wish you were here to see me marry. I love you. Please forgive what I'm about to do. And dear Lord, I'm going to need your understanding too.*

She didn't expect the marriage to go smoothly at first. There would be awkward moments, especially when she told Walker the truth—but that moment would come later. Sarah couldn't think of a single thing that could spoil this day, short of the wedding not happening at all. Walker could relax. She wasn't going anywhere but down those stairs at the appointed time.

The two women turned when they heard the door down the hall open again. Sarah held her breath until two pairs of booted footsteps echoed toward the stairs. She glanced at Flo.

"Just remember, honey, it's your wedding day no matter how unusual it appears. The good Lord is watchin' after you."

Sarah frowned. What an odd statement. Unusual? The housekeeper clucked as the clock in the hall chimed, signaling the appointed hour. Sarah straightened, holding still as Flo adjusted the crown of flowers around her forehead. "You go out there and take away their breaths, young'un."

Midafternoon sunshine streamed through the stained-glass window at the end of the hallway when Sarah stepped out of the bedroom with Flo carrying her train. The musicians struck up a tune and Sarah paused, cocking an ear to identify the song. It wasn't the wedding march. She crept down the hallway, Flo close behind. Her petticoats rustled as she halted at the top of the stairs, drawing a deep breath. Laughing voices floated up the staircase, and boots scraped back and forth across the floor. Music swelled as she stepped down onto the top stair.

"Remember," Flo whispered, "don't let nothin' bother you today. It'll get better, given enough time."

Sarah glanced over her shoulder with a hesitant smile. Was that "Turkey in the Straw" the musicians were playing? Gathering her skirts around her, she continued her descent.

Halfway down, Sarah paused again, shocked at what she saw below. People dressed in everyday muslins and calicos were milling about with cups of punch in their hands. Others danced, unaware that the ceremony had begun. There must be a mistake. The reception was never before the wedding.

She spotted a group of men talking and laughing with a man wearing a black collar. The clergy—but his Bible was nowhere in sight. He seemed to be in the middle of a funny story. Shouldn't Walker tell him the service was starting? Shouldn't he know? Where *was* Walker, anyway?

She stepped down another two steps, assessing the crowd. Walker was coming toward her, hurrying to meet her at the bottom of the stairs. Now whispers made their way around the room, and people paused midsentence to stare.

The lead fiddler spotted Sarah, his bow dropping to his side while he looked on. Walker reached her at the steps as the music died away.

The silence became deafening. Sarah's eyes met bewildered gazes, all equally speechless. The musicians lowered their instruments to their laps.

"Keep movin', darlin'," Flo said, nudging her forward. Sarah started, forgetting for a moment that she was the bride—the center of attention. Her feet seemed to be frozen in place.

Walker attempted a smile but failed. Instead, he extended his arm with a hopeful look.

Navigating the final two steps, she slipped her arm through his, murmuring under her breath, "Why are they looking at me like that?"

"Keep walking. I'll explain later."

"Hey, Walker, who's the bride?" a voice called from across the room.

"Is this a wedding? You should have warned us this was gonna be a dress-up occasion. I'da worn my Sunday suit," a second male voice chimed in.

Sarah heard her own soft intake of air. Her heart raced as Walker maneuvered her through the crowded room.

"They don't know, do they." *Don't panic. You know it will take time for him to warm to you—but he hadn't told his neighbors? How did they know to come?*

"They're starting to suspect."

Obviously he wanted to make certain the bride showed up this time. She stiffened and willed her feet to keep moving. It didn't matter. The bride was here and more than able to overlook the slight. So what if folks didn't know they had come to a wedding? They knew now. The handsome couple drew closer to the stone fireplace, and faces gradually melted away until there was no one in the world for Sarah but Walker McKay.

She couldn't ask for a better man than he. Young, brash, wildly handsome, strong, smart, and ambitious. The road to matrimony had been long and at times seemingly endless. But now she knew what Wadsy had meant when she had said, "When that one man show up, baby girl, you gonna feel it clean down to your toes."

Well, Wadsy, what I feel at this moment goes clean down to China.

Smiling, she tightened her hold on Walker's arm and whispered, "Coward." She caught his boyish grin from the corner of her eye.

"Invited the preacher, didn't I?"

"Does he know he's about to officiate at a wedding?"

"He will soon enough."

Walker and Sarah stopped before the clergyman. Though smiling, the older man looked a bit confused.

"Got your Bible with you, John?"

"Er...why, it's in the buggy. Do I need it?"

"Yes, sir. We're about to have a wedding."

Cheers broke out as the startled preacher quickly made his way out of the room. Well-wishers gathered around Sarah, vying for introductions. Walker accepted good-natured backslaps and ribbing, his tanned face flushed by all the excitement.

"Didn't think you had it in ya, son!"

Women voiced mock complaints about how they weren't able to show off their newest dresses. Sarah promised there would be many more McKay parties in the future.

"There will be?" Walker asked as she passed him on her way to greet a group of women her age.

"That's all right, isn't it?" She hadn't thought to ask him, but the McKay house was big and roomy, ideal for community socials, and she loved to entertain. The Livingstons' Christmas parties had always been the talk of Boston.

Reverend John Baird returned with his Bible prominently tucked beneath his arm, and the rather unconventional festivities began.

"Good friends, we delight in the marriage of...uh..." The preacher paused and then leaned close to Sarah. "What's your name, dear?" he whispered.

"Sarah," she quietly replied. "Sarah Elaine Livingston."

"...in Walker and Sarah's marriage today, and let us never forget the seriousness of the vows this couple is about to exchange."

The crowd quieted. It wasn't the marriage Sarah had dreamed about. Outside the window, ranch hands turned roasting meat over open spits. Household help shooed hungry hands away from the steaming bowls of corn and parsley potatoes lining the long rows of cloth-covered tables. The smell of baking bread drifted in from the kitchen while children scampered about on the lawn, kicking a ball as Sarah and Walker repeated their simple vows.

The McKay parlor wasn't the church she'd attended since birth. And there weren't a lot of flowers, just a bouquet of winter berries that someone—probably Flo—had placed on the parlor table. Wadsy, Abe, and Papa weren't here to share this moment, their eyes brimming with love. But it *was* her wedding day—the happiest day of her life—and she would do everything within her power to erase the uncertainty in Walker's voice, the haunted look in those blue eyes. It wouldn't happen today or tomorrow, but in time he would love her. There was no doubt about that in her mind.

"Do you, Sarah Elaine Livingston, take Walker Edward McKay to be your husband?"

"I do."

"Do you, Walker Edward McKay, take Sarah Elaine Livingston to be your wedded wife?"

"Yes."

Then it was over. She was married. She had the prized gold band on her left hand. S.H. engulfed her in a bear hug, nearly squeezing the life out of her while a beaming Flo looked on. The whole room was buzzing with congratulations, everyone wanting a turn at the newlyweds.

"Can't say I've ever been more surprised," Tom Howell confessed, pumping Walker's hand.

Walker smiled. "Me neither, Tom."

"Walker." A young woman approached, her eyes warm with congratulations. "Walker, you rogue. Why didn't you tell any of us?"

He winked at her. "Seth Olson would nail my hide to the barn if I'd stolen you."

"Seth?" Her eyes shifted to a tall, rawboned farmer who was talking with a group of men. "He doesn't know I exist." But a speculative smile now lightened her face.

Walker moved Sarah on to shake hands with the other guests.

Her new husband introduced her to a man who was the exact opposite of the handsome rancher. Small in stature, balding, with pale skin, the man wore wire-rimmed glasses, which he had taken off to clean as Walker and Sarah approached. "Caleb, I'd like you to meet Sarah…" He turned. "What's your last name?"

"*McKay,*" Sarah reminded him under her breath, smiling.

"Of course. McKay," he acknowledged. "Sarah, my good friend, accountant, and banker, Caleb Vanhooser."

"Pleased to make your acquaintance," Caleb greeted her, returning his glasses to his face and then grasping her hand solidly. "You could have knocked me over with a feather when I realized Walker was getting married today."

"Yeah." Walker smiled again at his bride. "It all happened pretty fast."

Later, Sarah donned her calico dress and moved through the rows of tables outside, pouring coffee, offering pie, and being the genial hostess. When Walker noticed, he pulled her aside.

"What are you doing?"

She gazed up at him warmly. "Serving our guests."

"You're not supposed to 'serve our guests.' It's your wedding reception."

"Really?" She stood back, assessing the crowd. "Looks the world to me like it's a barbecue."

"Look, I guess this was pretty underhanded. If you like, we'll do it again later—"

"No, this is perfect." She smiled. "I love barbecues."

Taking her arm, he ushered her to a chair and sat her down. She hoped to share a few private moments with him, but that wasn't to be. Women immediately crowded around her, and her hopes were dashed as he moved on.

Walker could hear her fielding questions from their guests and guilt struck him. *That was a rotten thing to pull on her, McKay.* So far she'd been nothing but compliant. He should have at least warned her theirs would not be the traditional marriage ceremony. He turned to look back. She was still sitting, chatting with the women.

But would she be there an hour later? Could he blame her if she up and left without a by-your-leave? What woman welcomed a barbeque on her wedding day?

Dusk streaked the reddened sky and lanterns were lit. Musicians stepped to the wooden platform and began taking their instruments out of cases. The sounds of fiddles and guitars filled the air.

Standing beside the gazebo, Walker chatted with friends who chided him about the surprise celebration.

"What gives, McKay? All these months and you never let on you had something like her, you old fox!"

"Figured you was bound to stay single the rest of your life."

"Bull changed your mind, did it?"

The men chortled, one reaching out to tap an angry scar still evident on Walker's left cheek.

"Pert near got yourself killed. You're lucky to get a second chance."

"Where have you been hiding this little beauty?"

Walker's eyes followed his bride, who was being waltzed around the dance floor by yet another man. Bride. Wife. That was going to take some getting used to.

As the men threw jovial arm punches, Walker took the affable ribbing in stride, his eyes on a radiant Sarah. He couldn't dispute the fact that his bride was a desirable woman. Her eyes sparkled, her laughter filled the spring air. Something stirred inside him, something he hadn't felt in a long time.

Something he didn't want to feel.

"Folks, gather around," S.H. hollered. "It's time to cut the cake!"

Walker watched a smile light Sarah's face when Flo emerged from the house carrying a large, three-tiered wedding cake. He silently thanked Flo for her amazingly adaptable skills. She'd produced a wedding cake faster than the average woman could cut one. The smile faded. What kind of groom would have forgotten the cake?

The customary exchange took place between the happy couple. Sarah sliced the cake and fed Walker a bite. He did the same, his eyes meeting hers over the tip of the fork. The sincerity in her gaze puzzled him. She was like a breath of fresh air to a stale room. Why was she here? And why would a woman like her need to marry a stranger?

It was late when guests began departing. Parents loaded children into buckboards and wagons, while others, reluctant to give up the merriment, danced beneath the full moon. The musicians seemed ready to play all night, if necessary.

The bride had disappeared upstairs earlier. Walker stood beside the barn, his eyes focused on the lamp burning in the upstairs window. Sarah would be getting ready for bed, brushing her hair, putting on a white silk gown…

Desire rose in him. But a whisper of fear was there too. Sarah was an outsider. The trick would be to allow her into his life but still keep a safe distance emotionally, so he wouldn't fall too hard and be burned again. A man didn't have to love a woman to live with her. He could spend the next fifty years with her in the house and never give her his heart. The deed was done. He and Sarah Livingston were man and wife. There was no going back now, even if he could. He headed for the house.

When he tapped on the bedroom door, Sarah answered with a soft, "Enter."

Candlelight spilled over the pristine sheets. His bride was sitting in the middle of the bed, waiting for her groom, her hair falling to her waist. Sarah McKay's gaze fastened on him, issuing a silent but unmistakable invitation.

"Are the guests gone?"

"A few are still dancing." He glanced at her, unbuttoning his shirt. He was surprised when she watched, her eyes brimming with interest. Peeling the shirt off, he tossed it on the chair atop her wedding gown.

She slid out of bed, padding over to him. Meeting his gaze, she smiled. Then her fingertips skimmed featherlight over the scars on this chest. She frowned. "Do they hurt?" When he didn't answer, she looked up at him and said softly, "It's the wife's duty to be concerned for her husband, isn't it?"

"I believe it is." He reached out to take her in his arms.

"Am I too bold?" she asked, hesitancy creeping into her voice.

"No, ma'am," he whispered.

"Good," she whispered back. "I only want to please you."

He was aware of the sounds of "The Missouri Waltz" drifting through the open window. He doubted he'd ever hear the melody again without remembering this night and this woman. Their mouths met, and his last coherent thought seemed odd.

For the first time in my life, S.H.'s nagging makes sense.

Chapter Nine

Stirring, Sarah shielded her eyes against the sunlight as she reached for Walker. Morning rays fell across the empty pillow where he'd lain beside her all night, his breathing slow and even. She smiled, quietly humming "The Missouri Waltz," which had unofficially become their wedding song. She was a wife—and hopefully she would be a mother soon. She lifted her head and her sleepy gaze scanned the room. She was alone.

Her wedding dress lay next to Walker's rumpled suit. It was hard to imagine that a day earlier, in this very room, Flo had been helping her dress, careful that every hair was in place. She smiled at the thought of Walker's "barbecue" wedding, recalling the sights and sounds, the guests celebrating long into the night.

At least that part of her dream had remained intact. The only thing more exciting than the wedding had been the wedding night—her first night as Mrs. Walker McKay.

The door opened softly and Walker came in carrying a tray of steaming coffee and cinnamon rolls from the kitchen. When he saw that she was awake, color crept up his neck and he mumbled a good morning.

"I thought you might want to sleep in," he said, setting the tray on the cedar chest at the end of the bed. "Yesterday was a big day."

She eyed the tray. "Do you cook too?"

"Flo left the rolls for us. I made the coffee. Hope you like it strong, with cream."

A man who didn't like his coffee black. That was a refreshing change. Propping herself up on her elbows, Sarah tucked the sheet under her arms.

"I like it any way you do." When she first came to Spring Grass, she could barely drink the coffee that was thick enough to spear with a fork. Over the past few days she had grown used to the murky black liquid and actually started to enjoy her morning cup with Flo.

She muffled a weary yawn. "Yesterday was quite a day, with the barbecue and all." Their eyes met and she grinned impishly. Walker sat down at the foot of the bed, his shirt open just far enough to reveal his thick thatch of curly, dark brown hair interspersed with red scars. Her throat closed, realizing how close he'd come to death. Flo had said it was a miracle that the bull hadn't killed him.

God had spared him for her.

"Sorry. I wanted to make sure—" he began.

"The bride showed up?" She sipped her coffee, watching his reaction over the rim of the cup. At least he had the decency to look apologetic. "Wild horses couldn't have stopped me from being there. There was one tiny problem, though."

Walker frowned. "What's that?"

She leaned toward him and murmured, "I felt a little overdressed."

Walker responded, meeting her halfway. Their mouths were mere inches apart. "How do you feel right now?"

"Happy. Incredibly happy." She closed the distance for his kiss, sighing with pleasure.

Later, Sarah returned the cold coffee and untouched cinnamon rolls to the kitchen, and decided that she would enjoy married life. Immensely. Immeasurably.

Chapter Ten

I don't want to be underfoot, but that chair would look much better by this window."

Flo, a hand on her hip, stood by as Sarah bustled around the room cleaning up the final reminders of the previous day's wedding. She'd been as busy as a one-armed wallpaper hanger all afternoon, dusting, polishing, and rearranging. Considering the pinched look on Flo's face, she was getting on the housekeeper's nerves.

"Can't understand all the fuss. I've cleaned for the McKays all these years. I don't know why all of a sudden things need changin'." Flo side-stepped as Sarah eased past, clutching a broom and a dustpan. "I dust the parlor every morning, but with the extra work lately, getting ready for the wedding, I hadn't had time—"

"Oh, Flo, I don't want to interfere. I know you've kept this home forever, but it's my home now, and I'd feel dreadful having you do all the work." She swatted an imaginary dust bunny. "Really, don't you think the chair would look better over here?" She stood by the side window. "We can go into town and look for material for new drapes. Then we could change out the lamps—"

"Whoa! Walker's a generous man, but he likes his home the way it is."

Sarah frowned. "But the drapes are faded—and those old lamps are outdated." She didn't understand Walker's modest lifestyle when he apparently had all the resources he'd ever need, not to mention her wealth—which he didn't know about yet. How much could a new pair of drapes and a new lamp cost?

Flo dropped into the chair in question—a large brown leather monstrosity positioned in front of the fireplace. Sarah knew it was Walker's favorite because he sat in it every evening to read.

"Walker likes the drapes—and his mother bought his father this chair for a wedding present. Walker's happy with the way things are, young'un. He won't want you to change anything."

Sarah cocked her head. "Papa says the house is a woman's domain."

"Walker ain't Papa."

Sarah couldn't understand why Flo was being so stubborn about moving a silly old chair a few feet across the room. The more she tried to help, the more Flo vetoed her ideas. How was she supposed to be a good wife if she wasn't allowed to *do* anything? Sarah stared at the chair, determined. It didn't look right where it sat. The light was better by the window.

"Flo, I'll take full responsibility for moving the chair. If Walker notices and says anything, we'll move it back, but I don't think he will, because it'll look ever so much better over here. He'll be so glad for the change that he won't mind that it's not in its normal place." Sarah touched the worn leather lovingly. "Men don't care about furniture."

Once, Wadsy had rearranged the whole parlor and Papa hadn't noticed for weeks. Of course, he'd looked a little cross when she lit in on his study.

Flo snorted, crossing her arms. "Walker'll notice."

"You can tell a lady by the mark she leaves on her home." Sarah began pushing against the back of the chair with Flo still in it. "Now… please…help…me…move…this."

Flo got up. "Move it, then. But you'll have to do it yourself. I'll have nothing to do with it." Muttering something Sarah couldn't make out, the housekeeper left the room, confiscating the broom and dustpan along the way.

With a newfound resolve, Sarah shoved the chair to its new place by the window. After several tries at pushing and pulling and coaxing, she got it where she wanted it. Then she lugged a table from the opposite side of the room and placed it just so next to the chair for Walker to set his coffee cup on.

"Fresh-cut flowers this summer," she murmured, "and it's perfect." She stood back, assessing the newly arranged room with a satisfied smile.

The rest of the day she scurried about the house, polishing, adjusting, and putting her touches on Walker's home. Flo had barricaded herself in the kitchen so Sarah couldn't consult her about further domestic possibilities. There were so many things she could do to convert this house from a bachelor's hideaway to a family home.

She eventually braved her way into the kitchen to see if Flo had started supper. The housekeeper was standing at the sink chopping something green, and she refused Sarah's help when she offered it.

"Two is one too many in the kitchen," Flo said.

"I just thought I should be cooking for Walker on our first night together."

Flo paused, giving Sarah an exasperated look. "I've got most of it done, but if you insist, you can make the corn bread. Be sure to watch that it don't burn. I'm going to see if the men are back before I set supper on the table."

Sarah opened the back door for her, bidding Flo a pleasant goodbye. A minute later she was dumping cornmeal, flour, eggs, buttermilk, salt, pepper, and a wad of bacon grease into a ceramic bowl. Blending the thick mixture, she scraped it into a hot skillet and carefully slid the pan into the oven. Then she hurried upstairs to freshen up before Walker came home. She only had the one calico dress, but she could send for all her clothing once she informed Papa...she paused. She'd been so caught up in wifely duties she hadn't made a trip into town to send Papa a wire.

※

Walker strode into the parlor, stretching his aching shoulder. He thumped loudly across the room, leaving a trail of boot scuffs across the freshly polished floor.

Engrossed in a letter, he headed for his favorite chair, toeing off one boot and then the other as he walked. It had been a long day. He and S.H. had worked on both fences in the back field. The cattle were being moved to greener pastures, so today he'd had one problem after the other. After hours of hard work, the coolness of the wooden floor felt good to his sore feet.

He held the spring issue of his favorite seed catalog tucked under his arm. One of the ranch hands had picked it up at the mercantile just this morning. He'd read it through after dinner, but first he'd peek inside. Pausing in front of the fireplace, he folded the letter, flipped open the catalog, and sat down. Before he could read the first ad, he was flat on his back and seeing stars. The seed catalog flew into the fireplace, where it rested on ashes. Not yet able to grasp what had happened, he heard footsteps coming down the stairs two at a time.

Sarah appeared in the doorway. "Walker? What happened?"

"Where's my chair?"

"By the window."

Walker struggled to sit up and Sarah hurried to assist him.

"Goodness. Are you injured—"

"Who moved my chair? Flo!"

"Don't yell at Flo. I moved your chair. I thought you'd enjoy more light when you read, so—"

"I want my chair left where it was—Flo!" He shot Sarah a disbelieving look. "Does Flo know you're moving furniture?"

Sarah nodded. "Change does a body good. You need—"

"I want my chair *right* here." He pointed to the spot where the chair had previously sat. "Not by the window."

Sarah bristled at his tone.

"Where's my seed catalog?" he demanded. Sarah's eyes switched to the fireplace and his followed. He grunted and reached for the flyer.

"You're getting everything dirty!" she cried, trying to intercept the sooty catalog before he ruined a whole day's work.

Snatching it free, Walker started to shake it clean.

Irritated, Sarah took it back and swiped it across the front of her dress, leaving a black powder mark but saving the rest of the room.

Walker glared at her for a moment before proceeding to move the chair to its original spot. When he turned back, he saw tears hovering in her eyes as she clutched her dirty dress, and his anger cooled. "Look, I'd rather you leave things as they are."

Blinking, she lifted her chin. "I'm sorry. I was trying to be helpful. I just thought you might enjoy more light."

Walker uttered something under his breath. Women and tears. He'd forgotten how easy it was to hurt their feelings, especially about womanly things. He fell into his chair, removing his hat. "I didn't mean to hurt your feelings, Sarah, but at the end of the day I want to come home and sit down in my chair in its usual place." He paused, waiting for the tears to let up. "Flo knows I don't want the furniture moved."

"Even if it's a better arrangement?"

"I like my furniture kept in the same place, okay? If you want to move something, move the porch furniture."

"Who cares about porch furniture? A woman leaves her mark on her house—"

"Please leave things alone," he said, more gently this time. "Flo knows how I like things kept."

Sarah's brown eyes snapped. "*Flo's* not your wife. I am."

"Flo has taken care of me for twenty-eight years. You're going to have to live with that." When he saw a tear roll down her cheek, he mentally kicked himself. Marriage was going to take some getting used to. "I'm not spoiling for a fight, Sarah. I only mean…" he paused, sniffing the air. "What's burning?"

Sarah's jaw dropped. "The corn bread!" She raced out of the room and into the kitchen, where smoke was rolling out of the oven. Walker followed her, pitching the smudged seed catalog onto the table.

Grabbing an oven mitt, she opened the door and reached for the pan of corn bread. A plume of smoke billowed out of the oven, and she jerked back as a blast of hot air and flames assaulted her and burned her arm.

"Here, I'll get that." Walker stepped in and took the mitt away from her, and she moved away to smear butter on the burn. He extracted the corn bread, tossed the skillet on top of the stove, and beat out the flames with a dish towel. "There. Fire's out."

Sarah sank onto a kitchen chair and buried her face in her sooty hands. "I'm so sorry." She was more than sorry, she was mortified. What wife didn't know how to bake corn bread?

Hands coming to his hips, Walker shifted stances. "Did you burn yourself?"

"Yes."

He reached for her arm and examined the burn. "It's not bad."

"Flo told me to watch the bread and not let it burn, but I was busy arguing with you about that silly chair."

He glanced at the smoking skillet and sighed. "I like burned corn bread."

Flo came into the kitchen, fanning smoke with her apron. "What's goin' on?"

Walker pointed to the smoldering pan.

Flo focused on Sarah, who dabbed butter on her arm. Flo's eyes switched back to Walker. He shrugged. "Land sakes," Flo said, eyeing the damage. "I'll stir up a new batch."

"Set the food on the table, Flo." Walker winked at Sarah. "Tonight's corn bread will make a man appreciate good cooking when he gets it."

"Sarah."

Sarah opened one eye to see Walker inches from her face the following morning. He shook her shoulder again lightly.

"Get dressed. We're going to town."

Sarah propped herself up on one elbow. He seemed in an unusually good mood, especially after the humiliating incidents of the night before. After supper, Sarah had gone to their room and pretended to be asleep when he finally came to bed. She'd been Mrs. Walker McKay one day, and already she'd stirred up enough trouble to last a month.

Maybe Walker wanted her to get up so he could send her home—was that why they were going into town?

"Why?"

"Errands. Put on something presentable. We'll be leaving in half an hour."

Walker left the room and Sarah rolled onto her back. Wadsy's amused face danced in front of her. *Done cut off your nose to spite your face, haven't ya, baby girl?*

Sarah spotted a cup of coffee and some toast on the bedside table. Walker couldn't be too furious with her if he was bringing her breakfast in bed. Of course, he hadn't stayed to eat it with her.

Sarah consumed the buttery toast and the scalding coffee, hungry from not having eaten much dinner the night before. She slipped out of her nightgown and into her only dress. The fabric now had black soot across the front of it. She brushed her hair, nimble fingers braiding the mass into a thick plait.

In spite of the first blush of marriage, her concern over Papa's certain worry cast a heavy shadow. His health would be sure to suffer. Sarah scowled in the mirror and bit her lower lip. A quick telegram to Boston would suffice. Turning from the dressing table, she hunted through the nightstand until she found pen, ink, and paper. Perhaps it would be wiser to let him know she was safe and well but not inform him yet about the marriage. He might try to have the union annulled, though she was Walker's wife in every sense of the word.

> Dear Papa,
>
> I am sorry for my hasty departure. Be assured that I am quite content and well, but please don't look for me yet. I will send more information later. Please also give my love to Wadsy and Abe.
>
> Your loving daughter,
> Sarah

She folded the note and shoved it into her pocket. All she needed now was a chance to go to a telegraph office alone. How likely was that to happen? And would Papa be able to trace it?

When she came downstairs, both Flo and Walker were sitting at the dining room table.

"Well, she is awake!" Flo said, smiling.

Sarah wondered if Flo's happiness came from the thought of having her out from underfoot for a day. But the woman was good; Sarah knew that. She studied her Bible first thing every morning, and Sarah had heard her praying aloud while she dusted and cleaned.

"Thank you for the toast and coffee, Walker. I enjoyed it very much. I'm ready to go when you are."

Walker tossed down the last of his coffee and got up. "We may be gone all morning, Flo."

"Don't worry about me. You two have a good time." The housekeeper accompanied the newlyweds out to the front porch, where S.H. had the buggy hitched and waiting. "Gotta bake a cake for Mrs. Snyder. She's been ailing this week."

"Aren't we going for supplies? Shouldn't we take the wagon?" Sarah wondered what would make Walker take a day off just to go to town.

"We don't need the wagon today."

S.H. helped Sarah into the buggy and Walker reached for the reins. His secrecy about the unexpected outing puzzled her, but she was relieved he hadn't asked her to bring her valise so he could put her on the train back home.

"Your father founded Spring Grass?" she ventured, unsure of what topics he would be willing to discuss. She held her head high as other buggies passed, proud to be sitting beside her strong, handsome husband.

"Some forty years ago. He and Ma came to Wyoming with a group headed for the far West to find work. Ma loved the land, and Pa bought it for her. Used every penny he had. S.H. and Flo live in the original homestead."

"You were born in Flo's cabin?"

"Guess I was. Pa built the new house for Ma years later."

"It must have taken a great deal of money." Sarah colored at her forward remarks. She cared not a whit about Walker's bank account. Being a Livingston meant that she had more money than she could spend in a lifetime. "It's a lovely home," she amended. *A young couple in love, building a home together on the wild prairie. How romantic.*

"They earned every cent. And they paid a high price for the land. The hard work killed Ma, and Pa was gored by a bull and died at the scene." Walker fell silent, and she wondered what memories darkened his thoughts. They rode for a while listening only to the clicking wheels.

Finally Sarah ventured to speak. "You were in an accident involving a bull recently?"

Walker nodded, his jaw tightening. "I was luckier than Pa."

"Your folks had a good marriage?"

"The best."

Sarah watched his tanned, masculine hands flick the reins against the horse's flank. She wanted to know everything about him, including his life before he met her. She longed to ask a dozen things more about him, but the buggy had rolled into town before she could voice them. The newlyweds caught everyone's attention, and once in a while Sarah would see someone point and turn to the person he was with, no doubt talking about the "barbecue" at the McKay ranch.

The buggy pulled to a stop in front of the mercantile. Sarah took in the row of weathered buildings, and her excitement grew when she saw a telegraph office not far from the livery, a general store, and a miller to the west. The bank where Caleb Vanhooser worked sat across the street from the train station. Overshadowing the other buildings, it was easily the largest structure in town.

Springing from the buggy, Walker helped Sarah down. Though her feet were now planted firmly on the ground, he still kept hold of her hand. His touch sent off all kinds of dizzying sensations. Squeezing his arm, she whispered, "Have I mentioned how happy I am?"

With a smile she couldn't quite read, he patted her hand. "Look around in the store. I need to talk to Caleb for a minute."

"Is there anything I should get?" she asked as he started across the street, wondering why he'd brought her with him if he only needed to talk to Caleb.

"Just look around. I'm sure Martha will be happy to help you."

She stood until he disappeared into the bank. When she was sure he couldn't see her, she scanned the street for buggies and hurried across to the telegraph office. Using money she'd taken with her from Boston, she ordered the telegram to be sent and gave explicit instructions that the persons on the end of the line were not to be told where the telegram had originated. The request caused raised brows, but the clerk promised to adhere to her wishes. "It's your money," he said. His eyes lit up when she added an extra dollar, which he stuck in his pocket.

After that she crossed the street again, and a lively bell jingled her entry into the mercantile, bringing a tall, slight man with two missing front teeth from the back room.

"Can I help ya, miss?" He glanced at the wedding ring on her finger. "I'm sorry. Can I help ya, ma'am? We got some—" He stopped and scratched his head. "Wait now…yer the new McKay missus, ain't ya? Didn't recognize ya there for a minute."

Sarah smiled and blushed. This was the first time she had been referred to as a missus. She liked the salutation.

"Yes, and you are?"

"Denzil. Denzil Logan. Only got ta meet ya for a second at the barbecue—I mean, weddin'. Quite a surprise for us all."

"Denzil! Denzzzzzil! Who's there?" a sharp voice barked from the back room, startling them. Sarah turned in search of the source.

"It's Mrs. McKay, Martha! Walker's new bride." The shopkeeper looked apologetic. "It's the missus," he whispered, as if the marriage were a secret and he'd like to keep it that way.

A large, tall woman lumbered out of the back room, wiping her hands on the front of her apron. She looked to be a little younger than Flo, but Sarah was no good at guessing ages. Martha Logan's round red face gave Sarah the impression she had been in a smokehouse, with the sweat rolling down her forehead and plump cheeks.

"Well, so it is. Morning, Miz McKay."

"Good morning. Please, call me Sarah."

"All right, and you can call me Martha." Her greeting faded when she glanced at Denzil, who was leaning on the counter and admiring Sarah's red hair with an ear-to-ear grin.

"Denzil! Go thread the machine. And be quick about it!"

The henpecked spouse excused himself and disappeared behind a curtain. Martha turned back, a friendly smile replacing her frown. She looked Sarah up and down as if she were a ham laid out for Christmas dinner. Her open appraisal made Sarah uncomfortable.

"Well, let's see," she said, taking Sarah by the arm and turning her around to study her back side. "Whoever made this dress knew what they were doing. Wasn't you, was it?"

Sarah shook her head.

"No, suppose not if you're here. Well, let's get to work, then. Do you know your measurements, or should I take them myself?"

Sarah stared at the woman in disbelief and then glanced out the front window. Where was Walker? And why would this woman be interested in her measurements?

Martha Logan came around the counter and pulled out a tape measure. "I bet that waist ain't much more than sixteen inches. Hmm... last time I had a waist that tiny was right before I married Denzil. Hon, married life will change that waist. Hate to mention it."

Sarah smiled lamely. "Yes, ma'am."

"Call me Martha, hon."

"I'm sorry, Martha, but I'm not sure what you're talking about. I came in here to..." Why *had* she come in here? Because Walker had insisted, that's why.

"Don't know what I'm talkin' about? Why, I'm talkin' about when ya have babies. You can't expect to keep that figure if you're gonna be birthin' McKay young'uns. Look at me." She patted her round stomach, the apron's fabric stretched full. "Had five before Doc told me not to have any more."

Sarah's gaze moved through the store for signs of children, but there were none.

"They're in school," Martha clarified, as if reading her mind.

Sarah considered backing away from the strange woman and leaving the store, but just then the bell jingled and Walker came in, his hat in his hands.

"You almost done?" he asked.

"Walker, you got a stubborn little lady here. I asked her for her measurements, but she doesn't seem to want to tell me." The woman grinned and brought her hands to her ample hips "Never seen a girl so fidgety when it comes to getting measured for dresses."

Sarah shot Walker a puzzled look. "Dresses?"

"Oh, honey, didn't your man tell you? You're here to get a mess of new dresses. Seems Walker don't want you running around in calico. Never found anything wrong with the fabric myself, but some folks are more picky than others, I suppose." She faked a frown and shook a finger at Walker. "Some are too rich for their own good."

"New dresses?" Sarah turned to face her husband.

"I noticed you only have the one. I had one of my ranch hands ride into town late last night to see if Martha would be willing to make a few." Amused blue eyes rested on hers. Sarah opened her mouth to deny that she needed dresses. She had closets full—but then the garments would need explanation.

"Can't have a McKay wearing the same dress the rest of her life."

She clasped her hands together in front of her and turned to Martha. "So you wanted my measurements because you're the town seamstress." Except for her wedding dress she had never, ever worn anything that Wadsy hadn't sewn with her own hands, but she guessed that was about to change.

"The best in town and don't you forget it!" Martha said, beaming. "Of course, Bessie Higgins will swear she is, but don't believe her."

Martha ushered her into the back room, shooing Denzil back to the front with a wave of her beefy hand. Among a variety of dressmaker's forms and material, the storekeeper's wife took Sarah's measurements.

When she was finished and Sarah emerged from behind the curtain, Walker was browsing the store, looking at farm implements and supplies.

"Martha said I'm to pick out fabric for my dresses. How many should I choose?"

"As many as you want. Just don't break the bank."

She smiled at her husband, hoping he knew how much she appreciated his generous gesture. Of course, when her secret was out and she told Papa about the marriage, he would send her wardrobe to Spring Grass and she would be buried in dresses.

Most of the samples on the table were plain, everyday fabrics, with none of the fancy taffetas and silks the dressmakers back East carried. She looked up to see Walker watching her. She blushed and picked up a bolt of brushed cotton.

"Do you like this?" She held it up next to her face.

"Fine."

She held the bolt at arm's length and studied it. The fabric was a deep crimson. "I think it may be too red for me."

She held up another, a light yellow. "How's this one?"

"Fine."

"I don't know...maybe it's too bright." She smiled. "Why don't you come over here and choose one for me?"

Walker hesitantly came over to the table and shuffled through the fabrics. He picked up a bolt of light rose.

"This one." He held it up to her. "It looks all right."

"Not pink. I have red hair."

"So?"

"Redheads don't usually wear pink."

He picked up a bolt of black.

"Black? Widow's weeds?"

"Okay—you choose," he said, laying the fabric back on the table. "Order what you want from Martha's selection or special-order something if that suits you better. I'll be out front." He turned to Denzil. "Put it on my account, Denzil."

Denzil glanced up from restocking canned tomatoes on a shelf. "Sure thing, McKay."

Sarah scolded herself for being so picky. She'd asked Walker to help and then criticized his choices. Martha came out from the back and approached Sarah, who was reconsidering the pink fabric.

"I think I've hurt his feelings, Martha. I didn't like what he chose for me."

"Honey, men aren't worth a hoot when it comes to fabric. Especially Walker. I'm surprised he didn't pick a saddle blanket." The women laughed, and Sarah was reminded of the new saddle and blanket her father had bought for her one Christmas. It was truly awful.

"Honestly, I don't know what to choose," Sarah admitted.

"Why don't you look through the samples I have in the back and see if you want to order something special? I have a feeling your man'll pay for anything you ask."

In no time Sarah had chosen five fabrics and patterns she liked, thanked the woman, and left to join her husband, who was now chatting with a group of elderly men on the front porch.

"Ready to go?" Walker asked.

"Whenever you are." She smiled back, nodding to the men as she stepped lightly to the buggy.

For the first time, she felt truly married.

Chapter Eleven

I s there any way to trace where it came from?"

Lowell set Sarah's telegram aside, his face lined with worry. Two weeks had passed, and the only sign of his daughter was the telegram that had arrived that morning. He was plain put out that Allan Pinkerton himself hadn't found time to work on the case. Perhaps he should wire the head of the agency and explain exactly how urgent the matter was. Would this female detective be able to handle the case as well as Allan?

Kate Warne was a pale woman, and Lowell wondered if she suffered ill health. Her eyes flashed from Mr. Livingston to Wadsy, who said she couldn't imagine where else Sarah might be. Lowell's initial irritation had blossomed into fear that his daughter might have met with ill fortune.

"Your daughter, or whoever sent this wire, put a block on it. We can't know for sure where it came from. We've checked with everyone on the list you provided and found no one who has either seen or heard from Sarah, including her friend Julie in New York." The detective accepted a cup of tea from Wadsy. "We checked the records on all outbound trains the day of your daughter's disappearance and every day for a week afterward."

"She wouldn't take a train. She'd know I could trace her whereabouts."

"She could have done so under an assumed name. She may have gotten a ride to the station in a passing buggy, although that seems unlikely from what you tell me. She isn't bent on harm, just headstrong. I've spoken to the clerk who was working the early morning shift on the day you discovered her missing, and he said that only one girl boarded the train that morning. He was quite certain that the young lady's parents accompanied her to the station. He said she seemed to be greatly upset about something."

Lowell eased to the edge of his chair. "Could it have been my Sarah? What did this girl look like? I wouldn't put it past her to have hired someone to act as chaperones. When she's upset, she's likely to do whatever it takes to accomplish her goal."

Like the time she had set off to Philadelphia. He'd found her selling flowers on a street corner. He shook his head. "Laverne, I've tried."

"Pardon?"

"Laverne. My deceased wife. I was telling her I have tried to raise our daughter properly."

"Yes, sir."

Wadsy twisted and untwisted her apron. "Oh, my. What's happened to my baby girl?"

Kate opened a folder and flipped through the pages. "Do you recognize the name Lucy Mallory?"

"No." Lowell sank back in his chair. He watched Miss Warne scan her notes.

"The station clerk reported that the girl boarding the train had brown hair and brown eyes and was wearing a light blue dress, to his best recollection. An older man and woman purchased her ticket. He assumed they were her parents."

"Don't sound like our baby girl. Who'da gone with her?" Wadsy asked.

"No," Lowell said. "Sarah has red hair. The clerk would have recognized that mane."

"I talked to several station clerks, and they claim that neither your daughter, nor anyone else matching the young lady's description, bought a ticket to board the train the week of her disappearance. I can check again if you would like."

Lowell got up and moved to the window. *Where has she gone?* He didn't want to think of what might have happened to her. She could have run away with anyone—or, even worse, she might be dead. He rubbed his temples. Neither he nor Wadsy had slept much over the past couple of weeks. "Are you sure there wasn't anyone else? Maybe someone they couldn't readily identify?"

Miss Warne checked her notes again. "The only other person boarding on the morning of your daughter's disappearance was a young man. The conductor said he looked to be less than twenty years old, but he couldn't be certain."

Lowell turned from the window to meet Wadsy's hopeful eyes. He knew they were thinking the same thing.

"Sarah has dressed like a boy to escape before. She used Blue Boy's— Abe's grandson's—clothing. Why didn't we think of this earlier?" Striding back to the desk, Lowell sat down. "That's it. Sarah dressed like a boy. That's why no one noticed a redheaded young woman leave that morning."

Kate frowned and checked the files again. "According to the conductor, he says the boy was young, wore a hat, and kept his head down. He boarded with only one small valise."

"Was it brown with a gold clasp?" Wadsy asked.

"The report doesn't say. If you give me a detailed description of the bag, I'll talk to the conductor again and see if he recalls. You believe this person could be Sarah?"

"I can't be sure, but I want you to explore every option. My daughter…" Lowell paused and turned away, momentarily overcome by emotion. "We have to find her, Miss Warne." He glanced back at her. "She means everything to me."

The woman's sharp features softened for a moment. She made a few notes in a small black book as Wadsy described Sarah's valise. Meanwhile, Lowell summoned Abe into the room.

"Abe, is it possible that Sarah got into your grandson's clothes? We're thinking she might have dressed as a boy that morning."

Abe's gaze drifted toward the window. "Blue Boy ain't said nothin' 'bout it, but I could check if you want."

"Do that, Abe. It's the only lead we have."

The detective closed her notebook. "We'll talk to the clerk again. Perhaps we've overlooked something." She covered her mouth with her handkerchief and coughed.

"That's a nasty cough, Miss Warne. Ya want some of my cough remedy?" Wadsy asked.

The detective smiled. "Thank you, but I'm afraid syrup won't help." She got up to leave. "We'll try to locate this Lucy Mallory and her parents, Mr. Livingston. Perhaps they saw someone who fits your daughter's description on the train or in the surrounding area that morning."

"If Sarah was still in Boston, you would have found her by now," Lowell said. "I'm offering a twenty-five-thousand-dollar reward for anyone who can lead us to her whereabouts. Someone must know something. I'd give up my railroad to have my daughter safely back home."

Miss Warne extended a hand to him. "I'll make this my first priority, Mr. Livingston. We'll find your daughter and return her to you."

Lowell rose and shook her hand. "Thank you, Miss Warne. Please keep me informed of any further developments, however small."

Wadsy escorted the lady detective from the study, and Lowell returned to his desk and gazed at Laverne's picture. "Don't worry, dear. We'll find her. I will stop at nothing to bring her home." Tears that had been threatening to fall all afternoon finally rolled down his cheeks, and he swiveled his chair to face the window. Every day he sat here, looking out at the street in the hope that he'd see Sarah walking up the sidewalk. But weeks had passed, and still there was no word of his daughter's whereabouts.

God, bring my child home. I know you have a right to turn away from me. I've not always been as faithful to you as I could have been. Forgive me.

Don't let me lose both Sarah and Laverne. Don't break this weary soul completely, Lord. I'll do better. I'll be a more obedient child myself, Lord. Just bring my little girl safely home.

He wiped his eyes when Wadsy returned.

"Sarah can't believe I won't try to find her regardless of this sketchy news. How do I know that she sent this? What if some no-goods are getting ready to extort money from me?"

"The telegram don't say nothin' about a payoff, does it?"

"No, but that doesn't mean I can trust this message. I'll keep Kate on the case." He awkwardly reached out to take the servant's hand. "We're getting closer, Wadsy. We'll find her any day now."

"Yes, sir." *Good Lord, let him do jest that. Mr. Livingston isn't lookin' so good these days. Got those worry lines around his eyes. Appetite's gone.* "Let me have Will fix you somethin' to eat. Jest a bite to fill your belly. You ain't et a decent meal in weeks."

Nodding, Lowell turned away. "Maybe some chicken—and bread and butter. And a few of those pickles I like. Maybe a slice of blackberry pie too. Tell Will not to forget the cream."

"Yes, sir." Pleased, Wadsy walked away.

That telegram must have set Mr. Livingston's mind to rest. He's askin' for cream and butter again. He must be feelin' powerful relieved.

Chapter Twelve

The McKay kitchen blossomed with Sarah's chatter. Her mind worked faster than Walker could think. *She's nervous,* he told himself as he ate breakfast and absently nodded at her cheerful prattle. Once she settled in she'd quiet down.

Having two strong-willed females in the house wasn't easy. Flo complained about having Sarah underfoot and that she took her "wifely" role too seriously. He wasn't sure how he should handle the dispute, but if he let them establish their territories on their own, he figured he'd be far better off.

Sarah broke through his ponderings. "Walker, do you think we could have a party? A real party that is not a wedding pretending to be a barbecue?"

He kept his eyes on the seed catalogue he was reading. "I don't mind."

"Wonderful. I was thinking maybe a lavish event? Everyone could wear their finest attire. A nice formal dinner with rich satin tablecloths—and maybe one or two of the ranch hands could serve so Flo doesn't have to work so hard. We could serve coq au vin—"

"Whoa!" Walker frowned. "We're simple country folk. Don't serve anything fancy and keep the list to a hundred folks. Beef and potatoes and none of that French stuff. Besides"—a flicker of a smile broke through—"you'd put a dent in my herd trying to feed all of our friends."

Sarah fell silent and he felt her gaze on him.

"You said 'our friends.'"

Walker sipped his coffee. "Did I?"

"You did. You said 'our friends.' I can't tell you how much that pleases me." She stepped closer to rest her hand on his shoulder. "Thank you for making me feel so welcome in your home."

"It's your home now." He hoped she wasn't going to go all womanly on him and cry.

"Yes, it is. Thank you again. It's a lovely thought."

Late that afternoon, Flo filled a jar with lemonade and wrapped it in a heavy cloth. Walker and S.H. were moving cattle nearby, and Sarah thought they would appreciate a cool drink. Though the distance wasn't far to walk, she asked a ranch hand to saddle one of the mares anyway. It had been months since she'd ridden, and she looked forward to the outing. She skipped upstairs to put on the new riding skirt Martha had made her.

Fifteen minutes later she was astride the mare and galloping to the south pasture. She missed her horse, Samson, and wondered if he missed her. They had ridden together nearly every day in the past few years. Once she'd cleared the air with Walker, she'd ask him to send for the animal.

The lemonade swished in the saddlebag. The mare's shod feet clipped merrily along the fields. Sarah's heart sang as she perched on the polished saddle. She was married to the man of her dreams. Other than not being able to see or talk to Papa or Wadsy, her life couldn't get any better. Soon she would tell Walker about the ruse, and then she would invite her family to come visit.

She spotted a shirtless Walker bent over a calf, and her pulse quickened. The heifer bawled for its mother, which S.H. held at bay.

Sarah approached quietly in order not to startle the men. Her gaze skimmed her husband's torso, resting on the vicious scars marring his olive skin. Reining in, she quietly admired him.

S.H. glanced up and grinned when he saw her. "That you, Sarah?"

Walker turned at the mention of her name. "What brings you all the way out here? Are you and Flo at it again?"

"No, I'm…" She struggled to remember the purpose of her visit. "I…"

"Came to see ol' Bessie here?" S.H. teased, slapping the cow on her side.

"No." Sarah felt her cheeks turn hot. "I thought you might be thirsty. I brought lemonade."

Both men chuckled and Walker released the calf, which ran bawling back to its mother. Then he lifted Sarah down from the mare and their eyes met and held for a long moment. Shivers raced down her spine. Was he beginning to love her a tiny bit?

He released her and then took the lemonade from the saddlebag and removed the lid. "Will you join us?" he asked, pouring the liquid into the tin cups she held for him.

"I'm not thirsty." Sarah could smell sweat and a mixture of shaving soap and musk.

S.H. took a long swallow. "Think I'll find some shade down by the creek."

Walker took a drink and then admitted, "Sounds like a good idea. It's warming up." When the foreman wandered off, her husband glanced her way. "Sure you won't have some?"

Declining the invitation, she dabbed perspiration off her brow. She didn't want to delay his work or be a hindrance to him.

His eyes skimmed her lightly. "Is that one of your new outfits?

She performed a mock curtsy. "Do you like it?"

He shrugged. "I don't know much about women's clothing. If Martha likes it, then it's fine."

Martha? What about me?

Walker sauntered to the stream, picked up a stone, and skipped it across the water. Sarah wished that S.H. weren't there so they could be alone. As if reading her mind, the old ranch foreman wandered farther downstream.

"It is really warm today," she observed.

Nodding, he washed his face in the stream, and then ducked his head underwater. Coming up, he shook his head, water flying everywhere.

Standing back, Sarah admired him, overcome with contentment. That's what she loved about her new husband. He was comfortable around her. He didn't act like a besotted fool—though a little more affection would be welcome. But that would come in time. They were growing closer every day.

Lifting her face to the sweltering sun, she silently prayed. *Dear Lord, I know I acted foolishly and unwisely, but it's turned out well. So well that I'm giddy with happiness. Thank you. And Papa will thank you once he meets Walker.*

Sarah doubted that even Wadsy could find fault with this man.

Chapter Thirteen

Sarah stepped out the back door that evening, drawing her wrap tighter around her shoulders. The air had cooled tonight, reminding her of Boston. Martha had included this beautiful soft wrap as a wedding present with the first dress she'd finished, and Sarah was thankful for its warmth.

Somewhere nearby, a wild animal called to its mate. Wolf? Coyote? Ordinarily she'd be curious to learn the source, but tonight she was just too tired to care. Sinking down onto the porch swing, Sarah thought about the long, exciting week, the wedding, then the days following when she'd acquainted herself with the rules and ways of ranch life. Papa would be quick to tell her she'd made her bed and now she'd have to sleep in it, but what a lovely bed it was. Walker was still detached in his new role, but she hoped that would change.

A smile raised the corners of her mouth and she shivered from thoughts of the tenderness Walker showed in the marriage bed. He was mindful of her innocence. She knew little of a man's way, but Wadsy had told her that all men were not alike. Some were good, and others were just plain inconsiderate. But not Walker. He was perfect.

Afraid he might read her thoughts, Sarah quickly looked away when the screen door creaked and her husband walked out. He paused, gazing up at the star-studded sky.

"Thought you'd be in bed by now."

"No." She fussed with her wrap, determined to ignore the powerful set of his shoulders. "Care to join me?" She patted the seat beside her. "It's a lovely evening."

"I didn't plan on staying out long. Just needed a breath of fresh air."

"Please. Sit." She scooted aside, making a place beside her. He eased down, the swing creaking beneath his added weight. The aroma of soap and the sunshine scent of his freshly ironed shirt drifted to her. Flo took care with his clothing, pressing each garment with a hot iron. Sarah had stood before Walker's open closet for a long time that morning, familiarizing herself with her husband's taste. He liked blue, with just a hint of starch in his collars. Denims were his choice of work clothes, but for social occasions he favored khaki, white shirts, and brown suits. Walker McKay was fastidious about his appearance, and that suited her fine.

The swing moved quietly back and forth. Moonlight bathed the honeysuckle trail along the front porch. Sarah could see a light burning in the bunkhouse. She'd yet to become friends with the ranch hands, but she would make it a goal to get to know them all soon. She intended to be a vital part of her husband's life in every way.

"Are you settling in comfortably?"

Sarah shifted at the sound of his voice, pulling her back to the present. "Yes, thank you. As long as I stay out of Flo's way."

"I take it you haven't had much experience in the kitchen."

"No…well, a little." She'd watched Will cook. And Wadsy had tried to teach her the finer arts of homemaking, but the lesson had not sank in. She much preferred reading magazines, wedding notices, or stories about faraway lands. Someday she wanted to go to Ireland, but Papa was always too busy to travel. Once he'd promised to take her, but he never had, and he had frowned on her going alone.

"I thought your letter said you cooked," Walker said.

"I do. A little." Very little.

"It doesn't matter. Flo is going to be rattled if you don't let her take care of the house and meals."

Sarah didn't intend to move in and abolish Flo's position in Walker's home, but she would like the freedom to consult with the housekeeper about food and furniture placement. She wanted to fit in, and part of fitting in meant being a wife and performing wifely duties, but she also knew she couldn't storm in and demand that everyone change for her. Eventually Flo would allow her into the kitchen, and she'd be careful not to overstep her bounds.

The hypnotic sound of the creaking swing blended with the sounds of the early spring evening. *This is what I've wanted all my life. Husband and wife enjoying each other's company at the end of the day.* And soon, if the good Lord blessed them, there would be three of them. A real family. Her life was finally perfect—with the exception of two small, niggling doubts. What she'd done was deceitful. And poor Papa. She *must* write the letter informing him of her marriage, but to do so meant telling Walker of her deception, and she wanted to be very sure there would be no retribution when she confessed her ploy. Fear that he would find the silly switch anything but what it was—a solution to everyone's problems—troubled her. He did not seem the type of man to find a ruse amusing. The lie was the only fly in an otherwise blissful ointment. Papa would forgive her peccadillo, but would Walker forgive her? Especially after Trudy's deception?

"Nice evening."

"Yes, lovely." Certainly he must be tired. He'd left the house shortly after sunup and hadn't returned until supper. Flo said Walker wasn't afraid of work. Like his father before him, he put in twelve to fourteen hours a day.

"Are you tired?" she asked.

"Tired?"

Color flooded her cheeks, so aware was she that the question sounded more like an invitation than casual conversation.

"I know you work very hard."

He smiled. "Are you?"

"Somewhat."

"Is this another one of the new dresses?" His fingers lightly toyed with a lock of her hair, playfully tugging it.

"Do you like it?"

"It's real flattering on you. Will you wear it to church in the morning?"

"Yes. Thank you."

Sarah sighed with contentment. If she hadn't met Lucy Mallory, she would be in New York now, hiding from Papa and searching for a man who filled her dreams and expectations. God had dropped Walker McKay in her lap.

Turning, she smiled. "It is getting late," she whispered. "And you do need your rest."

Chapter Fourteen

Sarah decided that no time was to be wasted arranging her first McKay social. She couldn't wait to plan her first husband-wife event for the ranch.

The day before the party, Flo invited her back into the kitchen on a limited basis.

"Darlin', you're trying too hard. If you'll let me do the work and just help instead of taking over, we'll move faster."

Today the two women were baking apple pies. Flo tried teaching Sarah how to make a crust using flour, a pinch of salt, lard, and a little water. Sarah's attempts turned out tough and doughy compared to the light and flaky works of art Flo eased from the oven. With each failed attempt, Sarah grew more flustered. She had watched Will prepare everything from tea biscuits to roasts. How could a simple piecrust defeat her?

"No, no, no." Flo stopped slicing apples and reached over to where Sarah was attempting to roll out another batch of crust. "You're pressing too hard. The crust won't be thick enough." The housekeeper confiscated the rolling pin and ran the pin back and forth until the dough was the right thickness. "I never saw the likes. Didn't your mama teach you how to cook?"

"Not really." Actually, she'd never seen her mama cook a single dish.

Will had cooked for the family forever. She sighed. "I want to be a good cook for Walker, but maybe I'm just not made for cooking."

"Don't give up. Cooking takes time and practice." Flo handed her the pin and returned to the apples. "You need to relax and enjoy your marriage. In time everything will fall into place."

"I'm trying, but it seems like I'm going backward instead of forward."

"Why don't you take a little break? Maybe if you took a nice walk, you'd feel better. When you come back, we'll start over." Flo pushed a bowl of bruised apples across the table. "Stop by the barn; the mares will appreciate a treat. There's nothing they like better than apples, and gettin' out of the kitchen for a few minutes will do you good."

Sarah had the strong feeling it would do Flo even better. She formed her apron into a cradle and Flo dumped several apples into it. Sarah smiled. "I suppose I could check on Diamond."

"She's with foal, isn't she?"

"Yes. She was bred late so she has a few more weeks yet."

She and Walker had taken a moonlight walk one evening, and they'd stopped at the barn to check on his personal stock. Diamond—Sarah's favorite—was Walker's prize mare, and Walker was anxious to see the foal delivered safely.

Flo shooed her out of the kitchen and into the midday light. Sarah savored the heat of the warm earth in the fields. A dozen ranch hands would be planting hay tomorrow. Walker had talked about it all week long, hoping that the rain would hold off until they could get the crops into the ground. Clutching the apples to her, Sarah sauntered toward the barn.

It took a moment to adjust to the dim light of the moist interior. Mares stuck their noses over their gates to sniff at Sarah's treats as she walked by. The breath from their big, round nostrils stirred up dust when they snorted.

She offered an apple to the first animal, a large roan. Long lips felt around the treat and enormous teeth split it in half with a crunch. Sarah jumped, laughing as the mare withdrew to chew with noisy satisfaction. She held up the second half of the apple and the animal made soft nickering sounds in her long, sleek throat. Patting her head, Sarah offered the other half and moved to the second stall.

Diamond's stall was larger than the others. The horse raised her muzzle from the water bucket when she heard Sarah approach. Diamond was a full sixteen hands high, coal-black with white markings on her forelock and front fetlocks. Sarah could see why she was Walker's favorite. She had enormous brown eyes that kindly asked what Sarah had brought.

"Here you go, girl." Sarah lifted an apple. The horse sniffed and took it from her hand in one bite, leaving a trail of water and saliva in her palm. Sarah wrinkled her nose.

"It's very unladylike to drool. If I couldn't see that you obviously have found a mate, I would remind you that men don't appreciate this kind of thing. Of course, horses may be different." Balancing on tiptoes, she stroked Diamond's mane while the mare crunched contentedly. She ran her hand up and down the long nose. "Now, Diamond, you are a lucky lady. You don't have to cook or clean or worry about not being able to cook or clean, right, girl?" Sighing, Sarah stepped back to move across the aisle to the next mare suddenly overcome with guilt. These beautiful creatures reminded her of home. Papa had been ecstatic when he'd given her Samson.

"You shore nuff are a purty one," a kindly voice said from behind her.

Sarah started, dropping the remaining apples into the hay. Leaning around the stall, she spotted a small, grizzled-looking man, holding a bowl of potato peelings. Potster. She'd seen the bunkhouse cook around, but they had not spoken

"I didn't hear you come in," she said.

"Sorry. I wasn't expectin' to find a little redheaded filly in the barn." He turned and spat into the hay. "I was enjoyin' your speech to Diamond there. And it sounded like Diamond was enjoying it, too, wasn't ya, girl?" He moved to the mare's stall, reaching into the front pocket of his vest for a lump of sugar.

Color sprang to Sarah's cheeks. "You shouldn't have eavesdropped. That's not polite."

A tobacco-stained grin widened. "Sorry if I offended ya, Mrs. Walker." Removing his battered hat, he made an old-fashioned, sweeping bow, dislodging some of the potato peels. "But I always speak my piece."

Sarah relaxed. "You're the bunkhouse cook."

"Potster. Bunkhouse cook and all-around maid. Closer to a mother hen sometimes." He wheezed a dry laugh and returned the hat to his head. "These boys need lots of lookin' after."

Sarah held out a hand. "It's nice to meet you, Mr. Potster, sir."

He frowned. "Mr. Potster, *sir*? You must be from the East. Round here I'm just Potster or Potsie." He bent down and picked up the scattered apples. "I believe you was in the process o' feeding the girls?"

Sarah took the remaining apples and tossed them into the stalls. "I should get back to the kitchen. Flo's teaching me how to bake pies, but I'm having trouble with the crust."

Potster threw his head back and laughed, slapping a thick thigh. "Flo's crust cain't hold a candle to mine. You come with me and I'll teach ya how to make a pie that will make Flo cry."

The last thing she wanted was to make Flo cry. "Thank you, Mr. Potster, but—"

"Just plain Potster, honey. No 'mister' to it." Potster spat into the hay and rubbed his chin. "No offense, ma'am, but from what I hear, Flo don't want you underfoot in her kitchen."

Sarah bristled. How dare he insult her…her…her what? Her rights? Actually, she didn't have any yet. Nobody had given her run of the house, especially Flo. *Face it, Sarah McKay. You can't boil water without burning it.* Potster's rough honesty disarmed her.

"It's not that I haven't tried. Honestly, I have. I just don't know how to cook."

"People ain't born knowin' how to cook. Ya gotta learn the skill."

"I'm trying. Flo's been working with me, but I'm afraid I'll never be able to make a decent piecrust or pan of corn bread."

"Why, corn bread's th' easiest thing on earth. Here." He reached for her arm. "Help me scatter these potato peelin's to the chickens, and we'll go back to the bunkhouse and make corn bread for the hands' supper."

"I'd better not." Sarah shook her head, thinking about the last pan of corn bread she'd tried to make. Walker had to beat the fire out with a dishcloth. "The men would starve if I cooked for them. Besides, I promised Flo I'd be right back."

"If I know Flo, she's doing fine without ya, and I could use yer help. I got thirty-five hungry men to feed! You'll learn a thing or two about fixin' vittles, an' I'll have a pretty face in m' kitchen for a change."

Sarah considered the request. She supposed any advice would be helpful. "I should tell Flo where I am in case she needs me."

Potster winked. "You do that, an' I'll meet you at the bunkhouse."

He chuckled a few minutes later when Sarah told him that Flo seemed relieved that Sarah would be spending the next few hours in his kitchen instead of hers.

Chapter Fifteen

Sarah settled on a tall stool and watched Potster slice potatoes with deft precision. In front of her was a large bowl and an assortment of cornmeal, eggs, flour, a mixture of cream of tartar, baking soda, and clabbered milk, buttermilk, salt, and bacon grease.

"I mix all of this together?" Sarah asked when Potster urged her to get to work. "How do I know how much to add?"

Potster winked at her. "Just start mixin'. I'll help when you get stuck."

Sarah lifted a dollop of bacon grease and flipped it into a heavy iron skillet. It seemed very odd to her that she should be taking cooking lessons from one of Walker's ranch hands.

"Enough?" she asked.

Potster glanced up from his potatoes and craned his neck to peer at the skillet. "Good enough. Now stick the skillet in the oven and let the grease get good and hot afore you add the cornmeal mixture. Remember, yer cookin' for hungry men. We'll need four skilletfuls."

Nodding, Sarah carried the pan to the woodstove.

Potster's laugh rang out. "You got spunk, girl. Ain't no doubt about that. I can see why Walker hitched to your wagon."

Sarah's cheeks flamed when the ranch hand slapped his knee with his free hand. "Can you open the oven door for me?"

"You gotta do this yourself or you'll never learn." He wiped his hands on a cloth and set the potatoes to boil.

She eased the skillet to a table and then opened the oven door. "I'm planning our first party as man and wife. There will be around fifty guests. How much meat do I need?" She slid the pan in and closed the door.

"Fifty, huh? That's purty small for a McKay gatherin'."

"I don't want to overstep my bounds, especially on my first event."

"Well, then I'd say five turkeys and four hams, and you'll need a pan of dressing for every five folk."

Sarah's face brightened. Arithmetic was her best subject. The numbers began ticking in her head. She quickly scooped another thick lump of grease from the can. "So cooking is all about math!"

He chuckled. "Never thought of it that way. My ma taught me. There were fourteen of us young'uns, and we all had to pitch in and help or we didn't eat. Ma was a pinch and smidgen cook."

"A what?"

"A pinch o' this, a smidgen o' that." He grinned. "That woman could cook for a king—imagine she is right now. She died ten years ago." He paused. "I suppose a body could write all these things down, but I never took the time."

"Just a pinch and a smidgen and you can produce edible meals?"

"Never had a man leave my table complainin' or hungry. As for learnin' to cook? After a while, you'll do it without thinkin'."

Sarah set to work. "Potster, you've worked for the McKays a long time, haven't you?"

"Since I was a knee-high to a grasshopper."

"Then you knew Walker when he was a little boy?"

"Helped deliver him." Potster poured water over cut potato chunks. "It was rainin' cats and dogs that day."

"What was my husband like when he was a small?"

She saw glimpses of "boy" still in him. The way he loved cookies and milk, and how he'd find humor in the oddest things.

"Oh, he was the typical little boy. Had more energy than a kid ought to have." The cook chuckled. "Got his backside tanned real often."

Sarah glanced up. "His father was a strong disciplinarian?"

"He was when you set his hayfield on fire."

Sarah grinned. "Walker did that?"

"Twice. Both times when he wasn't supposed to have a match any-where near him."

The afternoon flew by as Sarah ladled yellow batter into heavy iron skillets and talked about Walker's youth. The more she learned about Walker McKay, the more she loved him.

"Now," said the cook with a grand flourish, "the secret of making corn bread is…" He slid the pans into the hot oven and closed the door.

"Putting them in the oven?" Sarah peered over his shoulder.

"No," he said, his voice a gravelly whisper. "Taking them out at exactly the right time. The Potster's secret."

Sarah grinned, thankful she'd accepted this delightful man's invita-tion. Walker would be surprised!

Along with stories about Walker, Potster shared his cooking secrets and kept Sarah transfixed with tales of the West—the outlaws, cow-herds, dust, and ponies that dotted the beautiful, wide-open land. Be-fore she knew it, supper was ready, including four beautiful batches of perfectly browned corn bread.

She jumped when she realized the late hour. Flo would think she'd gotten lost! Throwing her arms around a startled Potster's neck, she squeezed. "I must leave now, but thank you so much."

Potster nodded. "Time shore got away from us."

She smiled. "Thank you for the cooking lesson. May I visit again?"

"Yer welcome as rain. It's been a real pleasure, Mrs. Walker."

"Call me Sarah."

His features turned bright red. "Yes, ma'am. Sarah."

"And you will be at the party this weekend?"

Potster frowned. "Would I have to wear my fancy duds?"

"Others will, but if you're more comfortable in your ordinary duds, then wear them." She had yet to adjust to these folks' peculiar vernac-ular.

A smile lit the cook's face. "Then I'll be there. Wouldn't miss it for the world!"

Chapter Sixteen

Wagons, horses, and guests eager for another McKay event crowded into Spring Grass on Saturday. News of the latest gathering had traveled faster than Sarah's invitations. Mild breezes and blue skies greeted the guests.

Walker leaned against a porch railing, keeping away from the party-goers filing through the house and out into the yard. In the midst of the attendees, his wife made sure that everyone had punch as they drifted around, chatting before retiring outdoors. Flo and Sarah had the place shining. Walker had been so busy planting the past two days that he had barely seen his bride.

Toward the end of the week, she had been up earlier than he was, preoccupied with the party and cooking lessons. He had heard Potster was tutoring her culinary skills. Cooking lessons from Potster. The two seemed an unlikely pair.

Music from guitars and banjos filled the air as guests mingled. He watched Sarah carry trays of smoked ham and cheese to the table. She suddenly turned from her task and met his gaze. "Why, Mr. McKay, what a pleasure to see you here. I'm so glad you could join the festivities." She playfully curtsied.

Walker conceded his absence with a nod. "I know I've been scarce lately. Planting season is a busy time."

"Hey, McKay, nice party," a voice called out.

Acknowledging the comment with a wave and a smile, Walker moved to join a growing group of ranchers on the opposite side of the porch. Sarah melted back into the crowd.

"So, Walker, how's ranching been treating you?" Blake Slayton asked.

"Looks to be a bumper year, Blake."

The remark brought a low, appreciative whistle from the other men. Every rancher there knew the pitfalls of a bad year, and they were quick to rejoice when one of them pulled off a good profit. Walker searched the faces of the men around him, many of whom were close friends. Rusty Johnson and his family had been on the same wagon train with Walker's parents. He and Rusty's sons had grown up closer than kin.

"Looks the same way over at the Circle J," Rusty offered. "We shore need it after the last few." Every man nodded in agreement.

"Maybe Walker should have married sooner." The men turned to see Caleb Vanhooser approaching. The accountant looked small and out of place among the ranchers. The men parted and welcomed him into their circle. He smiled nervously at the group.

Walker clapped the accountant on the shoulder affectionately. "I'd venture to say that this man and the good spring rains are partly accountable for the encouraging outlook."

Caleb removed his glasses and cleaned them with his handkerchief. "I think Walker's hard work deserves the praise."

Walker didn't know how he would have made it through his parents' deaths if Caleb hadn't been there to help him with the financial end of things. Walker was better with cattle than figures.

The group moved on, leaving Walker and Caleb alone on the porch. They spoke about the ranch and cattle prices until Sarah approached with punch. Caleb nodded and accepted a cup. "Lovely party, Mrs. McKay."

"Thank you." She extended the tray to Walker, who also accepted a cup. Inside, the first few notes of "The Missouri Waltz" drifted out.

"Very nice gathering," he commented. Was she aware of the song? Did it bring back memories of her wedding day?

"Thank you. I hope it isn't too large?"

"No." He took a sip of punch. "Looks to be about right, but I'm going to have to excuse myself. I have work to do in the barn before it rains."

"Today?" Her expression fell.

"I expected to be free, but unfortunately—"

"Can't your ranch hands do it?"

"No, Sarah. They're busy attending a party."

A strained silence formed. Caleb lifted his cup and swallowed some punch.

When she stiffened her back and walked away, Walker frowned. "What's wrong with her?"

Smiling, Caleb said, "You know women."

No, Walker didn't know women, but this one was starting to seem different. As he watched his wife walk away, he found himself wishing that he could stay a bit longer.

Chapter Seventeen

It was rare for Walker to take a day off, but the hay was taken care of, fences restored, and the push of work before and after the party left him needing a day of rest. Leaning close to the mirror, he slowly ran his razor down a cheek as he wondered what Sarah was up to this morning. She'd left the bed earlier than usual, murmuring something about baking biscuits.

He grinned when he thought of her in the kitchen. Potster had worked a miracle. His wife could now cook a skillet of corn bread that even Flo admired.

Sobering, he faced his image. Was that contentment he saw on his face? How could that be? He'd been married less than a month, and the tight lines around his eyes were gone. He studied the change, surprised at the transformation.

Whistling, he dressed and went downstairs, sniffing the air, which was laced with the smell of burning bacon. Potster couldn't change a moth into a butterfly overnight. Sarah's voice drifted to him from the kitchen.

"I don't think we should wake him. He was up very late last night." Her voice trailed off as she disappeared into the pantry.

Walker paused for a moment at the top of the stairs. Through the front window he saw Flo working in her early vegetable garden, so whom was Sarah talking to?

"What do you think, Brownie?" Sarah's voice came from the pantry, and Walker realized that she'd lured one of the cattle dogs into the kitchen. His grin widened as he pictured the old coonhound a captive audience, head cocked to one side, trying to decide what the female was saying. "Should I use white napkins or the blue ones? White is more practical, but blue matches his eyes…" Sarah started as Walker entered the room.

"You're awake. I was going to bring you breakfast in bed." She crossed the room and kissed him good morning. "I didn't wake you up, did I?"

Walker merely shook his head before sitting down at the table and watching her put the finishing touches on a breakfast tray, which she then carried to the table. He surveyed the damage before him and lifted a fork to run through undercooked eggs. Jagged pieces of eggshell floated in the gelatinous whites. Black specks dotted the heavily buttered toast. Four charred strips of what appeared to be bacon took up the rest of the plate. *Please, God, let "breakfast cooking" be on Poster's agenda.*

She sat down across from him. He couldn't escape. He had to eat this.

"Where's yours?"

"I'm not hungry. I've been too busy to think about eating." She grinned, propping her chin on her tented hands. "I'll just watch you enjoy your meal."

Walker took a bite of egg and toast and quickly chased it with a swallow of tepid amber liquid.

He peered inside the cup. What was it? Coffee? Hot tea? "Where's Flo? How come she didn't fix breakfast?"

Sarah smiled. "I gave her the day off. Since you're not working today, I thought we might spend some time together. You've been so busy with planting that we've barely had a moment to talk about the baby."

He glanced up. "Are you…?"

"I don't know—but if not I will be soon."

"Isn't it too early…?"

"Becoming parents doesn't require any specified length of time."

He never thought much about being a father, so he'd never contemplated the length of time it took to become one. He picked up a piece of bacon and studied it. "Time will tell. Once you conceive we'll talk about it."

"All right. We'll just spend a nice, relaxing day together."

Before they had gotten married, he hadn't thought about what it would mean to have someone underfoot most of his waking hours. What would it be like when babies screamed to be fed, toddlers raced up and down the hallways, and older kids banged doors shut, yelling back and forth?

Sarah stared at him expectantly, and it dawned on him that she was waiting for an answer. To what? He didn't have the slightest idea. His mind raced. *What had she been talking about? Babies? The house? New dresses?*

"Is that okay with you?" she said, still waiting. "For us to spend time together today? You said you were taking the day off."

"Oh." *That's* what she'd asked. "Yeah. Give me half an hour to catch up on my book work and then I'll join you."

"Take all the time you need."

He took a bite of runny eggs and forced himself to swallow. "Your cooking is getting better every day."

A smile broke across her features. "You think so?"

"Considerably better." He excused himself a moment later.

"I'll be free as soon as I wash the dishes," she called. "We can walk down by the river if you like."

Walker entered the study and picked up his cattle register. Rubbing his eyes, he edged toward his chair, listening to the third chorus of "Amazing Grace" as Sarah washed dishes. He smiled when he heard the back screen door flap. Brownie had escaped to the porch.

Walker kept careful track of all his stock in the register: when they were born, bred, and sold. Caleb insisted. Easing down, he suddenly flapped his arms wildly, searching for a seat. He fell backward as the register dropped to the floor. He lay motionless for a moment, stunned. Then...

"Sarah!"

She darted out of the kitchen.

He glared up at her but asked in a calm voice, "Did you move my chair again?"

"Yes, I moved it this morning. The light is so much better by the window, Walker. I know you like the chair in its regular place, but I thought if you'd just sit in it once by the window, you'd love it." She started picking up the scattered mail. "See how much better it is?"

Groaning, he shut his eyes. "I'm moving it back and, Sarah, don't, I repeat, don't move it again."

"I don't know what you're so upset about. Why don't you look before you sit down?"

"I don't want to look when I sit. I want to know my chair will be where I left it."

Sarah offered a hand up, which he refused as he pushed himself up from the floor. Giving her another short look, he moved the chair back to its usual place, sat down, and motioned for her to hand him the register.

"Do you need something?" she asked

"The register. It's on the floor."

"I see it, but I'm not a dog. All you have to say is, Sarah, please hand me the register."

Burying his face in his hands, he said in a tight voice. "Sarah, please hand me the register."

"Of course." She bent and retrieved the book.

When he had found his place and began again, he noticed she was still there. He lifted his head.

"Can I get you another cup of coffee?" she asked.

"No."

"Do you need your slippers?"

"No."

She sighed. "Can I get you anything?"

"My chair. In its proper place."

"I'm *sorry* about your chair—but really, Walker, you ought to look before you sit down." She turned and went back to the kitchen, and for a blessed two full minutes, silence reigned. Walker sighed, settling deeper into the chair cushion.

Before he had finished reviewing the information in the register about the new calves, she was back.

"Are you going to the barn today?" He could see that she had something nestled in her apron.

"I'm going to check on Diamond later."

"Good. You can take these." Sarah opened her apron to reveal four bright red apples. "There's one for each horse." She dropped the fruit in Walker's lap. He stared at the deposit.

His wife turned and went back to the kitchen. Walker, holding the register and four apples, watched her disappear through the doorway. A few moments later, she returned.

"I'm ready to go when you are, okay?"

Walker nodded.

When her singing started up again, he quickly shut the register and rose quietly, creeping to the hat rack. He needed a little space. Some time with the horses before they began their time alone.

He slipped his boots on soundlessly, keeping an eye on the closed kitchen door. As the singing rose in pitch and intensity, he quickly grabbed the apples and sneaked out the front door to find shelter in the barn.

He brushed all four mares and put them back into their stalls with an extra ration of hay. Spending time in the barn calmed him. Here he knew what to do; with Sarah, he didn't. But he couldn't spend the rest of his life hiding from his wife. He hung the picks and brushes back on the wall and then removed his hat and wiped his forehead, recalling his life before Sarah. Uncomplicated. Quiet.

He walked toward the bunkhouse, his mind on Spring Grass now. The ranch had been his father's pride and joy. The verdant, rolling hills stretched for miles. He inhaled the warm air, sweet from newly turned soil, and realized that regardless of the change in lifestyle, he was happy. Sarah's ways were different, but for some insane reason she didn't bother him most days. If she would just leave his chair alone they would get along fine. It was nice to have her around in the evening. She tatted while he read. He'd never thought to ask her about her former life, where she was raised and educated. Were her folks still living? Did she have brothers and sisters? So far she hadn't offered a scrap of information regarding her private life, and he knew little more than that she came from Boston.

He reached S.H. and Flo's cabin as S.H. was leaving.

"Where are you off to?"

"Flo's supplies are runnin' low. What are you doin' today?"

"Sarah thinks we need to spend the day together."

The old man winked. "Now, what can newlyweds find to occupy their time?"

Flo's voice sounded from the kitchen. "Git on with yer business, S.H. Quit teasin' the poor man!"

"Morning, Flo," Walker called. Inside, he found the housekeeper busy making new curtains. Bolts of shiny checked material were spread across the kitchen table. The woman looked up. "Thought you and Sarah planned to spend the day together."

"We're going to. I wanted to check on Diamond."

"By the way, Sarah moved your chair again this morning."

"I noticed."

Flo shook her head. "She wants to help, but she don't know how."

"I don't understand it, Flo. The ad promised an experienced house-keeper. Either her pa lied, or the Mallorys have a different idea of experienced than we do."

"Well, now. She's not a Mallory. She told you so the day she got off the train."

"Yes—I forgot. Some sort of mistake at the agency."

"So she says."

He glanced up. "You don't believe her?"

"I ain't got a problem with her other than she's underfoot. She cramps my style, but I can live with it if you can."

Walker frowned. "Her name isn't important."

"If that's your feelin', Walker, then I'd stay with it for a while." She bit off a thread. "Can't never tell how soup is going to turn out until it's done."

For a moment, silence dominated the room. Walker took off his hat, absently tapping his forefinger against the crown. "Given time, she'll improve, won't she?"

"The poor thing tries hard enough." Flo bent close to the table, her scissors rhythmically cutting the fabric. "Don't suppose you've taken a likin' to her."

Walker turned toward the counter and poured a cup of orange juice.

Eyeing him, Flo grinned. "Not going to answer?"

"Flo, do you have any dime novels? Sarah said something the other night about liking to read them."

"I may have a few." She laid the scissors aside and disappeared into the bedroom. Walker heard her sorting through the trunk at the foot of the bed, and a few minutes later, she returned with a stack of books.

"These ought to keep her busy."

Walker studied the covers, frowning. They looked like love stories. He took one off the top, read part of a scene, and then snorted and threw it back. "Got anything else?"

Flo laughed. "Men. Not a romantic bone in their bodies."

Walker took the books, thanked Flo, and walked back to the main house.

Strains of "Amazing Grace" met him at the door. He was tempted to ask Sarah if she knew any other hymns but thought better of it. She was making her way down the stairs with a basket of Walker's clothes tucked beneath her arm.

"You're back." She spotted the books. "What are those?"

"I thought you might like to read these. They're dime novels. They belong to Flo—"

"Love stories?" She took the last steps easily and then set down the basket. "That's so thoughtful of you, Walker. I love to read."

"You actually read this stuff?"

She frowned. "I have a romantic side. Does that bother you?"

"No, of course not. I wouldn't have brought them for you if it did."

Sarah scanned the covers. "I mostly read magazines back in Boston, when I had the time."

"Flo says to keep them as long as you need. She's read them all twice."

Sarah reached for a book and thumbed through it. "Thank you again, Walker. That was most thoughtful."

"I'll be ready to go shortly."

"I packed a picnic lunch. We can eat by the river."

"Fine. I'll be ready when you are."

Chapter Eighteen

That evening Sarah and Flo washed the dishes while Walker and S.H. escaped to the front porch. The sun hung low as it found its bed for the night, bathing the two-story home in a golden light. The men sat quietly, Walker on the swing and S.H. in a wicker chair with his feet propped on the ledge. Neither spoke at first, surrounded by the soft chirrup of crickets and the horses' nickers as they settled in their stalls.

"Been quite a day," S.H. said.

Hat tipped over his face, Walker murmured, "Can't remember a harder day off. Not since I was a small boy and Ma made me spend Saturdays working in the house. It's going to take me a while to get the hang of marriage." Sarah was good company, but Walker wasn't accustomed to doing nothing. Didn't suit his nature.

S.H. chuckled, settling deeper into his chair. Inside the house, dishes clattered and the melody of the women's conversation drifted to them.

Walker sat up and reached over to set his hat on the railing, barely missing a caterpillar working its way along the edge. He watched it reach the end of the post and inch up the side of the house. As it paused, a flutter of white caught the corner of his eye from the direction of the barn.

He straightened, squinting against the setting sun. "S.H., is that a chicken over by the barn?"

S.H. sat up for a closer look. The men watched the chicken get up, take a few steps, and flop back down.

"What's wrong with it?"

"Don't know."

The bird staggered back to its feet, wobbled in a wide circle, and then hit the ground again, occasionally ruffling its feathers.

The men got up and leaned over the railing for a better look.

Three more chickens staggered out of the barn.

"Are they sick?"

"They weren't an hour ago."

Walker stepped off the porch as the coop door swung open, spilling a dozen more hens and the rooster, all flapping and squawking. S.H. followed him down the steps, frowning.

"I'll be. Ain't never seen anything like it. It's almost like they're— uh-oh."

Walker turned to look at him. "Uh-oh? What's 'uh-oh' mean?"

S.H. lunged for a chicken and the bird hopped away, stumbling out of reach.

Wading into the flock, Walker tried to snare one. "It's like they are drunk."

"I think they are. Sarah was wantin' to help earlier, so I told her she could feed the horses. She must have gotten into my mash." S.H. grabbed for a hen and missed.

"Moonshine mash? S.H., I've told you I don't want you making or drinking that stuff on my property. Flo's going to have your head on a platter someday."

"I know. It's a powerful bad habit, one the Lord don't approve of, but this hankering comes over me...If Flo finds out I'm makin' moonshine, she'll nail my hide to the outhouse."

The two men sneaked up on the inebriated chickens one at a time. The fading light made it difficult to see, and Walker stumbled over a grain bucket, startling a hen he was about to nab. She bolted away, eyes glassy, sides heaving. He made a dive and caught her, and then he put her back in the coop.

"If Flo sees us, I'm dead." S.H. grabbed another hen by the leg and pinned her to the ground. The bird stared at him in wonder. Then feathers flew and she squawked as he carried her to the pen.

The men froze when Flo lifted the kitchen window and shouted, "S.H? What's going on out there?"

"Just settling the chickens," S.H. shouted back. He shot Walker a desperate look.

"They ain't gone to roost yet?" Flo yelled.

"They're gettin' there!"

Two hens had made it all the way to the porch and were assessing the steps. Their heads wobbled precariously on their feathered shoulders. Walker quietly approached the closest one.

"You take the other one," he whispered. S.H. reached for the first hen just as the porch door flew open.

"S.H., why are my hens putting up such a ruckus?" Flo stood in the doorway, Sarah peering over her shoulder. "S.H.?"

He straightened with a sheepish grin. "Nothin's going on, sugar. We'll be there in a minute."

Flo eyed the hen flapping behind his back.

"Why aren't those hens roosting?" she asked. "It's nearly dark."

"Well, they don't seem to be feelin' too good," he said. The hen set up another squawk, feathers flying the air.

Stepping onto the porch, Flo put her hands on her hips. "S.H. Gibson, what's goin' on out here? You two look like naughty boys caught with a hand in the cookie jar."

Walker caved in first. "They're drunk, Flo."

S.H. glared at him. Then he and Walker both faced her wrath, each holding a chicken that, apparently thinking it had successfully roosted, appeared to be asleep.

"Drunk!" she bellowed.

"Drunk?" Sarah echoed. "Chickens drink hard liquor?"

S.H. tried to absolve himself. "Now, Flo, honey, I know you're not going to like it, but I bought a little mash in town today—it's my last, sugar pie. Bought it from Babe Jensen, and I was gonna tell ya, but I didn't want ya to yell at me." He glanced at Walker pleadingly. "I don't know how the chickens got into it."

"Of all the—" Flo began. "Did you feed it to them?"

"Me! No, I wouldn't make a mistake like that, honey bunch."

Three pairs of eyes swiveled to Sarah.

Sarah's hands flew to her cheeks.

Walker eyed her. "Sarah?"

"What does mash look like?"

His eyes narrowed. "Why?"

Sarah swallowed. "S.H. allowed me to feed the horses earlier and…"

"Oh, mercy." Walker dropped his chicken. Squawking, she rolled onto her side. "Not the horses too!"

"No!" Sarah exclaimed. "I know I fed them oats. I know what oats look like." Color flooded her cheeks. "But when I was looking for the oats, I opened another barrel and…I may have forgotten to shut the lid."

S.H. was in the doghouse with Flo, and Walker had a coop full of drunken poultry.

Sarah's bottom lip quivered. She looked at the unconscious chicken under S.H.'s arms and the one lying peacefully in the dirt. "Are they going to die?"

"Mash isn't going to kill them, but they're gonna have a mean hangover come morning." Walker bent to pick up a limp bird. "I wouldn't use the eggs tomorrow, Flo."

Whirling, Flo marched back into the house and slammed the door. Sarah sank onto the porch swing, stunned.

"Guess I know where I'll be roostin' tonight," S.H. grumbled. He adjusted his hen and started for the barn.

Sarah glanced at Walker. By the look on his face, he was ready to buy her a train ticket back East. She had taken pains not to crowd him today, had done everything she could to make the outing successful, and now this happened. Granted, it had been foolish of her to leave the lid off that mash barrel, but it wasn't a hanging offense. She was getting a little tired of feeling inept. She might not have been born and reared on a ranch, she might not be the most experienced cook or housekeeper, but she tried, and Walker should be grateful that she loved him enough to want to learn. Tears welled in her eyes, falling unchecked down her cheeks.

She was in the kitchen feigning reading by the oil lamp when Walker came through the house and went upstairs. She heard the thump of heavy boots down the hallway; then their bedroom door opened and shut.

Tucking a bookmark into her book, she wiped away her tears and then crept up the stairway, straining to hear his activity. Was he so angry that he wouldn't talk to her?

She heard first one boot drop and then the other. When the bedcovers rustled, she walked into the room. Walker, sitting in bed, looked up from the journal he was reading.

"What are you crying about?"

"Nothing." She marched to the closet and removed her dressing gown.

Laying his reading aside, he sighed. "Anyone could have left the lid off that barrel."

"No, it's my fault and I'm sorry. I don't pay enough attention to what I'm doing." She crossed the room and sat down on the bed, determined to stay calm. She knew he hated it when she cried.

"Don't worry about it. You'll learn. You've only been here a short while." Softening, he asked, "Would a hot bath make you feel better? I'll have Flo heat some water."

While the thought of soaking her cares away was enticing, she knew a bath wouldn't solve the problem. They had to communicate on an emotional level. They needed to talk. The marriage would never grow otherwise, and she dearly wanted it to bloom, to thrive so that eventually, solving little problems like the chicken fiasco would be as automatic as breathing.

"We need to talk, Walker. I'm sorry if I get in the way. I only want to help."

"I'm sorry I make you feel that way. Your efforts are duly noted, but I'm not a talker, Sarah. Afraid I never will be. If you need something, just ask me but don't expect me to read your mind."

Sarah thought that was a little harsh, yet he was right. It would take years to learn each other's way, to develop trust and communication. But she *would* learn. She would show them all that she could be a sterling wife and helpmate. Ranching was second nature to Walker, and Flo had cooked for S.H. for forty years. How could she expect to master in a few weeks what had taken others a lifetime to perfect?

She swallowed the lump in her back throat. "A bath would be nice."

"Hey." His eyes gentled. "It's not the end of the world. You made a mistake. I make them all the time."

"Thank you." Tears welled in spite of her promise to not cry.

"Just be more careful next time."

"I promise I will. I know what mash looks like now."

And she wouldn't likely mistake it again.

Later, Sarah ran a finger over the cover of her dime novel.

"Are you going to turn out the light?"

She gave her husband an absent love pat. "In a minute. I want to read a few pages of my book." She met his gaze. "Thank you for being so thoughtful. I love to read. I even thought about writing a book someday."

He turned to his side. "That's nice."

An hour passed. She sat up and slammed the book shut. "Walker!" She rolled toward him and he grunted. "I'm going to write that book." She didn't know a wit about ranching, but she was well educated. She could write. She knew she could. And get the work published.

Opening an eye, he stared at her. "You're going to what?"

"I am going to write a love story." After all, she was living one—somewhat. But their union would grow year by year, and one day she would realize that what others thought was pure folly would be prove to be good judgment. She felt sorry for Lucy. This could have all been hers... "I can do it. Will you permit it?"

"You want to write a book?"

"Yes. A romance."

He wadded his pillow beneath his head. "Have you ever written anything before?"

"I've written letters, and once I wrote a short poem that took second place in a contest. May I use your den?"

Walker frowned. "Why my den? Can't you write in the parlor or the kitchen? Or even up here, where you wouldn't be disturbed?"

His hesitation puzzled her. She questioned him with a look. "Do you mind? The kitchen and parlor are noisy, and this room is so stuffy in the daytime."

"My study is my place, Sarah. A man's place."

He rolled over and adjusted the covers, and she knew he was thinking about his furniture. She wouldn't touch his furniture.

But she decided not to push him. She still felt guilty about the chicken incident and she didn't want to completely spoil the day.

She could picture the article in the monthly paper now:

> Sarah McKay's (wife of local rancher Walker McKay) first novel, *Love's Eternal Flame,* has broken all sales records. The fascinating and brilliantly written romance novel has swept fiction circles from Boston to Wyoming with a vengeance, and Mrs. McKay's fans are demanding that she write faster. When asked what her secret for penning riveting love stories was, Mrs. McKay says she's living her own romance, and cannot write any less.

She dropped a kiss on Walker's forehead, then leaned over him and blew out the lamp. Settling back onto her pillow, she sighed. A novelist. *Love's Eternal Flame*—or *Flaming Love*. *Love with a Handsome Stranger* wasn't bad—no, *Love Burns Brightly*…

Forever Love had a nice ring to it.

Chapter Nineteen

Sarah eyes skimmed over the gleaming parlor. There wasn't a hint of dust on the cherrywood tables, moss-colored drapes, or hand-hewed oak mantel. The open window carried the scent of lemon oil throughout the immaculate room. It was clear her dusting services wouldn't be needed here.

She'd woken thinking she would most definitely write Papa this morning and tell him that she was married and about to pen her first book, but the idea quickly dimmed. She had thought it would be so easy to confess what she'd one, but she was finding the ruse easier and easier to perpetrate with each passing day. If she told Papa she would have to tell Walker, who would tell Flo and S.H. The list went on and on. She'd wait a while longer before stirring that hornet's nest. *Forgive me for worrying Papa, Father, but at least he knows I'm safe. I hope he isn't too concerned, but he probably is. What father doesn't worry about his child when he has no idea where she is?*

Strolling into the room, she paused at the open window, sniffing. Mouthwatering aromas drifted from the bunkhouse kitchen. One glance at the mantel clock assured her that the old cook would be up to his elbows preparing dinner and wouldn't want to be bothered, but she fairly longed to tell someone about the book. Walker had not been impressed, but that didn't surprise her. His praise was hard to come by. As she left the parlor and started back upstairs, she noticed that the door to her husband's study was closed. Was he working at home this morning? She'd overslept, and by the time she'd read another chapter of the dime novel, dressed, and come downstairs for breakfast, Flo informed her that Walker had been up for hours.

The closed door lured her back down the stairs. Obviously, if he was in, he was busy, but too busy for a brief visit from her?

Stepping off the last stair, she edged toward the study door and rested her hand lightly on the door handle.

"Sarah! You're not to go in there!"

Sarah jumped, hastily withdrawing her hand. Rubbing her palm on her skirt, she turned to face Flo. "I was only going to say good morning."

"You know Walker doesn't like anyone to bother him when he's in his study."

"But I was just—"

"You'd better stay clear of Walker when he's in there, honey. His patience goes only so far." Flo eyed her sternly on her way back to the kitchen.

Sarah sighed and then followed the housekeeper, looking for a notepad and pencil. She was eager to start her book. A little while later she was settled in the parlor and jotting down plot ideas when a ruckus in the kitchen drew her attention. S.H. burst through the doorway, heading for Walker's study in a dead run.

Sarah listened as the foreman explained about a bull being down in the north pasture. A minute later, the two men left the house with a flurry of boots on the wooden floor and the slamming of doors.

Sarah sat until the sound of galloping horses left the barnyard. Laying the book aside, she stepped into the hallway. Her gaze swept the deserted foyer. She was relieved to see that Flo had disappeared too.

The open door to Walker's study beckoned to her. Edging along the length of the foyer table, she argued with herself about the inadvisability of entering sacred ground. Walker had forbade her to rearrange the furniture, and he didn't want her writing her book in his study, but he hadn't said anything about taking a peek inside. Besides, from the sound of things, he and S.H. would be tied up with the lame bull for most of the morning. Her slippers eased along the polished floor. If Walker's study was anything like Papa's, it could use a little attention. Papers, books, and journals would be everywhere. Sarah didn't think it would hurt anything to just step in for a moment and look the room over.

In a flash she entered the study and quietly shut the door. Leaning against the wooden panel, she paused to let her racing heart catch up.

A delicious sense of expectancy washed over her as she waited for her pulse to return to normal. Her glance slid over the masculine lair with its rich furnishings: the massive desk, burgundy leather sofa, and wingback chairs before a cold fireplace. Heavy gold damask draperies opened to reveal a large picture window that overlooked the unkempt rose garden. Closing her eyes, she released a quick breath. She was in.

Hurrying to the window, she feasted on the garden's fountains pouring water from the large vases perched onto a lovely, lily pad-covered fishpond. What an exquisite sight it would be if only it were tended. Maybe one day she would be able to convince Walker to allow her to plant new flowers in the spring.

Turning back to the room, she walked among the furniture, touching each piece and admiring the quality. This room would please Papa greatly, but nice things meant nothing to her. In many ways, she wished her husband were a struggling farmer who needed a young wife to help him make his way in the world. Money made people independent. Maybe if they were poor, Walker would need her more.

Sitting down in his chair, she leaned back, closing her eyes. Walker's scent surrounded her: leather, soap, and musk. Opening her eyes, she spotted an open ledger and a stack of unpaid bills. Today must be the day Caleb came for dinner. Every two weeks he and Walker combined business and pleasure over a plate of Flo's fried quail and hot biscuits.

Caleb Vanhooser was a strange little man. If he weren't Walker's friend, Sarah wouldn't like him. He'd done nothing to her personally, and he was ever the perfect gentleman, yet her instinct kept her reserved. There was something odd about the way he had avoided her at their party, as if she were an outsider and would never be anything more.

Shifting the ledger ever so slightly, she scanned the columns of numbers. Spring Grass's handsome profit impressed her, as well as Walker's generous tithes to the church. She sighed. Walker was her dream husband, and this was an area in which she could offer competent help. If there was one thing Sarah knew, it was numbers. A teacher had once told her she could keep books for the government if she wanted. Cooking and housekeeping came hard, but she excelled in mathematics.

Scanning the ledger, she felt a twinge of conscience; she hadn't meant to snoop, but she wanted to skim Walker's books and make sure they were accurate. He wouldn't have to know—not until he felt more comfortable with her delving into his business.

Sarah heard the back screen door open. Hurriedly shoving the ledger back into place, she arranged pencils the way they had been. Today wasn't the best time to start her fact-check, but the next time the house was empty, she would begin.

At least writing *Love's Eternal Flame* and rechecking Walker's figures would give her something productive to do.

Chapter Twenty

Agents Kate Warne and Frank Roche stepped onto the Mallory porch and knocked on the shanty door. A crowd of towheaded children from toddlers to teenagers ceased their play in the front yard to stare at the newcomers. *All boys,* Kate thought.

The door opened, and a man with his thumbs hooked between his suspenders and undershirt met their unsmiling gazes. The tall, thick man eyed the strangers coldly.

"Jack Mallory?" Kate asked.

"Might be. Who wants to know?"

Kate flashed her badge. "Kate Warne, Pinkerton National Detective Agency." She waited for the usual response.

"Woman detective?"

"Yes, sir. We'd like to talk to you if you have a minute."

Mallory opened the door wider, allowing them to enter. Sleeping pallets were spread across the dirt floor of the small sod shack. A long table sat at the south end of the room. "Frank Roche, my partner," Kate said.

Jack nodded toward his wife. "This here is Naomi—the missus."

Kate smiled. "Ma'am." The two detectives sat down.

"What is it?" Naomi frowned. "Has something happened to Lucy?"

"No, ma'am," Frank said. "We're just here to ask a few questions regarding your daughter's departure."

"What about it?" Jack asked, sitting down across from them at the table.

"Have you heard from your daughter recently?"

"No. We sent her a letter, but we ain't heard nothing back. Why?" Naomi glanced from Kate to Frank, concern etched in her eyes.

"I assure you there is no reason for alarm. We're hoping that your daughter will be able to help with a missing person's case we're investigating."

"That right? What would our Lucy know about a missing person?"

"We understand you were with your daughter in the train depot the morning she left. Is that right?" Kate said.

Jack nodded. "Me and the missus took Lucy to the station to catch the five forty."

"Did you see anyone other than your daughter in the waiting room that morning?"

The man pursed his lips in thought, his dark brows drawn tightly against his weathered features.

"A young boy," Naomi supplied. "There was a young boy waiting for the train."

"Anyone else?"

The conversation lagged. Outside, the children's squeals filtered through the open doorway. It was several moments before Jack said, "No, jest the boy."

Kate frowned. "Are you sure the other person was a boy?"

Frank leaned forward and added, "Could it have been a young woman dressed like a boy?"

Shaking his head, Jack said, "Don't rightly know. I suppose it could have been. Me and the missus weren't lookin' at other passengers. We were too busy trying to convince Lucy to get on the train."

Kate and Frank exchanged glances.

"She didn't wanna go. Got it in her head to marry some no-good neighbor boy, Rodney Willbanks. Kids." Jack snorted. "Got her set up to marry a wealthy rancher and what does she do? Tries to run off with a man who can't give her a roof over her head, let alone a decent life. Me and Naomi told her she was marryin' Mr. McKay whether she liked it or not. Girl's got a streak of orneriness in her a mile wide, but we weren't about to let her ruin what we got goin'."

"In what way?" Kate asked, taking notes.

"This McKay feller's got enough money to burn a wet mule. Lucy's not gonna ruin that for us. She's a looker, like her ma. I told her she needed to put that to use. The McKay feller wants an heir, and Lucy's born for breedin', just like Naomi here."

His wife's face flamed.

Frank sat closer to the edge of his chair. "You want your daughter to marry for money?"

"We want her to be happy, and money goes a long way toward happiness." Jack's rheumy eyes wandered the squalid shanty's cramped interior. "Ain't nothing wrong in wantin' the best for our daughter."

"No, sir." Kate closed the notebook. "You haven't heard from your daughter since the morning she left?"

"Like I said, we've sent a letter, but we ain't heard nothing back yet. She'll write any day now. So…who's this missing person you mentioned?"

"Sarah Livingston. Are you familiar with the name?"

"Livingston? Her papa the one who owns the railroad?"

"Yes, sir."

"I've heard of her. Hear she's a real handful."

Kate smiled. "Thank you for your time. We'll check back in a few weeks to see if you've heard from your daughter." She scribbled an address on a piece of paper and handed it to Mallory. "Meanwhile, if you hear from Lucy, please let us know."

"We'll be hearing from her any day now." Jack got up to walk them to the door. "Mail's slow. You know how it is. I ain't lookin' to hear anything for a while, but by now Lucy's married to McKay. Should be gettin' money anytime."

"Yes, sir."

"Lucy's our only gal. We got them five boys out there in the yard and the little one. My health ain't so good. I hurt my back and ain't been able to work steady for months. It'll be a real comfort to know someone's lookin' after us."

"Yes, sir."

On that note, Kate motioned to Frank and the pair said their goodbyes.

Walking back to the buggy, Kate glanced at Frank. "Isn't love grand?"

"Sounds like it," he replied.

Chapter Twenty-One

Lowell Livingston prowled his study, lighting and relighting a cigar. Kate took out her notebook and consulted it. The telegram at first had given them hope, but their inability to trace its sender left Kate frustrated. If it was from Sarah, she was taking precautions not to be found.

"Our next step is to check with McKay and Lucy in Wyoming," Kate said. She knew that Lowell didn't want to involve the rancher, but despite an intensive search, the agency had failed to turn up anyone who had seen or heard from Sarah since her disappearance. They were all hoping that Miss Mallory—now apparently Mrs. McKay—had observed more in the train station than her parents.

Kate closed the notebook. "What do you think, Frank?"

"We could send Fox and White up there and let them poke around."

Kate nodded. John Fox and John White were two of the agency's best. Short of Allan Pinkerton himself, there weren't any better.

"There'll be an additional thousand-dollar bonus for the man"—Lowell glanced up—"or woman who brings my daughter home."

"That's generous of you, Mr. Livingston, but it's not necessary." Kate straightened in her chair. Allan Pinkerton hired his detectives for their character rather than for their experience. He insisted on incorruptible, courageous men, dedicated to the law: men with strong personalities and keen powers of observation. Kate was the first woman Allan had hired, and she had talked hard and fast to convince him she was capable of filling the position. A woman could worm more secrets out of a reluctant male witness than any man could.

Women also observed what men couldn't, and they were able to form friendships with the wives and girlfriends of suspected criminals. She'd convinced Pinkerton of these facts and had gotten the job. Now she was among his top four agents along with Frank, John Fox, and John White.

Chewing on the tip of his cigar, Lowell stared out the window, a wisp of smoke playing through the worry lines on his brow. Kate could see that his daughter's disappearance weighed heavily on him. Her heart ached for him.

"We'll find her, Mr. Livingston. I understand you're a man of great faith. Use that now to calm your fears."

"If only I had listened closer, tried to reason with her…" Kate could barely make out the railroad tycoon's voice—it was filled with pain and regret. He spoke more to himself than to her. "I'm so afraid that something tragic has taken my little girl."

"You would have heard," she reminded him softly. "No news is good news."

"If I were to lose Sarah…" He shook the thought away. "Send the wire, Kate. Send McKay a wire and ask him to have Lucy Mallory get in touch with us immediately."

"Yes, sir."

"And tell Allan I want him in on this."

Frank spoke up. "I'll tell him, sir, but he's busy with another case."

"Hang the other case. Tell him he can name his price if he'll drop everything and help with the search."

"I'll tell him, sir."

Kate shook her head. It was unlikely the boss would comply with Livingston's wishes for any amount of money. Allan had been on the other case for months, consumed with apprehending the criminal. He wasn't going to be happy about this.

Kate rose, signaling Frank that the conversation was over. The two detectives left the Livingston study a moment later.

"Think we'll find her?" Frank asked.

"She has to be somewhere. We'll find her," Kate replied.

The Eye That Never Sleeps. The Pinkerton motto. For Kate, it meant more. She considered it a personal pledge.

Chapter Twenty-Two

Sarah finished lacing her boots and glanced up when she heard Walker come into the downstairs foyer. Her hair was pinned in a bold new upsweep, and she wore a burgundy dress of Martha's own design: rich polished linen that fit her nicely. The Johnsons' first spring barn dance was only hours away, and Sarah felt her spirits lift. Weeks had passed, weeks when she'd made no real advances in strengthening her marriage. Walker was polite but detached. She didn't feel the warmth and love she longed to feel. *In time,* she reminded herself. *Allow things to move slowly.* Every day he talked more, and he had even taken her for a buggy ride two nights earlier.

"Sarah?" Walker called up the stairway. "I'm home. Are you ready?"

She checked her appearance in the mirror one last time and then descended the staircase in time to catch Walker easing into his parlor chair. She noticed that he was careful these days of where he sat, looking behind him, no longer taking his seat's placement for granted.

"Hello," she said, entering the room. "What do you have there?"

"S.H. picked up the mail in town this morning," he told her. He paused, his eyes fixed on an envelope. "This must have been sent by mistake. It's addressed to *Lucy* McKay."

Her heart skipped a beat. A letter from Lucy's parents! Willing a

122

steady hand, she casually reached for the missive. "I'll take care of that. I'm sure it's from my father. He must have lost the address and sent it through the agency, but they seem to still be mixed up regarding our names. I'll write and correct the mistake."

Turning away, she stared at the envelope. Her fingers smoothed the seams of it thoughtfully. The letter inside bulged. Did she dare open and read mail meant for another? She glanced at Walker.

"Aren't you going to open it?" He finished sorting through his correspondence and threw it on the table. He stood up and brushed past her on his way upstairs.

"Yes...of course."

He paused and turned to look back at her. "When?"

"Now, while you change." She smiled. "You'd better hurry. We don't want to be late for the dance."

"I'll only be a minute." His eyes skimmed her lightly. "You look beautiful tonight."

"Thank you."

"I won't be long." He turned and left the room as she sat down in his chair.

The letter lay like a coiled rattler in her hands. Had the Mallorys discovered what the girls had done? They couldn't have. It wouldn't be addressed to Lucy if they had, and Lucy would never inform her parents of the switch—not for months. Sarah's mind calculated the time. She'd been at Spring Grass eight weeks. No, Lucy wouldn't have told anyone yet. She would be still basking in her honeymoon with Rodney. *Remain calm, Sarah. This is only a reminder that you need to tell Walker about the ruse.*

She lifted the envelope to the light but couldn't make out the writing.

She had to open it.

No, she couldn't.

Her hands quivered and she rested the letter in her lap, pressing her fingers to her temples. Opening it would be an invasion of privacy—Lucy's. Leaving it unopened prevented her from knowing if the Mallorys suspected their daughter's ploy.

But what if the Mallorys were on their way to visit and the letter informed her of their imminent arrival?

Picking up the letter, she gingerly played with an edge of the envelope, wiggling a finger under the flap and trying to loosen the stubborn seal. She dangled the envelope by one finger, shaking it. Finally, she tore the seal away and scanned the contents quickly.

Walker started down the stairs and she sprang to her feet, cramming the letter into her pocket. When she streaked past him on her way up to their room, he reached out and grabbed the hem of her dress.

"Whoa—what's your hurry?" He turned her around by the shoulders.

"We're going to be late," she murmured.

"We have plenty of time. Everything all right back home?"

"Perfect. Walker, I really don't want to be late." Could he see the guilt in her eyes? The deception blacker than sin? Papa's words rang in her mind. *Sarah, your sins will always find you out.* The ploy was over. She must tell Walker the truth—now, before he discovered her deception on his own.

But the mere thought made her ill.

Walker let her go and went over to check his appearance in the staircase mirror. "When you write back, invite them for the holidays."

"Oh. Yes. I will. Thank you."

"I'll bring the buggy around."

"Yes. I only need a minute."

She waited until she heard the back door close, and then she took the rest of the stairs in a rush, Walker's smile etched in her heart and the letter burning a hole in her pocket.

A few minutes later, she climbed into the buggy and sat beside her husband. It was a beautiful evening; the sky was a variation of blue, crimson, and orange. Sarah looked forward to their carriage rides. She and Walker attended church every Sunday, and she rode to town with him occasionally for supplies. Everywhere they went, someone stopped to comment on what a handsome couple they made. Sarah loved the attention. Little gray-haired women patted her hand and assured her that she and Walker would make beautiful children. Rugged men from neighboring ranches slugged Walker on the arm as they walked by, still chuckling about the wedding barbecue.

Had it been two months already? It seemed only days. She snuggled closer to Walker on the buggy seat, and he pressed back against her warmth. Tonight she felt him relaxing. Maybe he was beginning to open up, little by little. He often watched her when she walked across a room, and one night when she was doing the dishes he helped, splashing her with soapy bubbles until she retaliated and they both ended up soaking wet on the kitchen floor.

Self-reproach brought her back to reality. It was all a ruse, a scam. Her marriage was founded on a lie, and the Mallorys' letter confirmed it.

She straightened away from him and retied her bonnet strings. If only she knew how he would react to her confession. Had she earned his respect—if only a tiny bit? Would they both laugh about the switch in their old age, the way the townsfolk chuckled about the wedding?

Or would he send her away, forcing her to return to an empty life in Boston or, worse, to a cheerless Uncle Brice? Who would want her, now that she had been with a man? The ruse would spread throughout Boston, and no amount of Papa's money could buy back her reputation.

Walker glanced at her. "You're going to make that pretty lip bleed," he said.

Pretty lip? He'd never once said anything that personal to her. Hope rose and then fell. Sarah realized she was biting her lip so hard she could feel the broken skin.

"Something bothering you tonight?"

"I'm just nervous." She hoped her face didn't reflect her anguish. "The Johnsons didn't talk to me much at our party, and I'm afraid Mrs. Johnson doesn't approve of me."

"Nonsense," he said, dismissing her concerns. "And why would you care what they think of you? It's a simple party. The Johnsons most likely didn't mean anything by their oversight." He switched the reins to his left hand and patted her knee with his right. "Stop worrying about every little thing and enjoy yourself."

Would he be so kind if she blurted out her secret?

The carriage rolled up the drive of the Johnson ranch. Ahead, she saw rows of buggies and surreys lined in front of the sprawling farmhouse. Tantalizing smells greeted them when they drew closer, and Sarah's pulse quickened. She adored dancing, especially with Walker. She'd forget about the letter until after the party and deal with it later. For the next few hours, she was going to enjoy her husband's company.

The carriage came to a stop amid a swarm of servants and party guests waiting to greet guests. Two tall, burly friends of Walker's swept her from the carriage. Walker disappeared into a flock of women who had convened to drag him into the party the minute his boots touched the ground. Before she could sputter yes or no, the men whisked Sarah across the yard and into the open barn alight with lanterns. More neighbors moved to welcome her, and for the first time since she came to Wyoming, she felt at home.

Sarah promised the first dance to Buck Whitley, a school friend of Walker's. His height and gawky legs made him an awkward partner. He hunched over, trying to accommodate Sarah's diminutive frame and carry on a conversation. His bumbling but sincere attempts amused her.

"If you don't mind me saying, ma'am, you sure are a pretty sight. I'd venture to say about the prettiest I've ever seen around these parts."

Sally Hinter danced by close enough to overhear Buck's comment and swatted him on the arm. "You'd better be nice to us trolls"—she winked at Sarah—"'cause she's taken." Her sizable bulk forced her partner to crowd Buck. "You don't have a chance, Buck. Not when she has Walker McKay waitin' at home."

The two couples parted with good-natured laughter. Buck blushed and handed her to one of Rusty Johnson's red-haired sons, who whirled her away.

The sweet strains of fiddles and revelry pushed unwanted thoughts of the Mallory letter aside. Sarah tried to bow out when the couples lined up for square dancing, but Mac Maze, whose name aptly described his dancing style, wouldn't hear of it.

"Just follow the directions," he said, leading her to the line, "and keep your eyes on me."

The dance began and those gathered in the middle separated from their partners. They folded over in a bow and Sarah did the same, bowing to her left. She righted herself to see Mac doing the first step, something called a do-si-do. Her feet flew, trying to keep up with the music. After a few spins and bows and different partners, she began catching on and lifted her skirts to prance lightly around a man she'd never seen before whose grin was as wide as Texas.

She traded partners again as the dance ended and she found herself face-to-face with Walker. The crowd clapped when Walker caught her up in both arms and swung her around, his gaze centered on his bride.

She laughed as she flew through the air, holding tightly to him. She'd watched him all night and been rewarded with only brief glimpses of him dancing with other women, chatting with friends, or being slapped on the back by ranchers. Now she was in his arms, and the evening took on a magical glow. Pulling her close with one hand around her back, he met her eyes, and the desire she saw there took her breath away. He was starting to fall in love with her.

"You're the belle of the ball," he teased.

"And you're the prince," she teased back. He kissed her briefly and then twirled her around for a promenade.

The fiddles slowed and Sarah recognized the first strains of a waltz. As Walker moved her easily around the floor, his gaze met hers. It was as if she were the only woman in the world, and he the only man. Pressing his mouth against her ear, he whispered, "You're beautiful, Sarah McKay."

She floated in a warm cocoon. Later, Walker brought punch, and they sat on the sidelines holding hands, watching the merriment. Other men stood back, now that Walker had openly claimed his bride.

Sarah observed occasional glimpses of envy from the local girls, but for the most part the single women in town had accepted her. One by one they stopped to say hello and offer their best wishes. Rolene Berry invited her to the quilting bee the following week, and, smiling, Sarah accepted.

Lanterns burned low when Walker finally said it was time to go home.

Sarah's feet throbbed from hours of dancing, but she felt hope on the buggy ride home. Hope that Walker was falling as deeply in love with her as she was with him. Hope that when she told him about her silly ruse, he would forgive her. How could he not? They were a match made in heaven, and after tonight, even he knew it.

"That wasn't so bad," he bantered.

"It was wonderful. The best dance I've ever attended."

"And I'll bet a pretty woman like you has attended her share."

"I've had my share, but never anything serious," she admitted. *Oh, thank you, Wadsy and Papa, for your protective love and care. If it weren't for you, I'd be married to*—the possibilities astounded her. If she had recklessly married anyone but Walker, would she have ever felt this kind of love? Papa's watchful eye was starting to make sense, and so was the Lord's. He had protected her, and now she could see how reckless and destructive her impatience could have been.

S.H. had waited up for them. He took the reins as Walker lifted Sarah off the buggy seat and kept her in his arms.

"Have fun?" the foreman asked. He glanced at the couple, and then a blush crept up the sides of his face and he hurriedly looked the other way. "'Pears so."

❖

Later, Sarah smiled in her husband's arms. Walker's defensive guard was starting to lower. Slowly but surely he was starting to trust her, and trust was the cornerstone of marriage. And she was going to tell him she was untrustworthy.

Stirring, he opened his eyes and traced his fingers lightly along her jawline. "What did the letter say?"

"Letter?"

"From your father."

The letter. She had forgotten about it.

"Oh…nothing much. He misses me and hopes everything is going fine."

Rolling onto his back, he leaned over and lit the lamp. "I just realized that I know nothing about you—or very little. Tell me about yourself."

"Walker, it's so late, and you have to get up early in the morn—"

A finger to her lip quelled the protest. "Hey." He gazed at her, a smile touching the corners of his mouth. She loved it when he smiled. It softened his features and made his eyes even bluer.

"Tomorrow we'll have more time—"

"Tonight. I want to know everything about you."

"All right." Now was the appointed time to reveal her treachery. Taking a deep breath, she began. "I was born Sarah Elaine Livingston. I'm twenty-five years old—really old to not be married and have a family of my own. My mother died when I was seven and my nanny raised me." She slid down on her pillow and pictured Wadsy—dear, sweet Wadsy. How she loved that woman. "Wadsy has been a second mother to me. I love her dearly."

"What about your father?"

"He's an entrepreneur. He has a head for business."

"Oh, yeah? What does he own?"

"Own?" Her mind reeled. "Steel." *Tracks.* "And…buildings." *Train stations.* "Lots of buildings."

"Then you come from a privileged childhood?"

"Yes. Papa spoiled me dreadfully except for one thing." She paused, thoughtful. "I longed to go to Ireland, and he never found the time to take me."

"Is there something in Ireland you would especially like to see?"

"No, but the country just sounds lovely, and I would love to explore it with someone I love."

"I see. Siblings?"

She shook her head. "Only child."

"That's rough, isn't it."

She grinned. "Maybe for a man who has to produce an heir, but not for me. Papa never forced me to do anything against my will." Her eyes softened. "I know you feel obligated to have a child, but I don't mind. I never wanted anything more than to have children to care for."

A blush tinged his cheeks. "I…my original motive appears shallow, that I had nothing in mind regarding marriage except to produce an heir. When I sent for you, that was my main goal, but…"

"But?" She teased, tracing the outline of his strong jaw.

His gaze met hers in the soft light. "There have been times lately when you have made me lose track of that original goal." Something passed between them. Silent but unmistakable…Fondness? Love? Did she dare even think the word yet?

Sitting up, Walker assessed her. "Sarah, why would you want to be a mail-order bride?" Suspicion crept into his eyes. "I would think you would have had more suitors than you could handle."

"Not really. Oh, I had plenty of suitors, it's true, but none were ever good enough for Papa." She met his eyes. "That's why I decided to take the matter into my hands. The way things were going, I would die an old maid before the man came along that my papa would find suitable."

"What does he think of your life now?"

"Hmm. Well…Walker, I'm sure he will love you when he meets you and sees how happy you've made me."

Grinning, he tugged on a lock of her hair. "You're happy?"

"I am. I never dreamt that I could be so happy. I knew marriage would be special, but God has more than fulfilled my expectations."

Gently leaning over her, he kissed the tip of her nose. "You make a man feel mighty good."

"I want to make my husband feel that way all of life. Feeling good is an important part of living." She knew the angst he'd suffered with Trudy and she would not repeat it. She would never hurt this kind, generous man.

✿

Much later, while Walker slept, Sarah opened the letter and hurriedly read the contents.

> Dear Lucy,
>
> We hope this letter finds you well. We are
> worried about you. Has the wedding taken
> place? You have had plenty of time to become
> Mrs. Walker McKay and get that dreadful
> Rodney Willbanks out of your head. I'm sure
> you kin now see the wisdom of our decision.

Sarah read on, eyes widening. Mrs. Mallory told about the hard times on the Mallory farm, how Mr. Mallory had to sell some of his chickens at market to buy supplies for planting and now they were low on eggs. Mr. Mallory hadn't found work in months, and they were about to lose the homestead.

The entire letter was little more than a plea for money and a demand for Lucy to supply it.

The six pages showed little concern for their daughter's happiness. The final lines read:

> We deeply hope that this letter finds you well
> and that you have come to adjust to your
> situation in a manner befitting a lady.
>
> yore Ma and Pa

Sarah rested the letter in her lap. Lucy's parents had sent their only daughter to marry for money, caring nothing for her happiness. Relief filled Sarah. She'd saved both Lucy and Walker from a deplorable arrangement.

She consulted the missive again. " 'P.S. We purchased a new cow

last week.'" A new cow. She felt steam coming from her ears. Purchased
with money they felt sure would be replaced by Walker. Shoving the
letter back into the envelope, she put it under her pillow, crawled over
Walker, and blew out the lamp.

A *cow*.

Chapter Twenty-Three

Stirring, Sarah slowly opened her eyes the next morning. The force that could bring her world crashing down around her lay on the nightstand beside her. Swallowing against the tightness in her throat, she thought about getting up as the door opened and Walker came into the bedroom. She smiled when he bent and kissed her, nuzzling her sleep-warm cheek.

"Anyone ever tell you that you're beautiful first thing in the morning?"

"No, but I love to hear you say it."

Tell him, Sarah. Tell him now, while he's in a charitable mood. Last night he was so kind…he can't deny that the good Lord has brought us together.

"S.H. and I are going into town," he whispered against her lips.

"What about breakfast?"

Rumpling her hair, he gave her another brief kiss before he sat down on the side of the bed. "Breakfast was two hours ago."

"What time is it?"

"Eight o'clock. S.H. and I are getting a late start, so don't expect us back until supper."

Sarah lurched upright. Eight o'clock? How could she have slept so late?

She focused on him. "What?" she said, noting the warm expression in his eyes.

"It's just…I never thought…after Trudy, I figured I'd spend my life alone."

Her heart ached, treachery a bitter taste in her mouth. "And now?" she whispered, both fearing and desperately needing the answer.

Even as she asked, she knew the answer. But when he took her in his arms, she didn't have the strength to shatter his illusion.

After Walker left with S.H., Sarah dressed and then wandered downstairs in search of breakfast, the lie still embedded in her heart. Flo was standing at the kitchen counter, surrounded by butter, flour, chocolate, and eggs. "Thought you'd grown to the bed."

"It's shameful, isn't it? I read until late, and—" Sarah paused, color flooding her cheeks when she saw Flo's sly grin. "I'm starved. Is there any bacon?"

Flo motioned toward the warming oven. "Saved you a cinnamon bun. Had to nearly beat S.H. to keep him from eatin' it."

"Thanks." Sarah poured a cup of coffee and then moved to stare out of the window. It was hot this morning, barely a breeze stirring. Clouds were building in the west, telling of coming rain.

"Did you have a good time at the dance?" Flo scraped the thick, rich cake batter into two round baking pans.

"Wonderful. I learned to square-dance."

"That right? I'd have thought a pretty gal like you would have known how to square- dance."

"I spent most of my life ballroom dancing." Her mind skipped back to Papa's lavish soirees. Ladies dressed in dazzling gowns and sparkling jewels, men in black suits and ties. "I still don't understand why you and S.H. didn't go. You would have had a good time. Everyone asked about you."

"Me and S.H. cain't stay awake past eight." Flo slid the cake pans into the hot oven and closed the door. "Walker said there was a letter from your folks in the mail?"

Sarah lifted the cup to her lips, closing her eyes. "There was a letter, yes."

"They doin' all right? Must be hard on 'em, having a daughter living so far away. My pa woulda never sent me cross-country at your age." She chuckled. "'Course, Pa didn't necessarily want me marrying S.H., either."

Small talk was lost on Sarah as she berated herself for the lies that rolled off her tongue like honey. She had to tell Walker about the ruse—today. The sun couldn't set on the McKay household until he'd been told of the deception. Shivering, she brought the cup back to her mouth and drank without tasting. *Today, Sarah. When Walker comes home tonight, you will tell him and beg his forgiveness, and then you will get down on your hands and knees and pray that he will somehow find it within him to overlook your foolishness.*

Flo slid the cinnamon roll onto a plate and set it down on the table. "Guess you'll write your folks and let them know you got here safely. S.H. can post the letter for you when he goes to town next week."

"Yes, I need to do that," Sarah murmured. After she told Walker, she would write to Papa. She would end this awful treachery and prayerfully build a new future, one with Walker McKay. The conviction the Lord laid on her heart every waking moment was unbearable.

She ate the roll, thinking about the long day that stretched before her. She had officially started the book, a tale about a girl in love with a man she was deceiving. It shouldn't be hard to write; she knew the story by heart. The only thing she didn't know was the ending.

"Flo, where can I find a dictionary?"

"Walker's probably got one in his office. Want me to get it for you?"

"I'll get it." Sarah carried her cup and plate to the sink, excused herself, and left the kitchen.

She hadn't been in Walker's study since the day she saw his ledger. She opened the double doors to the large, manly room with its shelves of thickly bound books and rich leather furniture.

Moving quickly to the shelves, she searched until she found the item. Then she noticed that Walker's ledger lay on the desktop, open. Tomorrow was Caleb's day to come and reconcile the records.

Sneaking a hurried peak, she scanned the pages. The long, precise columns had grown. Habit made her want to check the additions and subtractions for accuracy. Caleb appeared competent, but Papa said a man should always know his personal business, especially in monetary matters. Her eyes darted to the open study door.

It would only take a few minutes to check the tallies. Flo would be occupied in the kitchen until the cake came out of the oven—the pleasant aroma of baking chocolate filtered through the air.

The foyer clock struck nine as she edged around the corner of the desk and sat down, drawing the ledger to her.

Row after row of entries filled the pages. Frowning, she studied the columns, occasionally encountering Walker's chicken scratches questioning Caleb about a certain entry.

She turned another page, her eyes running down the columns. The deposits never fluctuated, even though she had heard Walker talking to S.H. about how well the ranch was doing this year. Where were the receipts? Papa kept his receipts with his records for future reference.

The entries went back at least a year. She located the most recent additions and compared the totals to those of the accounts. The totals matched in all columns. The straight edges of the numbers showed how meticulously accurate Caleb was. Every month, the same deposit total, the same payroll deducted. Household expenses in one row, farm expenses in the next. Sarah smiled, proud of how well her husband managed the ranch. His earnings were consistent spring, winter, and fall. She frowned. Even with what little she knew about farming, the consistency didn't ring true.

She ran her fingers up and down the numbers. At the beginning of the entries for the past spring, she paused. Too consistent. Too even. Something wasn't right.

Sarah understood profit from her discussions with her father, and from her father's deliberations with others. She grabbed a pencil and started calculating.

In the kitchen Flo hummed under her breath while she browned a roast, and then checked on the cake. Good thing S.H. and Walker wouldn't be wantin' dinner on the table at noon.

She eyed the flies on the screen door. A body couldn't keep up in this house. In addition to everything else, she'd have to stop by the study and ask Sarah if she wanted chocolate or vanilla icing on the cake. Walker favored fudge and S.H. liked raspberry, but Walker had asked that the icing be Sarah's favorite. Lord, it was impossible to keep everyone happy. She picked up the basket of wash and glanced out the back door, frowning when she saw the boil of dust. How was a body expected to hang wash if Potster was gonna beat rugs on the clothesline?

Twenty minutes later, she'd shooed Potster back into the bunkhouse and hung the last of the towels to dry in the hot sun.

The kitchen was hotter than an August attic when she returned to the house. Remembering that she needed to ask Sarah about the icing, Flo went looking for her. When she saw Sarah sitting in the study, head studiously bent over Walker's ledger, she stopped dead in her tracks. As soon as the girl realized Flo was standing in the doorway, she offered a quick smile.

Flo frowned. "What are you doing?" Why was Sarah going through Walker's books? Caleb came to dinner twice a month to do the bookkeeping. There was no reason for Sarah to be prying—unless she wanted to know Walker's financial worth. Her gaze returned to Sarah's and the young woman looked away.

"Just trying to be helpful."

"Sarah...you know what happened when you tried to help feed the horses. Drunk chickens."

"Flo, if Walker gets angry—which he won't when he sees my accounting—I'll tell him it was my idea. I've discovered a few errors."

Flo frowned. Walker was finally adjusting to Sarah, but she doubted he had adjusted this much. Still, there was little else she could do short of locking Sarah out of the office.

"Land, girl, Caleb is mighty touchy about his work."

"They're small errors. I won't mention my work; I'll just adjust the figures. No one has to know I've seen the records."

"I don't know...I don't like it." Flo remembered the purpose of her visit. "Do you want chocolate, raspberry, or vanilla icing on that cake?"

"Pardon me?"

"The cake. Chocolate, raspberry, or vanilla icing. Walker told me to ask you, but I forgot."

"Chocolate...isn't that Walker's favorite?"

"Yes." Flo's eyes skimmed the young woman. "You need anything washed?"

"There are a few things in my dressing room. Do you want me to get them?"

"No." Flo backed up, uncomfortable with the encounter. Walker would have a fit if he knew that she was messing with his books. "I'll go get them myself." She left the room and started up the stairs.

She had no call to meddle in Walker's business, but he ought to know that his bride was snooping around the study. Entering the couple's bedroom, she started gathering clothes.

Walker was starting to trust again. It'd be a nightmare if his trust were misplaced a second time. Sarah seemed to be his perfect match, yet what did they really know about her? She came from somewhere near Boston, and her ma and pa must have been anxious to marry her off to have allowed her to be a mail-order bride. Flo threw a shirt into the basket.

She'd never seen Walker happier than he'd been with Sarah the past few weeks. His smile was back, and he walked with a lighter step. Marriage agreed with him. She'd hate to think Sarah was in the marriage for reasons other than honest ones. Could she possibly be one of those gold diggers out for Walker's money and nothing more? Spotting Sarah's hastily discarded dress flung on a corner chair, she stuffed it in the basket. Young'uns. Even though it was one of Sarah's new frocks, she figured it could use washing after the dance.

She moved to the bed, straightening the covers. Young folks these days weren't taught to make a neat bed. Nothing bothered her more than—She glanced over her shoulder when she heard something drop to the floor. An envelope?

She bent to pick it up. Mallory. Flo turned the envelope over in her hands as she studied it. The letter itself lay under the bed. Groaning, she got down on her knees to fish it out. Her eyes skimmed the body of the text. *This is none of yer business, Flo. Lay the letter on the nightstand and be about yer laundry.*

Getting to her feet, she refolded the papers. They were uneven, so she shook them out and tried to put them in order. Her eyes fell on the first sentence.

Then the second one.

A minute later she stuffed the letter into the envelope and laid it on the stand. Snatching the remainder of the dirty clothes, she stuffed them into the basket, steaming. It appeared that the Mallorys were schemers, but how was Sarah tied up with Lucy Mallory? Apparently there *was* a Lucy Mallory or her parents wouldn't be writing to her here. And they no doubt thought their daughter was about to put them in tall clover, but if the agency had a mix-up in names…How did Sarah figure in all this? More to the point, if Lucy thought she'd milk money out of Walker, why would she have consented to a switch with Sarah, if that was what had happened?

Flo tried to shake her mind loose from her fussy thoughts. Something sinister was going on here, but when S.H. heard about it, he'd either tell her to mind her own doins' or else he'd tell Walker.

Oh, precious Lord. What do I do now? She didn't have the heart to tell Walker the Mallorys were out to take him and witness his disappointment a second time, but she couldn't stand by and let strangers swindle him out of his money.

She was torn between anger at Sarah and pity for Walker. S.H. He'd know what to do. S.H. could talk sense into Sarah. The girl didn't seem materialistic; in fact, she was just the opposite. Maybe Walker wouldn't care about the switch. After all, he'd married Sarah to produce an heir. Maybe he was willing to pay whatever price she asked.

Then again, maybe Walker McKay didn't have an inkling that Sarah had married him to provide an income for her shiftless family. Sinking to the side of the bed, Flo stared at the basket of dirty clothes.

There was gonna be trouble over this or her name wasn't Florence Mae Gibson.

Chapter Twenty-Four

A box of pencils and two hundred sheets of white paper were tucked safely in the supply box for Sarah, so Walker guessed the whole day wasn't a wash. He smiled, liking the thought of having an author for a wife. Chances were, nothing would come of Sarah's efforts, but he was impressed with her writing goals.

He could smell supper as S.H. wheeled the buckboard into the barnyard.

"Pot roast," S.H. guessed.

"Meat loaf."

S.H. and Walker unhitched the team and walked them into the barn before heading for the house. They found Sarah curled up reading in Walker's chair. She paused to look up and smile when they came into the foyer.

"Research?" Walker teased over his shoulder as he climbed the stairs to wash up.

Sarah grinned. "No, I'm saving that for later."

"I have something you might like," he called.

"I like everything you have!"

He laughed at her almost childlike devotion, deciding that having a daughter with curly red hair might be nice. A boy would be fine, someone to carry on the McKay name, but he'd have no objections to a girl with Sarah's laugh. Or her smile. Or anything about her. Truth was, he was starting to like everything about Sarah. Maybe marriage wasn't so bad. Once a baby came, they would be a family.

Flo had supper on the table when S.H. and Walker took their seats.

"Flo, if you weren't already married, I'd marry you again," S.H. said.

"If I weren't married, you'd have a time of it catching me, S.H. Gibson. Get your elbows off the table."

S.H. spooned green beans onto his plate, winking at Walker. "You let Sarah talk to you this way?"

Walker grinned at Sarah as she put a couple of slices of roast beef on his plate. "My wife has respect for me, S.H."

"The meat should be delicious. I didn't go anywhere near it," Sarah said quickly, handing the platter to S.H.

Walker grinned. "I can see that. Thanks." The couples didn't ordinarily eat together, but that morning before they left for town, S.H. had suggested that they all eat together at their place that evening.

S.H. then took the bowl of potatoes Flo was offering him. "Why don't you fix my plate? Sarah fixes Walker's."

Flo ignored her husband and sat down. "S.H., it's your turn to say grace."

The meal proceeded with friendly chatter, except for Flo, who ate without looking up.

Sarah buttered a piece of hot bread, smiling. "How was your trip into town?"

"Wasted a whole ding-dong day," S.H. said. "Didn't get half done what we needed to do." He glanced at his wife. "You're awful quiet tonight, sugar bunch. Something put you in a bad mood?"

Picking up her fork, Flo met Sarah's eyes pointedly. "Just you, S.H. You always put me in a bad mood."

S.H. winked at Walker. "Tart little heifer. I wouldn't trade her for a California gold mine."

"A California gold mine?" Walker reached for the cream pitcher. "I'd have to think about that one."

After supper, the men insisted the women could wash dishes later. They led them onto the porch and handed them packages, which, by the look of them, they'd wrapped themselves. Walker couldn't take his eyes off Sarah as she shook the gift, trying to guess what the box held. She hadn't been far from his mind all day.

"Go on," S.H. urged Flo, his brown eyes sparkling with mischief. "Open yers first."

His wife eyed the ill-wrapped package. "S.H., what'd you do? Wad this paper up and stomp on it?"

"That's a first-class wrapping job, Florence Mae."

"It's downright disgraceful." Flo tore into her package, gasping with delight when she held up a new dress. "S.H., you old goat! We can't afford this."

"Honey bun, I'm rich in every way that matters. Just stuck a little extra money away in my sock each payday—weren't nothin' much." He reached for her hand and gave her a kiss as gallant as any knight would his lady. "Worth every penny to see the look in yer eyes right now," he said softly.

Flo's eyes misted and she leaned over and kissed him soundly.

Walker draped an arm around Sarah's waist. "You're next."

"Oh, Walker, you shouldn't have. You bought me all those lovely dresses—"

He silenced her with a brief kiss. Sarah squealed when she opened the parcel of pencils and paper. "Paper! Thank you so much." She jumped up and threw her arms around his neck. She glanced at Flo.

Walker watched the exchange, wondering why there was an underlying tension between the women tonight. "I love it!" Sarah hugged the paper and pencils to her chest. "Thank you. I've never had a nicer gift."

"Are you gonna write love scenes?" S.H. teased.

Sarah turned a deep shade of crimson. "Of course not, S.H. My books are going to be fun and inspiring and…well, I'd never—"

"Oh, S.H., leave her alone," Flo said. She gathered up the wrapping paper and headed back into the house.

"Hey, where ya goin'?" S.H. sat up in his chair. "Aren't you gonna model yer new dress for us?"

"Not tonight, S.H. Those dishes won't wash themselves."

The screen door flapped shut, and S.H. turned to Sarah. Shrugging, she handed the pencils and paper to Walker. "Guess I need to help her."

Walker glanced at S.H. when she disappeared into the house. "What's that all about? Did the two of them get into it today?"

S.H.'s features sobered. "Flo didn't say, but there's a definite chill in the air."

❖

Later that night, when she told S.H. about catching Sarah reading Walker's financial records and about strange the letter, he told her to stay clear of Walker's business. Said she didn't need to be stickin' her nose into other people's dealings, but Flo didn't like withholding information from Walker, especially this information.

If Sarah was up to something she shouldn't be, Walker needed to know.

Chapter Twenty-Five

When Caleb knocked on the door the next morning, Sarah invited him inside. As always, he carefully stepped around her, avoiding her direct gaze as he fiddled with his glasses.

"You're a bit early. Walker's not in from his morning rounds yet," Sarah explained as she escorted him into the parlor. "Would you like something to drink? Coffee or tea, perhaps?"

"Well, uh, yes, coffee would be nice." He smiled, but the effort seemed insincere. Sarah excused herself while Caleb sat uncomfortably on the couch. Flo wasn't in the kitchen when Sarah got there, but the coffee from breakfast was still warm on the stove. She poured two cups, placed them on a tray, and went to retrieve sugar from the pantry.

Playing hostess to Caleb was not exactly an ideal way to spend a morning, especially with her novel awaiting her. She sighed. Returning from the pantry, she placed the cream pitcher and sugar bowl on the tray and lifted it. With slow, sure steps, she navigated back into the parlor.

Caleb shot off his seat the moment she came through the doorway. His hat, which he had taken off and placed on the chair beside him, tumbled onto the floor and lay by the satchel he carried with him to each meeting with Walker. Sarah set the tray on the table.

"Here," she offered. "Let me take your things into Walker's study so you won't be tripping over them." She picked up the hat and reached for the satchel.

"No!" Caleb's tone startled her. Sarah straightened and delicately lifted her eyebrows.

He cleared his throat. "I…I prefer to keep it with me."

"Suit yourself," she said, taking a seat opposite him. The man certainly was an odd duck. She watched his hands fumble with the sugar spoon until he managed to tip a few spoonfuls into his cup. Rather than let him make a similar mess with the cream, she intervened.

"Allow me to serve you." She took the pitcher from his hand. Despite the warmth of the room, Caleb's touch chilled her. She poured cream for both of them and settled back into her chair. Why was the accountant so nervous? He had no way of knowing she had been snooping through Walker's books. And even if he did know, why would that knowledge make him uncomfortable?

She took a sip of coffee. She didn't want to accuse Caleb; she couldn't confront him with anything. All she had were suspicions of misconduct. Considering her own lies, Sarah realized she couldn't make bold statements until she had informed Walker of the truth about her situation. But that shouldn't stop her from finding out what the little man was about—for this little man *was* about something.

"So, Caleb," Sarah asked, "how long have you been taking care of Walker's books?"

The accountant took a moment to answer. Clearing his throat, he fixed his gaze on his crossed hands. "Your husband and I have been close friends since Mitch and Betsy died."

"You didn't keep Walker's father's books?"

"No. Mitch took care of everything. Cattle. Books. Everything."

"Strange." Sarah took a sip from her cup and silently chided herself for pursuing the questioning this far. *Go slowly. This isn't the Inquisition.*

"Pardon?" Caleb adjusted his glasses and then took a sip of coffee.

"Excuse me, I was musing out loud. I've seen Walker working on the books—or so I thought."

"He leaves notes. He may glance at the calculations once in a while, but there's no reason for him to concern himself with finances."

"That is so true," Sarah said, placing her cup back on her saucer. "Especially with the ranch making such a handsome profit these last few months."

Caleb smiled. "The growth of Spring Grass has been astounding. Mitch taught him well."

"But he didn't teach him everything, obviously," Sarah said with a feigned laugh, "or Walker would keep his own books."

Her meager attempt at humor fell, and silence took over. She wanted so badly to ask about the inconsistencies she'd found in the calculations, but she didn't. She had already overstepped her bounds by being in her husband's study in the first place, and most definitely she should not be nosing around in his personal business. The errors she'd detected had been small but puzzling. And yesterday she'd found a sizeable deposit that had gone unrecorded. Perhaps Caleb would catch the error today.

She glanced up when Walker came in through the front door, knocking mud from his boots.

"Caleb! Sorry I'm late. Things were a little hectic around here this morning." He smiled at Sarah and her heart fluttered. "Luckily you were in good hands."

"Yes, excellent hands," Caleb agreed. He immediately got up and reached for his briefcase. A moment later he disappeared into the study, no doubt relieved to be free from Sarah's prattle. Walker followed the accountant and Sarah slumped back in her chair.

What had gotten into her? Questioning Walker's best friend as if he were a common thief. Her teeth worried her bottom lip. She couldn't know for certain if the errors were incompetence or held significance.

That night Sarah climbed into bed with pencil and pad in hand. "Walker?"

"Mmm?"

"I'd like to read you part of my book."

"Okay."

"Are you too tired to listen?"

"No, I'd like to hear it." He rolled over to face her.

She paused, filled with curiosity. "How was your meeting with Caleb today?"

"Good. Why?"

"I was just curious. He always seems uneasy around me."

"He's got a shy nature. I thought you were going to read what you've written."

"Oh, yes. This isn't all I've written, but let me tell you a little about the plot. It's a story about a girl who wants nothing more in life than to be married. Her papa is overprotective, so no one who courts her is ever good enough. The men, in essence, are terrified of her father's reputation of smothering his daughter, and though he is wealthy beyond words, the smarter ones want nothing to do with her. She sets her cap for numerous men, but they are never the one God or her papa has planned for her life. She becomes more and more frustrated because she thinks that she will be too old to marry and have children by the time the Lord sends the right man."

Walker listened intently.

"So this girl—this foolish, foolish girl—decides to run away. She boards a train and on the train she meets…" Sarah paused, taking a breath.

Walker's eyes skimmed her. "The man of her dreams?"

"Yes. Definitely the man of her dreams, but I haven't reached that part yet."

"Then what? The train derails? That won't hold the readers' interest if she dies in the first chapter."

"No, the train doesn't derail." Sarah shuffled the papers. "That's about as far as I've gotten right now. I can't decide where to go from here."

"So," he offered, "maybe she meets the man on the train. Love at first sight?"

"Possible. Or perhaps she meets a young, desperate woman whose parents have insisted that she be a—oh, a mail-order-bride? And she doesn't want to marry a stranger because she's desperately in love with another man, one she feels God intends for her. So, perhaps there's another woman on the train who wants nothing more than to be married—"

"The heroine of your book."

"Yes...the heroine. What if she's on that train and she meets up with Elizabeth and—"

"Elizabeth?"

"Secondary character."

"Oh."

"Anyway, what if this woman and Elizabeth meet up and decide that since the woman wants nothing more than to marry, and Elizabeth wants nothing more than to be free of her parents' plan to marry her off to a stranger—" she glanced over when she heard Walker's soft snore.

"What if I decided to fill Lucy's place? And I love it and I love you, and S.H. and Flo. I love Spring Grass." Her tone trailed off, and she set the pencil and paper aside and slid down between the sheets. "And now I have myself in a dismal mess that I can see no way out of."

"Hmm?"

"Nothing, darling. Rest." She patted her husband's hand and closed her eyes.

Dear God, forgive me. If only truth wasn't stranger than fiction.

Chapter Twenty-Six

Walker was about to start up the stairs with a tray for Sarah the next morning as she stepped off them. He had planned on surprising her with coffee and muffins in bed. The only surprise now was Sarah's early rising.

"How nice of you!" She stood on tiptoe to kiss him. Her face glistened with soap and water and her smile melted him. "I'm sorry I spoiled your surprise," she whispered, kissing him again.

"Why don't we eat upstairs anyway?" he suggested

"What about your morning chores?"

"They can wait."

Laughing, she turned and sprinted back up the stairs, clutching handfuls of her dress before her.

In the bedroom, he set the tray on the nightstand. Sarah sat on the edge of the mattress and picked up a muffin and pulled a piece off the top, offering it to him. They fed each other bits of the sweet treat and tried unsuccessfully to twine their arms together as they sipped the scalding coffee. Eventually they burst out laughing.

"I'm so happy here, Walker."

He took her hands in his and began kissing bits of muffin from her fingertips. He had come so far in the last couple of weeks. So far…

"Sarah? Is something bothering you?" he asked.

She struggled to break free of her imposed prison. Now was the time to tell him. *Tell him, Sarah!* She started to speak but managed only a weak, "Well…" before falling silent again. If she told him he would make her leave. He was starting to trust her, to fall in love with her. He would accuse her of lying, which she had. Of being as bad as Trudy, which she was. She couldn't leave here. She loved him so desperately!

His gaze softened. "Nothing could be that bad. What is it?"

She searched for delay. "It's Caleb."

"Caleb?" He frowned. "What about Caleb?"

"I…I don't think he likes—no—trusts me."

Walker laughed. "Caleb? Why would you say that?"

"He seems…uncomfortable around me, Walker. Do you know why?"

Chuckling, he drew her to his chest. "That's what's bothering you? Honey, if I hadn't known him all these years I'd think he didn't like me, either."

Sarah pulled away to meet his gaze. "Actually," she bit her lip again, deep in thought, "I've been meaning to ask you something about Caleb."

"What is it?" He reached for his coffee.

"I know you trust him, but how well? I mean, how much attention do you pay to his accuracy with your ledgers?"

Walker's hand paused as he brought the cup to his mouth. "What makes you mention the ledgers?"

"Just wondering."

"I pay little attention to the books. That's what I pay Caleb for. Why the concern?"

Sarah felt her cheeks color. "No reason, really. It's just that my father always took care of our business…ledgers and all, so I was wondering how closely you watched them."

Walker grinned. "Well, you have nothing to worry about. I trust Caleb completely."

"I'm not worried," she scoffed. "Finances are the least of my concerns."

"Good," he said, "because I don't want you to have to worry about anything ever again."

She wished that were possible, but once again her nerve failed her. She couldn't lose this man. He was her whole life now.

Chapter Twenty-Seven

Potster cracked another egg into the bowl, eyeing Sarah. "Clean as a whistle."

"Cleaner," Sarah agreed. Sniffing the aromatic air, she wondered if she'd ever cook as well as Potster. She bent her head and sighed, and wrote another sentence in the notebook. After her morning talk with Walker, she'd thrown herself into writing, sickened that she had deliberately let the ruse continue. God had every reason to be disappointed in her. When Walker left for the fields, she'd sought refuge in Potster's kitchen.

"You spend all yer spare time workin' on that book. What's it say, anyway?"

"You wouldn't like it, Potster. It's about love."

He frowned. "What's that supposed to mean? Love's my specialty. I know a lot about the subject." He rolled a chicken leg in a bowl of flour. "Name me one stronger love than man and his food, and I'll eat my hat."

"God's love for you. And me."

"Shucks, that's a given. Throw me another one."

"The story is about a girl from the East who runs away to the West and finds the perfect man."

"Oh, *that* kind of love." Raising a cleaver, he split a chicken breast with one swift motion. "The lovey-dovey kind that makes the ol' heart go pitter-patter?"

Sarah laughed as the old cook picked up a whole chicken and started waltzing it around the kitchen, cleaver still in hand. He cooed to the plucked bird, giving it loud, smacking kisses and calling it "milady" and "madam."

Sarah shook her head at his shenanigans. "Go ahead and make fun of me. You'll be sorry one day when I'm a famous author."

Potster deposited the chicken on the counter and affected a sweeping bow. "If you think you can write anything more romantic than that in your book, Mrs. Famous Author, I'd like to hear it."

Sarah consulted the roughed-in chapter. She'd been working this morning on the part where the heroine switched places with the girl on the train. The more she wrote, the more the story became autobiographical, and she broke out in a cold sweat when she pictured herself carried off by an angry mob, publicly humiliated for her behavior. She'd plead with Walker to save her, but he would coldly turn away, saying she'd hurt him more than Trudy.

Then he would look her straight in the eye and say something derogatory about hats.

It didn't make sense, but then nothing in her life made sense, so why should her musings?

But writing came surprisingly easy to her, as if she'd been born to pen fanciful, romantic stories.

"Oh, this is much more romantic than that silly chicken dance."

"Then read it to me," Potster said.

"Are you sure you want to hear this?"

"Fire away. I'm all ears."

She took a deep breath and started to read.

> The train, a massive, domineering beast with
> an engine full of coal as black as Elizabeth's
> heart, crept through the hills and valleys, des-
> tined to reach the end of the track and take her
> to her one true love. But who was that love,
> that knight, that chivalrous man who would

be forever hers? The man who would whisk
her off on his stallion into the bright sunset?
Who was this man for whom she risked her
future to marry? She did not know, nor had
she any idea of his means or ways.

Once she had assumed the life of Emma
Lowery, she knew she could not turn back.
She could know but one life, a dreary existence of deceit, longing, desire, but also one
of true and unabashed love.

Sarah paused. The following paragraphs dealt with her arrival at
Spring Grass. The characters so closely mirrored Potster, S.H., and Flo
that she was afraid to read it aloud. She knew the wise cook would discover her guise.

Potster glanced up. "Ain't bad…a little rough around the edges, but
you can fix that. Go on."

Sudden tears welled to her eyes, blurring the pages. Potster was so
trusting, so gentle and kind; he had been her best friend since she'd
met him that day in the barn. If she lost his respect she would never
forgive herself. She'd had few close friends in her life, and she couldn't
bear to lose him. What would he think of her when he discovered that
she was deceiving Walker, that she had been all along? And Flo? Would
she regret the day she'd taken Sarah under her wing? Was the housekeeper beginning to suspect that Sarah was a fraud? She'd been distant since she'd caught Sarah looking at Walker's books. Sarah sensed
that Flo was suspicious of her intentions. With each passing day, she
could feel herself getting snared deeper and deeper in her web of lies.
She wanted more than anything for the deception to be over, but she
was powerless to stop the deceit. At first she had been frightened that
Walker would send her away, but now she worried more about hurt-
ing him badly, and she couldn't bear the thought.

Potster saw the tears and frowned. Laying aside his knife, he approached her, squatting to kneel beside her chair. "Here, now, it's not

that bad. I don't know anything about writin' books. You shouldn't take to heart what some ol' farmhand says about yer writin'. It's gonna be a fine book, believable or not."

His remark was more than she could bear. Dropping the pages, Sarah buried her face in her hands and whispered brokenly, "It's me, Potster. It's me, and it's all true! The story is about how I traded places with that girl on the train. I've meant to tell Walker—every day I think I will, and then something happens and I don't. I love him so much, and I truly think he has feelings for me—but I'm afraid that once I tell him what I've done, he'll be so furious with me that he'll send me away. Oh, Potster, I don't know what to do!"

Potster drew back, his eyes bewildered. "Whadda ya mean it's you? It's just a story."

"No!" Sarah cried. "The story is about me! I'm Elizabeth. I'm the one with the black heart. I'm only pretending to be the bride the agency sent."

Sarah related the whole story: running away from her father, meeting Lucy on the train, how they hatched their foolish plan. She told him about the Mallorys' letter, and how they wanted Lucy to marry Walker only for what he could provide them.

Potster sank into a chair opposite Sarah. "If that don't beat all. Have you told anyone else about this?"

"I can't tell Walker, and Flo already thinks I meddle too much." The sobs began again, unchecked. "Walker will send me away, Potster. I know he will. He'll never forgive me for deceiving him, and who could blame him? I should have told him the truth from the beginning, but I was foolish. So very selfish and foolish."

Potster awkwardly bobbed his head. "No one's gonna hate you, and no one's gonna send you away, but you're gonna have to tell Walker what you've done. The longer this goes on, the worse it'll be. He's a fair man. He'll be mad as a hornet, ain't gonna try to kid you about that, but he'll listen to your side of the story."

Sarah shook her head. "I can't. I love him, Potster, and if he sends me away I'll die. I didn't mean for it to go this far. I thought I would have been able to tell him by now. I thought once he fell in love with me, he'd find the ruse laughable."

Reaching across the table, Potster wiped her tears with the edge of the tablecloth. "Walker's had worse news—and he's got a heart bigger than you think. You got to tell him, young'un, and you got to tell him before another day passes." He bent to retrieve her fallen pages and put them back into her hands. "You got to tell him before he finds out on his own. That'd make things a heap worse, child—a whole heap of a lot worse."

Sarah knew Potster was right. Not another day could pass without Walker's knowing the truth.

How many times had she promised herself the same pledge, and when the day ended she still hadn't told him? But today was different. It had to be today.

She dabbed her eyes on the edge of her sleeve. "I'll go find him and tell him now."

"That's my girl." Getting up from the table, he went back to the stove and turned the chicken, casting worried looks her way.

Sarah felt surprising relief, and Potster's quiet reassurances gave her the courage she needed. Telling Walker wasn't going to be pleasant. She remembered what Wadsy always said. Correcting a lie was never easy, so it was far better to not tell one.

She got up from the table, grasping the edge when the room spun. It took a second for the setting to come back into focus. Potster glanced at her.

"What's wrong?"

"Nothing. I felt a little lightheaded," she said, her focus slowly clearing. The dizziness passed, but the smell of hot grease was making her queasy. "I'm all right now."

"You best go to the house and lie down a while. Flo'll fix you something cool to drink. I ain't got nothin' but coffee out here."

Releasing the table's edge, she tested her legs. "I suddenly feel very unsteady."

"You've overexcited yourself, young'un. Stop by the kitchen and have Flo give you a cool cloth before you go looking for Walker. Go on now." His smile gradually faded. "If you really don't feel good, maybe you ought to stay put until Walker rides in."

Sarah touched her head. "No. I want to tell him before I lose my courage."

"Sarah, if you need me, you come and get me, and we'll tell him together."

Sarah crossed the room to give him a grateful hug. "I'm glad you're my friend."

The old man awkwardly patted her back. "That's good, little gal. Because you're gonna need one."

Yes, she was going to need all the friends she could muster when she told Walker.

Sarah paused when she stepped out of the bunkhouse, allowing her eyes time to adjust to the bright sunlight.

A commotion in the barn caught her attention. She could hear the thump of sharp hooves hitting wood. When she walked into the barn, she discovered Diamond down in her stall, legs flailing against the wooden cubicle.

"What's wrong, girl?" Sarah peered over the stall to look at the mare. The animal gazed up at her, nostrils flared with pain.

Potster burst into the barn after her, wiping his flour-covered hands on his stained apron. "What's going on in here?"

"I think Diamond's trying to foal."

He quickly assessed the situation. "She's a bit early yet. We need Walker and S.H." Potster knelt to comfort the animal.

"I'll get him," Sarah flew out of the barn and raced toward the field on shaky legs. She spotted Walker and his foreman on horseback, riding slowly across the north meadow. Waving her arms wildly, she tried to catch their attention.

When Walker spotted her, he kicked his horse into a gallop. Sarah waited until he was close enough to hear her.

"It's Diamond! She's trying to foal! Hurry!"

Walker nodded and galloped toward the barn. Within moments he jumped off his saddle, dropping the reins. Sarah ran to catch up.

"How long has she been like this?" he asked.

Sarah struggled to match his long-legged strides as they entered the barn. "I don't know. I found her a few minutes ago and she was already down."

Potster massaged the horse's belly, trying to keep her from thrashing her head into the side of the stall. Diamond's eyes were wide, her mouth foaming.

"This ain't good," Potster warned as Walker came into the stall. "Poor girl's in a lot of pain."

"Easy, girl, easy." Walker knelt, running his hand down the animal's heaving sides. "Keep her still, Potster. Sarah, get me a bucket of water."

Sarah grabbed a bucket from the wall and rushed to the pump. Latching onto the handle, she pumped furiously, impatient with the small stream. Water trickled slowly into the pail, and she pumped harder, using both hands now. Flo came out the back door, shading her eyes.

"What's going on?" she hollered.

"Diamond's trying to foal!" Sarah stopped momentarily to catch her breath.

Flo approached, commandeering the pump handle. "Here, I'll bring the water. You go see if Walker needs help."

Sarah hurried back to the barn. On the way, she noticed black smoke rolling out of Potster's kitchen window.

"The chicken!" she cried. "The chicken's on fire, Potster!"

Potster darted out of the barn, his eyes following Sarah's finger.

"Go help Walker!" Potster sped off to salvage dinner as Diamond's whinnies filled the air.

Sarah ran inside to Diamond's stall, where Walker was calmly stroking the mother's back with one hand.

"Where's the water?"

"Flo's bringing it." Sarah's chest heaved. "How's she doing?"

"We need to cool her down and see if we can stop her labor." Walker spoke softly to Diamond and she nickered lowly, her eyes wide with fright.

"What can I do?" Sarah asked.

"It's all up to Diamond now. Come on, girl. Relax. You need to hang on a few weeks more before you have this foal."

The horse's sides heaved as Sarah climbed the side of the stall and leaned over the railing to watch. Diamond's sweat-slick coat shuddered under Walker's soothing hand. Diamond rested, panting. "Atta girl." Walker turned to maneuver along the railing, and she couldn't see his expression. A moment later he was crouched behind Diamond.

The mingled smells of sweat and horse filled Sarah's nostrils. Walker gently patted Diamond's side.

"Good girl, good Diamond." Sarah noticed that he had taken off his gloves and now ran his hand lightly over the horse's head.

The mare heaved and nickered, but she calmed as Walker continued to speak in soft tones.

The stall suddenly tilted, and Sarah lifted her hands to her head. She saw Potster enter the barn and say something to Walker, but the blood pounding in her ears blocked out the words. Potster placed the bucket of water beside Walker and glanced up at Sarah, mouthing words that looked something like "far too…"

What was he saying? Sarah scowled, shaking her head to clear the fuzz. The stall was spinning out of control. Spinning, whirling—then it went black.

Chapter Twenty-Eight

Walker strode through the back door, carrying an unconscious Sarah. Flo followed, shock registering on her face. "What happened?"

"She fainted. Send one of the men for the doctor."

"Doc's over in Dexter County visitin' kinfolk. Effie mentioned Sunday that he'd be there all week."

Walker took the stairs two at a time. Kicking their bedroom door open, he carried Sarah to the bed and gently put her down. Momentarily stirring, her eyes fluttered. Smiling, she lightly touched his cheek before sinking back into unconsciousness.

Flo hurried in with a pan of cold water and cloths. By the time she wet the compress, Sarah was coming around.

"Walker…"

He gently pressed the cloth to her forehead. "Hold still, sweetheart. You fainted."

She gazed up at him, eyes melting into his. "Swooned?" she murmured.

"You were looking over the stall one minute and out cold the next." He grinned, smoothing a lock of hair off her face. She tried to sit up, pushing his hands aside.

"Diamond?"

"She's quiet now."

Sarah wilted back to the pillow, her eyes drifting shut. "I'm glad."

"I'll get her something cool to drink," Flo offered, turning to leave.

When the door closed, Sarah looked at her husband. "I'm fine, Walker. Really."

"You don't look fine."

Reaching out, she traced the outline of his cheek. "Apparently breakfast didn't set well with me."

"Doc Linder's away visiting family, but if you think you need him—"

"I'm fine, really." After sitting up, she swung her legs off the bed and slowly stood. Moving to the washstand, she groaned when she encountered her image in the mirror.

"Potster said you felt faint earlier. What's going on?"

"It was too hot. The bunkhouse kitchen is always sweltering."

Flo returned with two glasses of lemonade. Placing the tray on the bedside table, she clucked. "What are you doing up? You should lie flat for a while."

"I feel better, Flo. There's no need to fuss."

"Well, young lady, you're not going anywhere until you've had something cold to drink and have been off your feet for at least an hour."

Sarah glanced at Walker, grinning. "Yes, ma'am."

"I have to check on Diamond," he said, backing out of the room. His eyes still locked with Sarah's. "I'll be back shortly."

"Walker…I need to talk to you," Sarah murmured.

"We'll talk later, sweetheart. Don't let her up, Flo."

"I won't."

When the door closed, Sarah lay on the bed and closed her eyes. She'd promised Flo an hour of rest, but she was having difficulty keeping still. Through the open window, she could hear the ranch going about its daily business. Walker was close to the house this afternoon. She had to tell him. She'd promised Potster and she'd promised herself. It was one promise she intended to keep.

She savored the last few blissful moments of Walker's innocence. After today, nothing would ever be the same between them, regardless of how he took the news.

Blinking back tears, she recalled the feel of his arms at the dance, the warmth of his hand on the small of her back as he helped her into the buggy, and the concern in his eyes this morning.

She kept her eyes closed against a swell of dizziness. Her stomach rolled, and she wondered if she needed to empty it. The breakfast muffin—she shuddered at the thought.

An hour passed, and she slid off the bed and washed her face and straightened the pins in her hair. The dizziness was gone, and her head cleared. She couldn't put it off any longer. Walker would probably be in the barn. They would have a few moments of privacy—enough for Sarah to tell him the truth about her identity and their marriage.

Flo was bent over the sink, scrubbing pots, when Sarah crept down the stairs. Unlatching the front door, she glanced over her shoulder as she slipped out, letting the door softly close behind her. She wondered if this was how men felt facing the guillotine. It couldn't be much worse than the mission she was about to embark upon.

When she turned around, she jumped as she came face-to-face with Lucy Mallory. Sarah stared at her but couldn't find her voice.

Lucy broke the strained silence. "Hi." She grinned. "Guess you shore didn't think you'd ever see me again."

Chapter Twenty-Nine

Sarah grasped the porch railing, staring at Lucy as if she were an apparition. "What are you doing here?"

Lucy set down her valise. "I didn't marry Rodney." She drew a deep sigh. "He turned out to be no good, just like Pa said."

This can't be happening. The dizziness returned and Sarah held on tighter to the rail. *Not now, when I was just about to tell Walker.*

The girl shrugged. "For a while everything was wonderful, but then he started going out every night drinking and coming home early in the morning, smelling of whiskey and women's perfume. He vowed that he loved me and was gonna marry me soon, but, well, money was always so tight, and then he quit his job at the dock because a feller cussed him out. I wanted to send Ma and Pa the five hunnert you gave me and tell them that McKay fellow gave it to me, but Rodney done spent it all afore I could say squat." She frowned. "Shore surprised me. He talked so sweet and all, but he was for sure a scoundrel. Once we were broke, they set us out in the middle of the street." She paused, her eyes perusing the large farm house. "Oh, my. This is so purty."

Sarah slumped against the railing. "Why didn't you go home? What made you come here?"

"I did go home." She drew another long sigh. "Pa was furious when he found out what I'd done. Said I couldn't skip out on Mr. McKay and that I had to come here and fulfill my duty." She reached out to touch a trailing rose. "This is 'bout the purtiest place I ever saw."

Sarah had to get rid of the girl before Walker discovered she was here. She couldn't let Lucy Mallory ruin everything! Collecting her wits, Sarah straightened.

"I'm sorry, but I'll have to ask you to leave. Walker and I married several weeks ago, and I won't let you walk in here and threaten our union."

Lucy shook her head. "Actually, I asked Pa about what would happen if I got here and you were already married. He said Mr. McKay ain't really your husband. Not legally. He's married to Sarah Lucille Mallory, right? That's me, not you."

"No, he's married to Sarah Elaine Livingston. I told him my real name, and he didn't mention a word about the change."

"Don't matter. Pa says he has a contract with me. Paid Pa a hunnert dollars for me—not you."

Heartsick, Sarah clasped her hands to keep from wringing them. "What do you want from me?"

"Why, nothing from you. You kin go on with your life, but we'll just have ta tell McKay the truth—you ain't told him about the switch yet, have you?"

Sarah shook her head, unable to think.

"I didn't think so. We gotta tell him. Then you have ta leave and I'll fulfill the contract."

"You can't—it's too late. Walker will be furious when he learns what we've done. He'll send us both away. You don't know him, Lucy. He was deeply hurt by a prior engagement, and he isn't a man who'll take lightly to being tricked by two women. He won't want either one of us."

The idea of Lucy replacing her in Walker's arms, in his heart, in his life, churned the rising sickness in Sarah's stomach.

"Pa says he kin annul the marriage. He still needs an heir, don't he? I'm sure he'll be mad as a wet hen for a few days, but that'll pass. He contracted for a bride, and I'm that bride."

Sarah stared at her, wondering how anyone could be so simplistic.

Lucy didn't seem concerned at all that Sarah's marriage was legitimate. "Pa says I ought marry Mr. McKay and live in this fine house." She stood back, openly enthralled with Spring Grass. "He must be plenty wealthy."

Sarah turned as the front door opened and Flo appeared, holding an armful of dirty sheets. Sarah could see from the look on her face that she had heard too much.

"What's going on out here?"

Lucy promptly extended her hand. "Lucy Mallory," she greeted with a bright smile. "I'm here to marry Mr. McKay."

Flo glanced at the extended hand and then at Sarah. Sarah felt tears welling in her eyes. She couldn't bear the look of shock and disbelief on Flo's face. Brushing past the bewildered housekeeper, she grabbed her skirts and flew into the house and up the stairs.

Nausea overcame her flight and she slumped on a step, not sure if she could go on. She laid her head down, sobbing. Part of her wanted to die. Then she wouldn't have to face Walker, wouldn't have to witness his anger. His pain. Gathering her strength, she stood up, climbed the last of the stairs, and ran down the hallway, slamming the bedroom door a moment later.

Flo listened to the flight, wondering if the world had gone mad. First Sarah fainting, now this person claiming to want to marry Walker—she turned to face the young woman standing on the front porch and looking very much at home.

"Who'd you say you were?"

"Lucy Mallory."

"Sarah is Walker's wife."

"Might be, but I have a legal contract that sez he's supposed to marry me." The girl smiled confidently. "I'm for sure Lucy Mallory."

"Mallory? Sarah said there was some sort of mix-up at the agency—"

"No, ma'am. No mix-up. I'm Mr. McKay's intended."

Flo's eyes swept over her. Where was S.H.? "You stay right here." She reentered the house and marched up the stairs, sheets trailing behind her. If Sarah wasn't the right bride, then whom had Walker married? She grimaced at the thought of Walker facing yet another deception. Pausing in front of the couple's room, she pressed her ear against the closed door. She could hear the sound of vomiting. Dropping the sheets, she entered the room without knocking.

Sarah was hunched over the chamber pot, heaving. Flo bent to help, holding the sobbing girl until the retching gradually eased. The old woman gently brushed the damp tendrils of hair out of her face. "Land sakes, this has been quite a day for you, young'un. What in the world is going on?"

Sarah slumped to Flo's shoulder, crying. "I-I've done a t-terrible thing, Flo."

Flo held her tight, gently rocking back and forth. "Is the girl downstairs really Lucy Mallory?"

"Y-yes."

Flo brushed her hair, fingers untangling wet strands off her cheeks so she could see the young woman's anguished features.

"I don't even pretend to understand what's going on," Flo admitted. "But you're only going to make yourself sicker if you don't get yourself under control. Whatever it is, God knows what's happening, and there's nothing in his eye that can't be forgiven." She sat Sarah up, wiping at the tears coursing down her cheeks. When the girl had gained control of her emotions, Flo said softly, "Now tell me what's happened and we'll see what we can do about it."

Sarah's story slowly unfolded, and Flo listened intently as Sarah revealed that she was the daughter of wealthy railroad magnate Lowell Livingston. There'd been an argument, and Sarah had run away. During the journey she'd met Lucy. At the last moment Sarah realized she couldn't marry Walker without telling him her real name. The change hadn't seemed to bother him.

Flo had never heard such a story. "Why did you run off? Certainly some fine young man in Boston would have married you. Your father is a wealthy man."

"I don't want someone to marry me for my father's money. I want them to marry me because they want me, because they love me!" Pulling out of Flo's arms, Sarah leaned over the chamber pot and emptied her stomach again.

"Lord have mercy on your soul, young'un. Your pa must be worried sick about you. Does he know where you are?"

"No...but he knows that I'm safe," Sarah managed to acknowledge between bouts of nausea.

"Mercy. You got a knack for gettin' yourself in powerful messes." Flo waited until the retching eased. She was thoughtful for a moment. Then she said, "Sarah, have you had your monthly?"

Sarah glanced up, pale and weak from the violent episode. She shook her head.

"How long have you been feeling sick?"

"It started this morning—well, maybe yesterday, but the dizziness started today."

"Could be that you're expectin'."

"I...don't know. Is this how a mother-to-be feels? Dreadfully sick?"

"Sometimes, honey. Are you prone to fainting spells?"

"Besides the barn, I had one in Potster's kitchen this morning."

"I think you're with child, young'un. You got to tell Walker."

Sarah sat back on her heels, closing her eyes in despair. "Even if I were, I wouldn't tell Walker—not until I've seen a doctor and confirmed the suspicion. He'd only think I was lying to him." Once he learned about her deception he wouldn't believe a word she said, and who could blame him? If only Lucy hadn't shown up today. By tomorrow she would have told him...

Flo shook her head. "The days following Trudy's departure were dark ones. Walker didn't sleep or eat, and he prowled about the house at night, snapping at anyone who crossed his path. This isn't going to be an easy time in the McKay household."

Covering her face with the cloth, Sarah murmured, "What about Lucy? She's downstairs. If Walker sees her—"

"Don't worry about her. I'll keep her out of the way until you can talk to him."

Sarah gave her a grateful look. "Thank you, Flo. I'll change my dress and go find him."

Flo turned to leave, absently gathering the sheets she'd dropped on her way out.

"Flo?"

"Yes, honey?"

"You know I love him, don't you?"

Flo nodded, smiling at her for the first time in days. "A body would have to be blind not to see that."

When Flo walked into the parlor, she noted that Lucy had made herself at home. Hands clasped behind her back, the young woman roamed the room, closely examining the craftsmanship of the clock Betsy had given Mitch fifteen Christmases ago.

She turned and smiled when she saw Flo come in. "This is jest the purtiest clock. It must be very expensive."

"Yes, it is. If you'll excuse me, I have to take these sheets to the washroom."

When she returned a few moments later, Lucy had moved from the clock to the mantel and was holding a porcelain vase in both hands.

"Are you the maid?"

Flo met her curious gaze before stiffening her back. "I've run this household long before you were born."

"That's nice. What's your name?"

"Flo."

"Flo. My pa had a dog named Flo." Lucy gently placed the vase back on the mantel. "Is Mr. McKay handsome too?"

"Too?"

"Well…he has all this money." The young woman's gaze roamed the room. "Pa says he could buy the moon if'n he wanted."

"He doesn't buy moons."

Lucy waltzed around the parlor, eyeing the furniture and running her hands along the polished tables. Clearly, life was looking up for her.

She sat herself down in Walker's chair, testing the comfort as she tilted her head at Flo. "Is he a kind man?"

Flo stepped over and jerked a pillow from behind the girl's back. "Always been decent to me."

Lucy seemed taken aback by the pillow's sudden departure. Touching a hand to her hair, she said brightly, "Is Mr. McKay available? I really should talk to him as soon as possible. My parents are expecting…" She paused, looking hesitant for the first time. "My folks expect to visit soon, and they'll for sure want me married afore they git here."

"Miss Mallory—" Flo heard the kitchen screen door slam shut and she quickly looked over her shoulder.

"Flo! You got any leftover meat loaf? I'm hungry."

Walker.

Lucy straightened her skirts, giving the housekeeper a hopeful look. "Is that him?"

"In the warming oven, Walker!" Flo turned back to Lucy. "That's him, missy." She bent close as she walked past the young woman. "A word of caution: He doesn't like surprises."

Walker had found the meat by the time Flo reached the kitchen. He bit into his dinner, washing it down with a swallow of milk.

"Let me fix you a plate. I have some beans and corn—"

"No time, Flo. I got to get back to work."

Walker cut a hunk of bread. "Is Sarah feeling any better?"

"Ask her yourself. She wants to talk to you."

Walker swallowed another bite. "Where is she?"

"Upstairs."

"She'll have to make it quick. I'm behind in all my chores." He quickly strode through the kitchen into the hall foyer.

Flo saw him glance into the parlor as Lucy got up from her chair, smiling. He nodded. "Afternoon."

"Good afternoon, Mr. McKay." Lucy's eyes turned bright with excitement.

Flo hurriedly diverted him toward the stairs. "Hurry along. Sarah's waiting for you."

As Walker proceeded up the stairs, Flo returned to the parlor to distract the visitor.

Chapter Thirty

"Sarah? You up here?" Walker paused at the bedroom door.

Sarah froze when she heard his voice, forcing back another bout of queasiness. "In here, dear..." Dear? She never called him "dear." He would know something was wrong.

The door opened, and Walker stuck his head in. "Who's the girl in the parlor?"

Sarah got off the bed and moved toward the washstand. "An acquaintance. Someone I met on my way here."

"Why aren't you in the parlor visiting with her? Still not feeling well?"

Sarah looked away, unable to meet his eyes. He would know all too soon that Lucy Mallory was no one's friend.

Entering the bedroom, he kicked the door shut with the heel of his boot. "Flo said you wanted to see me?"

Unable to find her voice now, she nodded.

He winked at her. "Lonesome?"

"No...not lonesome."

Concern clouded his features when he noted her flushed and tearstained expression. "Are you still feeling bad? Why don't I send one of the—"

"I'm not ill!" The denial came out harshly. She bit her tongue, willing her tears at bay.

"Okay," he said softly. "Maybe a kiss will put some color back into those cheeks." He walked over and bent to embrace her.

Any other time she would welcome his advances. But not now, not when she was about to destroy their world. She left the washstand to put distance between them. Why hadn't she told him sooner? Now she'd waited too long. Lucy was here, threatening to destroy the connection that had just started to form between them.

Following her across the room, he made a second attempt to take her into his arms, failing again.

Shrugging his efforts aside, she said shortly, "Please, Walker. There's something I have to tell you."

Their eyes met and locked. He smiled and said quietly, "I can think of better ways to spend my break than talking."

He had never been so forward, or spoken in such an intimate tone.

Fear flooded her. What if he insisted that she leave today, insisted he'd bargained for Lucy Mallory and that he was obligated to keep the commitment? Sarah knew in her heart that she was Walker's soul mate.

Foolish Sarah. Such thoughts are wishful thinking. Walker will be so furious when he hears what you've done that he'll order you out of the house and out of his life. He'll say you betrayed him as surely as Trudy betrayed him earlier.

But it wasn't the same. She wasn't Trudy, and she loved him with every fiber of her being. Would he see that?

Twisting the hem of her apron, she tried to organize her confession in a sane manner.

You're not going to believe this, but a funny thing happened to me on the way here—

No, that would never work. He'd see right through that.

I should have mentioned this earlier, darling—you'll laugh when you hear it, but the agency didn't send me. Isn't that hilarious?

He wouldn't find it even mildly amusing, let alone hilarious. The certain knowledge crowded her throat, threatening to cut off her air supply. Her head swam. *Please, God, don't let me faint now. Provide the words to make him believe that what started as deceit quickly turned into a deep love.*

Walker's voice came to her through a fog. "So what's so important that you need to talk to me about it in the middle of the day?"

Sucking in breath, she willed her voice steady. "I…you'll never guess…actually, I know you'll find this really odd, even amusing…" She paused, taking in another deep breath. How could she say it?

I tricked you. I played a cruel hoax on you and jeopardized what might have been a glorious marriage between us, all in the name of selfishness.

He would never forgive her. She knew that as surely as she knew her knees were about to give way again. Heading toward the bed, she swallowed against the rush of bile to her throat.

"Sarah?" New concern tinged his voice. "Are you going to faint?"

Grasping her by the shoulders, he eased her down on the side of the bed.

"Flo!"

"No!" She didn't want Flo to be here when she told him. One pair of accusing eyes was enough. "I don't need Flo," she murmured. "Please, Walker…let me say this."

Walker leaned close, his breath warm against her cheek. "What is it, sweetheart? Sarah…what's wrong?"

Tears brimmed in her eyes and she lay back on the pillow, aware it would be the last time he would look at her with love and caring in those blue, blue eyes. Never again would he see her as the woman who shared his bed, his heart, the one and only woman he'd dared to trust after Trudy.

"I don't know how to tell you this."

His eyes met hers, grave now, as if he knew their idyllic world was about to collapse. "Just say it."

Clasping his face between her hands, she said softly, "I'm sorry, Walker. I'm not your intended bride."

"What are you talking about?"

"I lied to you. There was no mistake by the agency. Lucy Mallory is the bride you sent for."

His penetrating gaze held hers as the words sank in. Long, agonizing moments passed. She saw fear, disbelief, betrayal, pain, and then gradual acceptance play across his features. Had she honestly expected him to laugh it off, to compliment her on her extraordinary theatrical abilities?

The moments between her revelation and his reply seemed to stretch into days. She couldn't read his eyes for the torrent of conflict that waged there.

Straightening, he released his clasp on her shoulders, and her hands slid away from his face. "Who are you?"

The coldness in his voice hurt, but she deserved it. The teasing was gone, the husbandly banter vanished. In their place she heard the voice of a stranger.

"My name *is* Sarah Livingston." When she saw confusion cloud his eyes, she prayed for wisdom. She lifted her arms, willing him to return. "What I've done is inexcusable, but I can explain if you'll only permit me."

For a moment she thought he might allow her a brief explanation. Her heart soared and then plummeted when his eyes hardened, his jaw clenched. "Why should I allow you anything?"

"Because I am your wife—in every sense of the word, Walker. I love you." When he swore, which he never did, she went on, "Our vows were legal. In God's eyes we are man and wife."

Uttering a black oath, he cupped the back of his neck and stood, pacing the room.

"I meant to tell you—I tried to tell you this morning. I was on my way to find you, to explain when Lucy arrived. Please, don't hate me…"

He paused before the window, staring at the activities below. Normal sounds drifted up, but the day was anything but normal. "Did Flo know about this?"

"No, she didn't. Not until this afternoon when Lucy showed up. She heard us talking, and I had to tell her what I'd done then."

He turned to look at her. "Lucy Mallory is *here?*"

"Sitting downstairs in the parlor. She's the...acquaintance I mentioned."

"I don't believe it." Resuming his pacing, he ran his fingers through his hair. She knew he was trying to make sense of what she'd told him. But if she couldn't, how could he?

She climbed off the bed and approached him hesitantly, as if she were cornering a wounded animal. Gently she put her hand on his arm. "I know it's upsetting, but all is not lost. All you have to do is void your contract with Lucy and nothing changes. She'll go home and we'll never speak of this day again. I'm happy being your wife. I'm deeply in love with you, Walker. You sent for a bride, and I want to be that woman."

He shrugged her hand aside and her heart broke. All the love and assurance he would ever need was in her eyes. Couldn't he see that? Didn't he know by now that she'd never pretended feelings she didn't have—that she adored him? No woman could ever respond to him the way she had if she didn't love him.

And he wouldn't have responded to her the way he had if she were merely a convenience, a broodmare, someone to bear his name and children. Love could be theirs again if only he could find a way to forgive her.

"I know this is upsetting—"

"Upsetting?" He could barely look at her now. "You *lied* to me, and you think it's *upsetting* to me?"

"Devastating," she amended.

He glared at her.

"Insidious," she murmured. "Judas-like, actually, and I'm so very sorry, but I did tell you my real name the first day we met."

His look nearly felled her. "I wasn't listening."

"You heard me and you acted as though one woman was as good as another."

"At the time, it was. But things have changed." He turned accusing eyes on her. "I trusted you. I believed that what we had was real."

"It is real! I love you with all my heart!"

"You've lived a lie for how many weeks?"

"I told a fib and I'm sorry, but what I've done is not unforgivable," she pleaded. *Please, God, he has to forgive me. I can't lose him because of one foolish mistake.*

Stalking to the door, he refused to answer. She followed him, begging now. "Not unforgivable, Walker. I know you're upset. I understand that I've betrayed you. First Trudy and now me, but I give you my word that I never intended to hurt you, and I don't want to leave you. I love you. You must believe me. You're the only man I want, the man I've dreamed about since I was a young girl. I believe that we would have never found each other if God hadn't planned this—"

"You're blaming God for this nightmare?"

"No! I would never—let me prove to you that I can be trusted. I shouldn't have lied, and I'm paying the price, but I've kept the bargain. I've looked after your house, tried to be of help, and done everything I know to make you happy. Please, Walker—"

"You've made a mockery of marriage, Sarah. How can you speak of God and how he would approve this…this insult?"

She stepped back as he slammed out of the bedroom, the noise jarring her teeth.

Blinking back tears, she bit her lip and sagged against the closed door. "Just say you'll at least think about it," she whispered brokenly.

❖

Lucy's fan paused, and she brightened as Walker came downstairs. Half rising out of her seat, she smiled. "Mr. McKay—"

The rancher strode past the parlor and disappeared into his study, slamming the door behind him.

As she sank back to the sofa, her fan fluttered harder.

Chapter Thirty-One

The foyer clock struck seven. Sarah sighed, her gaze returning to the study door. Walker hadn't come out, and the closed door was a stark reminder that her husband's anger had yet to run its course.

Lucy Mallory shifted in her chair, eyeing her empty plate.

Pork roast, boiled potatoes, and string beans sat untouched on the table. No one was going to eat until Walker took his chair, which he apparently didn't intend to do tonight.

The minutes ticked by. The women avoided eye contact, focusing instead on their plates. How long could Sarah keep up the pretense that Walker would join them? Supper was served at six. Apparently, if he wasn't speaking to her, he wasn't taking meals with her, either.

"I could eat a skunk," Lucy complained. "Is Mr. McKay ever going to come out of his den?"

How long did it take to starve a person? Sarah's gaze slid to Lucy, her thoughts anguished. Wadsy's voice flashed through her mind. *Shame on you, baby girl! You're as much to blame for this as that Mallory girl!*

The dining room felt as if every window was closed and air was a priceless commodity. Flo came to the doorway, glancing anxiously toward Walker's study. "No word from him?"

"None. Flo, maybe we should—" Sarah started to get up, but the housekeeper leveled a warning finger at her. "You stay put, young lady.

You've caused enough trouble." The older woman disappeared back into the kitchen.

Closing her eyes, Lucy said softly. "This is real puzzlin'. I honestly thought you wouldn't care if I showed up."

"Why would you think that?"

"Because it's an arranged marriage. How close could you get to Mr. McKay in a few short weeks?"

"Close enough to fall deeply in love with him."

Lucy sighed and closed her eyes. "Mr. McKay will have to settle the dispute. He sent for me, and all this—" her hand swept the lavish dining room—"should be mine."

"Walker is worth so much more than his bank account. He's good and honest, and I played a deplorable trick on him." A defensive note had started to creep into Sarah's tone. "And you shouldn't have traded him off like a goat."

"You shouldn't have accepted him like a rabid wolf—"

"Neither one of you have the sense God gave a goose." Flo came back through the doorway with coffee. "You both had better get on yer knees and ask the good Lord to settle this, and to forgive yer foolishness. One lie leads to two, and two to three, and before you know it you got a mess the likes of what yer facin'."

Lucy sighed and glanced at Sarah. "The housekeeper doesn't like you either, does she?"

"The name's Flo." The housekeeper thumped the coffeepot on the table and left the room.

Flo probably didn't like her anymore. Sarah stared at her plate, choking on remorse. She'd didn't need a lecture on lying. She knew full well the consequences.

Walker could be in his den this minute considering his contract with Lucy.

Clearing her throat, Sarah said quietly, "I wouldn't count my chickens before they hatch if I were you. Walker's just as upset with you as he is with me. Your family may want his money, but he's not a fool."

Lucy took a sip of her coffee. "How could he be? I didn't come here pretending to be someone else. I didn't marry him under false pretenses."

"You're as guilty of this lie as I am." How dare she insinuate this was all Sarah's fault? If she hadn't agreed to the ruse, Sarah couldn't have pulled it off.

"*You* suggested the switch."

"*You* wanted to marry Rodney Willbanks."

Both women sat up straighter in their chairs.

"If you think you can waltz in here and take my husband, *Miss* Mallory, you have another think coming!"

"He's not really yore husband!"

"He *is* my husband and I have a whole town of witnesses and a marriage certificate to prove it. We took our vows before God—"

"You lied to God."

"I did *not*!" Sarah would never lie to God. A scream of fury stuck at the back of her throat. She wanted this woman, this Jezebel, this home wrecker, out of Walker's house and out of her life. Lucy wanted him only for his money and what he could do for her family. Sarah would fight to the death before she'd hand him over to the scheming likes of Lucy Mallory.

"I want you to leave, Lucy. Now, this evening. S.H. or one of the ranch hands will find you a room in town. You can leave on the next train."

"You can't order me to leave. You ain't got no authority. Pa said for me to stay."

"I'm Walker's wife. This is my home."

"Not anymore. I have a bindin' contract."

"No judge will make Walker honor that contract. He's already married."

"We'll see."

"I'll make you leave." Sarah pushed back from the table, prepared to do battle.

Lucy snatched a biscuit and hurled it. Sarah gasped as the bread ricocheted off her right cheek. Gritting her teeth, she calmly reached for the bowl of gravy, hurling the contents at Lucy.

Pork roast flew, then china cups. Jam and coffee splattered the table-cloth, and the dining room erupted in a full-scale assault as the women threw dishes, screeched, hit, and pulled hair.

"Girls!" Flo burst from the kitchen and waded in to separate the warring factions, who were now rolling around on the floor. It took a minute for the housekeeper to get the girls back in their seats. Sopping gravy off the front of Sarah's blouse, she tsked.

"Never saw such goings-on in all my born days. What are you, a bunch of hooligans?"

"Flo, she just wants—" Sarah began.

"I know what she wants!" Flo left Sarah and moved around the table to see about the ugly stains dotting Lucy's blouse. The young woman's hair was loose from its pins, and she had a big gob of grape jam above her left brow.

"Lord have mercy. Have you two no learnin'? Throwing food like unruly children! You ought to be ashamed of yourselves."

Sarah reached for a napkin, wiping greasy spatters off her skirt. "She has to leave, Flo. This is an impossible situation. Walker will never come out of the study while she's still here."

"I'm not leaving," Lucy announced. "Not until I talk to Mr. McKay and tell him the truth." She brushed food crumbs out of her hair. "You think you're so smart. You'll be attendin' my wedding, Sarah Livingston."

"I hope you like barbecue," Sarah grumbled.

"What?"

"I want this catfight to stop, you hear me?" Crossing her arms over her chest, Flo glared at the two girls. "I'm going in that study and get this mess straightened out. You sit right here, and I don't want to hear a peep out of either one of you! Do you understand?"

The women nodded in unison.

Flo disappeared around the corner, and Sarah hazarded a quick look at Lucy, who promptly stuck out her tongue.

Ignoring the infantile gesture by looking in the other direction, Sarah licked jelly off her lips. It would be a cold day before she let that woman—or any other, for that matter—get her clutches into Walker McKay.

Chapter Thirty-Two

"W alker?" Flo tapped softly on the study door.

"I'm busy, Flo."

"You're not that busy, and if you're not decent, you'd better say so, because I'm comin' in." She waited for a moment and then turned the handle. Walker gave her a dirty look as she entered the room.

"Can't a man have his privacy around here anymore?"

"Ordinarily, yes, but these aren't ordinary times. And cowards don't get special privileges. Hidin' away in here ain't gonna solve a blessed thing." She walked to the window and opened the drapes. Fading daylight poured into the cluttered study. Walker sat at his desk, his hair tousled and his feet propped up.

"What was all the noise out there?"

"Your women, fighting like street brawlers."

"I don't have any women."

"Beg pardon, but you do. Two of 'em, and they are throwing food at each other."

He grunted. "Are they still here?"

"They're still here, big as life, sitting at your table waiting for you to come out."

"Inform the ladies they'll be sitting a long time."

Flo straightened a stack of books, absently wiping the desk's surface with her apron hem.

"I can't blame you for being upset. Who wouldn't be, under the circumstances? Marry one woman and find out she's not who you think she was. But the problem isn't going to be solved by you holing up here, refusing to even discuss the matter. I can't have those two girls sitting at my table all night. Got food all over my clean floor, the tablecloth's a mess…"

Giving her a questioning look, Walker tossed down a half glass of brandy.

She shook her head. "Yer not a drinkin' man. You think that brandy will solve your problem?"

His boots hit the floor, and he got up to prowl the room. "Why did she do it, Flo? Why didn't she just tell me about the switch? At the time, it wouldn't have made any difference. One woman was as good as another."

At the time, that might have been true. But not now. As much as Walker vowed he'd never fall prey to another woman's treachery, Sarah had wormed her way into his heart, and that made her actions even more painful than Trudy's betrayal.

"I can't answer for Sarah, Walker. She tells me she's sorry, that if she had it to do over again, she'd tell you exactly who she was. She's young. She goes on feelings instead of sound judgment. She realizes she's done wrong, and she tells me she prays you will forgive her and go on."

He snorted. "Who is she, Flo?"

"She said she is Sarah Livingston. Her father is a wealthy Bostonian railroad owner."

He shook his head wordlessly. "How blind can a man be? Then the next question is why, Flo?" Walker paused before the window, his eyes fixed on the rose garden, the disheveled flower bed yet another knife to the heart.

"She says she made the switch because she wanted to be married. She's stayed on because she loves you."

"She needed a stranger to fill her needs?"

"Does seem peculiar, a pretty little thing like Sarah. Who knows why anyone does anything? But she seems sincere enough. Still…"

Walker turned to look at her. "Still what?"

Flo hadn't wanted to mention it. She'd seen no need until now. But if Sarah was in the marriage for anything other than what she claimed, then Walker needed to know. "I found her going over your books here a while back."

"My financial ledgers?"

"She said she was trying to help you. Said she was good at math. When I mentioned it to S.H., he didn't think it was anythin' to get upset about. Could have been idle curiosity—you know how fascinated Sarah is with ranching. Besides, she comes from a wealthy family. I wouldn't let it overly concern you, but you need to know."

Walker turned back to gaze out the window.

"What are you going to do about the situation?"

He stared at the flower garden as if the answers lay somewhere between the roses and the fountains.

Flo said softly. "S.H. should have plowed that garden under years ago."

He remained at the window, staring.

"You can't just ignore the situation, Walker. It's not going away. Two women are sitting out there waiting on you to decide who is going to be your wife."

Snorting, Walker returned to the desk.

"She's gone about it the wrong way, but Sarah's suited for you, you know that. You're just hurt and you got a right to be."

"She deceived me. "

Sighing, the housekeeper replied, "You'd best eat a bite. It's late and you ought to be good and hungry by now." She edged toward the door. "Do you plan to stay in here all night?"

He returned to the desk. "I might."

"S.H has gone after Caleb. Figured you'd want to talk to him about this."

"Thanks, Flo."

She closed the door behind her.

Caleb arrived shortly before dark. S.H. showed him in. Both men looked worried, questioning Flo with their eyes when she answered the door. She shook her head and nodded toward the dining room. Lucy and Sarah still sat in their chairs, the length of the dining room table separating them. Caleb glanced at the closed study door. "Walker in there?"

Flo inclined her head. "He's expecting you."

When the accountant walked by the dining room he paused to tip his hat. "Good evening, ladies."

Cold silence met his cordial efforts. Sighing, Flo hurried on to the kitchen.

A second knock came not long after Flo's departure.

"Go away!" Walker bellowed.

"I'd like to, but you asked me to come."

"Caleb?"

"How many friends did you send for?"

The door opened a crack, and Walker allowed him entrance. Caleb stood by the doorway, his eyes skimming the jumbled room. "Have you been ransacked?"

"Worse. I've been lied to."

Walker slammed the door and resumed pacing.

The two men shared the same age, but the years had been kinder to Walker. Caleb's gray suits and dark shirts made him look sallow, washed out, and overly weary.

The accountant frowned. "You look awful."

Running a hand over the back of his neck, Walker muttered something about feeling awful, and then sat down at the desk.

"So, who's lied to you?"

Walker picked up a glass and tossed down the contents. Sarah's deception cut deeply, causing him to finally realize how much he had grown to love her. Love. The very thing he'd told himself he would never do. "Sarah," he said.

Caleb's eyes shifted to the open ledger on the desk. "Regarding what?"

Walker swiveled around to face him. "About everything. Who she is. What does she want?"

"Sarah?" The accountant sat in the wingback chair in front of the desk and removed his wire-rimmed glasses, absently polishing them on a hankerchief. "What's she done?"

Walker replied quietly, "She tricked me, Caleb. She took Lucy Mallory's place."

Caleb glanced up.

"The two women switched places. Lucy Mallory went off on some jaunt to marry a man she wanted, and Sarah agreed to stand in as my bride."

"Merciful heavens. What could they have been thinking?"

"That I was a fool and I'd never know the difference, and that even when I did, I wouldn't care." It turned his stomach to think of how easily he'd fallen for the trick. But he knew why. The moment Sarah Livingston got off that train, something had happened between them, something he hadn't wanted to acknowledge. If Lucy hadn't showed up, when would she have told him about the switch? Tomorrow? The week after? Never?

"How did you discover the deception?"

"She was forced into telling me today. The real bride is sitting in the dining room. Seems Lucy Mallory has had a change of heart and now she wants to keep her end of the bargain."

Caleb hooked his glasses behind his ears, repeating, "Merciful heavens."

The two men sat in silence.

"What does Sarah have to say about her actions?"

I'm sorry, Walker. I love you. Please let me be your wife. Let me show you I can be trusted. The knife twisted deeper. "She says she intended to tell me about the switch."

"When?"

"I don't know, Caleb. Does it matter?" He reached for the brandy container, but Caleb's hand stopped him.

"Why don't I have Flo bring in a pot of hot coffee?"

"Coffee won't help."

Replacing the stopper in the bottle, Caleb moved the liquor aside. "So Sarah lied. She could have done worse."

Giving him an impatient look, Walker got out of his chair and returned to the window.

"You didn't know Lucy Mallory. You didn't know Sarah. You were willing to marry a stranger in order to produce an heir, so I hardly see where you've been wronged."

"She *lied* to me, Caleb. And I trusted her."

"True, but she hasn't run off with another man."

Maybe it would have hurt less if Sarah had run off with another man. Then she wouldn't be waiting in his dining room. His gaze focused on the unkempt garden.

"Flo says Sarah's been going through the books, trying to help."

Caleb sat up straighter, color draining from his face. "Why would she do that?"

"Who knows why Sarah does anything?"

Loosening his collar, Caleb shifted in his chair. "There'd be no reason for her to look at the books. Do you suspect she's after your money?"

"She shouldn't be. Her father is one of the richest men in America."

"Could she be lying about her identity? Perhaps she isn't Sarah Livingston."

Walker turned to give him a wry look.

The accountant reached for the brandy and poured himself a drink. The burgundy liquid spilled on the desk and he absently blotted it with a piece of paper. "I'll recheck the books and make certain that she hasn't tampered with them."

The statement irritated Walker. "She hasn't 'tampered' with them.

She can't even manage a meal, much less swindle me out of money. She's not a thief."

"You didn't think she was a liar."

The observation was met with stony silence.

Sarah wasn't a thief. Walker would stake his life on that, although at the moment he was helpless to know why. She'd lied about her identity. She'd lied to him, lied to Flo and S.H. and Potster, but her explanation was so cockeyed he almost believed it. Before meeting her, he'd never known a woman who could get herself in so much hot water with so little effort.

Caleb downed the liquor, his eyes returning to the ledger. Sweat covered his thin upper lip. "I'll take the books home with me. Until this matter is resolved, you can't be too careful."

"That isn't necessary. You and I are the only ones with access to the funds." Walker thought about telling Caleb about Sarah's earlier questions about bookkeeping but decided not to. One crisis at a time was enough.

"Still, I want to go over them carefully." Caleb sat his glass on the desk, pressing the handkerchief to his upper lip.

"There is something you can do." Returning to the desk, Walker reached into the side drawer for the signed agreement between him and Lucy Mallory. "Can you read this thing and tell me what I signed?"

Caleb's brows lifted. "You don't know?"

"At the time I thought I did. Back then, I didn't think it'd make a whole lot of difference."

"I'll look it over." Caleb took the papers and the two men fell silent.

Walker leaned back in his chair and closed his eyes. Maybe the contract he'd signed with Lucy's father would take the choice out of his hands.

The thought was even worse than present circumstances.

Sarah watched the clock and then lowered her head to the dining table, nausea building again. The mere thought of food made her shudder, yet she knew she should eat.

Her head shot up when she heard the study door open. A grim-faced Walker and Caleb emerged. Her hand automatically reached out to touch Walker when he walked past her chair, but he brushed it aside.

The two men sat down at the opposite end of the table.

Walker refused to meet Sarah's eyes. "Where's Flo?"

"She may have gone to bed. Lucy is taking a walk."

"Caleb, tell Flo and Miss Mallory that I want to see them."

Sarah searched for a hint of forgiveness in his eyes and found none. He looked tired and disappointed, and she longed to take him in her arms and comfort him. But the look of desperation on Walker's face held her silent.

Caleb returned with Flo wearing a nightcap and Lucy in tow.

Lucy stood behind the seat closest to Walker, murmuring. "Mr. Mc-Kay. Ever so nice to make yore acquaintance." She dipped in a little curtsy before sitting down.

Sarah rolled her eyes but Walker acknowledged the greeting.

Flo took a chair next to Sarah, reaching for her hand beneath the table and giving it a squeeze.

Caleb flipped through the contract, scanning various sections. Pausing, he glanced up, clearing his throat.

"Walker has asked me to review the contract he and Miss Mallory signed prior to her arrival. Walker, is there anything you want to say before we proceed?"

Sarah slid to the edge of her chair, holding tightly to Flo's hand.

He pinpointed Sarah with his gaze. "You shouldn't have said the agency made a mistake and pretended to be the mail-order bride I was expecting. You should have told me who you really were."

"I was going to..."

The pain in his eyes penetrated deep into her heart. It was a devastatingly fit punishment for her betrayal.

"I was foolish," she said softly. "Please forgive me, Walker."

"Actually, it was my fault," Lucy admitted. "I shouldn't have agreed to the plan, but Sarah was so desperate. I'm terribly sorry, Mr. McKay. I wasn't thinkin' real clear, but once I realized we had a bindin' contract—"

"Miss Mallory, the reason doesn't matter," Walker said stoically. "I'm bound by what the contract stipulates."

Lucy looked momentarily flustered. "Pa says you got an obligation to marry me because of that there paper."

"Caleb, what are my options?"

"Well, it's rather complicated." Caleb studied the document. "Of course, there's no clause relating to the present circumstance, mind you, and I'm not a lawyer—but I believe, if I read this correctly, Miss Mallory is legally entitled to enforce the contract."

"That's not fair!" Sarah cried. "Walker is married to me!"

Caleb received the outburst coolly. "Technically that's true. But the contract indicates that he was bound to another woman. According to this document, Miss Mallory is the legal party who—"

"She forfeited that right when she allowed me to take her place." Sarah turned to Walker, her eyes silently pleading while Caleb continued to recite contract clauses.

The accountant's voice faded and Sarah was aware only of her husband. Walker couldn't let this happen. He had to put a stop to this madness.

Her gaze locked with his, and now she saw not pain but a kind of powerlessness he seemed to accept.

"Caleb ain't an attorney," Flo reminded them when the banker finished. "Might be that Estes Knolls would have a different opinion about the document."

Walker broke Sarah's locked gaze. "Estes won't be back from Portland until next month."

"That's right. He is away on lengthy business," Caleb said.

Flo squeezed Sarah's hand.

Relief flooded Lucy's face. "If he says the contract is bindin', then I guess we ain't got no choice. Sarah can either go home or go live with her friend in New York. You kin have this marriage annulled and then you and me kin git married, and then Ma and Pa kin come see us."

Flo's jaw firmed, and she cleared her throat. "It's none of my business who you choose, Walker, but before you make a fool of yerself a third time, you'd best take this into consideration." She took the Mallory letter from her pocket. Sarah gasped.

"Flo, no, don't—"

"Sarah, you may have lied to us, but it would be worse to have a thief carry on the McKay name." The housekeeper handed Walker the letter.

Walker scanned the missive and Sarah held her breath. Lucy's face flushed crimson when he finished and fixed angry eyes on her.

"Who wrote this?"

"I believe that would be Miss Mallory's mother," Flo said.

Tossing the papers on the table, Walker stood up. "Miss Mallory, S.H. will take you to the train tomorrow morning."

Lucy sprang to her feet. "Why? You cain't do this. We have a real legal-like agreement! Why...my pa won't hear of this! You'd best give this more thought, Mr. McKay." She whirled on Flo. "Where did you git that letter?"

The housekeeper shrugged.

Lucy whirled back to face Walker. "You can't do this. I'll tell Pa."

Walker met her eyes coldly. "You'll be leaving tomorrow. I'll see that your ticket is paid for."

"While we're on the subject of who's stayin' and who's goin'," Flo added, "there's another thing you should know."

The baby. Sarah shot the housekeeper a warning look. If Walker decided to forgive her, she wanted it to be because of love and not because of obligation.

"Flo, please don't. If Walker wants to send me away, I'll go."

Flo continued as if she hadn't heard. "You'd be a fool to send Sarah away. You're mad right now, but you'll get over it. Don't do anything until you're thinkin' straighter."

"Flo, I am capable of defending myself," Sarah murmured, her cheeks hot.

"Walker, the contract says—" Caleb opened it again.

Sarah glared at him. He was on Lucy's side. This didn't surprise her. Caleb Vanhooser sensed her suspicions. Caleb and Lucy argued with Walker, Flo chiming in with her opinion until the room rang with voices.

"Enough!" Walker threw his hands up. The room's occupants fell silent.

"Miss Mallory, you nullified the contract by not arriving when you said you would. Tomorrow S.H. will take you to the train, buy your ticket, and give you fifty dollars for your time and effort."

Lucy glanced from Sarah to Flo and then whirled and marched out. "You cain't do this. Ma and Pa are countin' on that money," she declared over her shoulder.

Flo shoved back from the table. "Now yer finally making sense. I'm going to go get her set up at our house."

Sarah slumped in relief, closing her eyes. Walker hadn't asked her to go, but he hadn't asked her to stay. He walked past her chair, hardly sparing her a glance. She opened one eye a moment later and found a tight-lipped Caleb staring at her.

"Don't you have somewhere you need to go?" she asked, weary of trying to win his friendship. Being polite wasn't possible tonight.

"I was about to ask you the same." With a foxlike grin, he stood up and reached for his briefcase. "I trust you'll sleep well tonight, Sarah. Rest up for your journey back to Boston."

❖

Early the following morning, S.H. reined in the team just short of the train station. Not a word had passed between the foreman and Lucy on the way into town.

Lucy reached for her bag before the wagon came to a complete stop. She was furious with Walker's decision and even more upset about facing her parents back home.

"I'll get that." S.H. set the brake and bounded off the wagon, coming around to help her. She gave him a cold look, stepping down on her own.

He shrugged before hoisting the bag and carrying it to the train platform. "Have a pleasant trip, Miss Mallory. Do you need any help with arrangements?"

"Jest leave."

Tipping his hat, he said, "May God grant you safe journey."

The buckboard rolled off and Lucy quickly crossed the street and went into the telegraph office. Approaching the counter, she pulled the fifty dollars from her purse, peeling off a bill.

"Can I help you, ma'am?" the man behind the window asked.

"I want to send a telegram."

"Yes, ma'am. Whom should I address it to?"

Lucy smugly glanced over her shoulder. The dust from the McKay wagon rose as it rattled out of town. "Lowell Livingston, Boston, Massachusetts."

Chapter Thirty-Three

Sarah? A thief?" Potster stared at Walker as if he'd lost his mind. "That little gal might use poor judgment occasionally, but she ain't no thief." He handed Walker a cup of coffee.

"Then why was she going through my books?"

"Cain't say, but I'd bet my last dime she don't care if you got a dollar to your name. I've known a few women in my day, and she ain't that kind, Mr. McKay."

Walker grinned in spite of his heartache. "I've heard rumors about your women."

Potster chuckled. "All true."

S.H. walked up to join the men. He slapped a strip of leather in Walker's free hand. "Notice you're a little testy these days. Haven't seen much of her lately, have ya?"

Walker hadn't seen Sarah at all since Lucy had shown up a week ago. Flo said she was under the weather. Finishing the harness he had been repairing, he reached for another one. What was ailing her? Guilt? Or was she really ill? For a split-second concern seized him, but then he quickly shook the emotion aside. Flo would have told him if Sarah were in any danger.

"Wouldn't hurt none to check on yer woman, would it? Flo says she's a pitiful sight, eyes nearly swollen shut from cryin'."

"She's not my woman, S.H. Not since she lied to me."

"Could be that yer bein' a little bullheaded about this. The girl's crazy about ya, Walker. Any fool can see it."

Potster agreed. "You won't find a woman like her on every corner. Now, if you'll excuse me, I gotta git back to the bunkhouse. I got meat cookin'." He turned and left.

Walker fiddled with the halter in his hands. "Implying that I'm one fool who can't see it?"

"If the boot fits."

Walker wanted to go to her. The nights were long without her. He missed her smile and the sound of her laughter, the way she looked in the early mornings, all tousled and warm. Sleeping in the spare room wasn't his idea of paradise, but every time he reached their bedroom door he remembered that she had lied. If a man couldn't trust a woman, all the lovemaking in the world was useless.

S.H. stroked the mare's neck. "You keepin' this hardhead company, ol' girl?" Diamond threw her nose up in the air and tossed her head as if denying any involvement with Walker's mulishness.

Walker gritted his teeth and bore down to tighten the finishing knot on the halter. "Maybe I should send her home, S.H." The thought had been at the back of his mind for days. He couldn't forgive her, and he didn't want to stay in the guest room forever. Sarah should be home with family, people who loved her. Yet that idea appealed to him less than facing her.

S.H. snorted and tore a piece of leather in two. "If that's what you really wanted, you'da sent her home with that other gal."

Walker threw the halter over a stall door and then reached for a saddle that needed mending. S.H. had a point. Trudy had left him with no choice; with Sarah he still had options. He could forgive her and move on. Until a week ago the marriage had been good, nearly ideal. Sarah was welcome company, easy on the eye and easy to be with.

A man didn't have to love a woman in order to live with her. He was in the marriage to sire an heir. Personal feelings hadn't counted when he'd ordered a bride, and they needn't count now. So why did her deceit stick in his craw? Why did he lie in his bed sleepless nights, his mind going over the way she had made him feel nine feet tall inside?

"So what are you gonna do? Refuse to speak to her until the baby's born?"

"There isn't going to be a baby, S.H."

"Open yer eyes, Walker." S.H. glanced up.

Walker's saddle slipped from the stanchion and into the hay. "What's that supposed to mean?"

Color dotted S.H.'s cheeks and he busied himself with the mare.

"S.H.?"

"What?"

"What does 'open your eyes' mean?"

Head bent, S.H. eased behind Diamond's flanks and began checking her hooves.

"Do I have to come over there and beat it out of you?"

"I cain't tell you, Walker. Flo would shoot me. I already opened my big mouth too much."

A chill ran up Walker's spine despite the extreme heat. Sarah's sickness, her wan features—a whole week spent in bed. Sarah was scatterbrained, but she wasn't sickly.

"S.H., is Sarah carrying my child?"

"Don't make me tell ya, Walker. I wanna be able to eat and sleep in my own house."

Walker leaned over to jerk the saddle back on the post.

"She can't be," he said. "If she was, she would have told me." She would have used it as a tool to trap him. What better way to bind him than to produce his heir?

S.H. took off his hat and wiped his temples, shaking his head. "Son, don't you know nothin' about havin' babies? The woman don't know right away but the signs are there. Ya could be in there rejoicin' about a baby together, but you're out here fixin' straps and sleepin' on an old bed in the spare room because of some misplaced pride ya think is more important than yer feelin's for her." The old man grabbed the cattleman's shoulders. "Do yourself a favor. Let it go. Ain't nothin' nicer than wakin' up to the woman you love in yer arms. Makes up for a heap of wrongs." His tone dropped lower. "Forgive her, son. Yer feelings are gonna get mishandled once in a while, but you can survive the hurts with a little more love. Take a page from the Good Book and forgive. You'll be a better man for it."

Chapter Thirty-Four

The sound of a carriage pulling up to the house drew Sarah away from the vanity, where she'd been absently brushing her hair. When she lifted the bedroom curtain aside, her heart sank. Papa was climbing the porch stairs. That rotten Lucy had wired Papa and told him where she was! Taking a deep breath, Sarah prepared for battle.

She quickly changed into her best dress, listening to the familiar murmur of her father's voice downstairs. When Lowell spotted her coming down the stairway, his face crumbled. Despite her resolve her heart ached for him. He'd aged ten years in the months since she'd last seen him.

"Hello, Papa."

Instead of the anticipated explosion, Lowell's shoulders slumped, his eyes bright with emotion.

"Dear God. I feared that I might never see you again."

Sarah stepped off the last stair and into her father's arms, hugging him tightly. It felt so good to hold him. "I'm sorry, Papa."

"Are you all right, child?"

"Fine, Papa. And you?"

"Better, now that I can hold you in my arms."

Stepping back, Lowell cleared his throat, eyes brimming with unshed tears. "You look lovely."

Sarah wrapped her arms around her papa's waist. "Let's go into the parlor—"

Flo cleared her throat from the stairway.

"Oh, I'm sorry, Flo. I was so happy to see Papa that I neglected you." Sarah introduced the housekeeper to Lowell.

Flo nodded. "You'll be needin' privacy. Use the study." She smiled at Lowell. "You must be dry as a bone. I'll fix a pitcher of lemonade." She saw them into the room and then hurried off, discreetly pulling the double doors closed behind her.

Lowell sat down on the sofa, rubbing his forehead. Sarah had witnessed the anxious gesture a hundred times over the years when Papa was upset.

"Sarah Elaine, what have you done?"

Standing behind Walker's desk for comfort, Sarah clasped her hands, gathering strength. She wasn't proud of running away, but given the choice, she'd do it over again for just one hour in Walker McKay's arms.

"I know you feel that I've done a foolish thing, Papa. I married a man I didn't know. He could have been cruel or a drunkard, but fortunately he wasn't—or isn't. He's a wonderful man, and I've hurt him deeply." Lifting her chin, she drew a lengthy breath. "I love Walker McKay with all my heart, but...he doesn't share my feelings."

"I know what you did! You took another woman's place and married a total stranger. You lied to McKay, betrayed me, and made a mockery of the sanctity of marriage. Are there no limits to your absurdity, Sarah?"

Focusing on her hands, Sarah forced back tears. "It seems there aren't, Papa."

Shaking his head, Lowell sank back against the sofa. He closed his eyes and she wondered if he wished he hadn't come. "You and this McKay are legally married?"

"We are."

Pain flickered briefly across Lowell's face.

"What do you intend to do about this situation?" he asked quietly.

"I'm not sure."

She had given the subject much thought—day and night—but she still had no solution. She didn't want to return to Boston. She wanted to stay here with her husband, her child, and the new life she'd begun. "I want to remain here, but Walker refuses to discuss the matter with me. When he is speaking to me again, we'll decide what to do."

Getting up, Lowell walked to the window. He stood there for a moment, staring at the overgrown rose garden.

Sarah watched his changing expressions. *It isn't fitting that Walker leave beautiful flowers unkempt to represent one woman's betrayal,* she thought. Surely each time he looked at the garden, the sight reopened old wounds. Why didn't he destroy the hateful reminder and cut it out of his life the way he had her pleadings? Sighing, she looked away. But then, had he ever truly opened his heart to her? Perhaps when she left he would simply plant another rosebush in honor of Sarah Livingston.

"You will come home with me, Sarah. Mr. McKay has been through quite enough because of you."

"No, Papa. I can't come home with you."

"You have no other choice, daughter." Lowell turned from the window, his face blotched with anger. "You can't expect Mr. McKay to go on as if nothing has happened. You lied to the man and misrepresented yourself. Surely you don't expect him to turn a blind eye to your whims."

"I don't expect that, but you don't understand. I've been a good wife. I've tried to be of help around the house, make friends with his ranch hands, and dutifully fulfill my wifely obligations—" She broke off, blushing when he winced at her openness. "Walker is angry right now, but he'll cool down, and when he does, I know that I can make him love me again."

"Your rosy perspective implies that he loved you before. Is this true?"

"I don't know if he loved me, but he liked me, and that's the first step to love. Given time I know I could have made him love me. You can't ask me to go back to Boston, Papa. I have to stay here until I know there's no other choice."

"I'll not have you throwing yourself at a man's feet, clinging like a pathetic, love-starved pup. You will come home, Sarah, and we'll find a way to rectify this mistake. We'll keep this distasteful episode quiet, and people will never know—"

"I can't do that, Papa."

"You can and you will."

Sarah paced the study. Everyone would be the wiser when she delivered Walker's baby a few months from now. She'd missed her second monthly. Flo was right, she was expecting a child—Walker's baby.

The McKay heir.

If she could only hold on long enough for Walker's rage to subside, she would tell him about the child, and his broken heart would mend and he would accept her again. If not—

"There's no other way, Sarah. Now, pack your things. We're leaving immediately. My private rail coach is waiting at the station."

"No. You don't understand, Papa. I can't leave because I'm expecting Walker's child."

A cannon shot would have been less explosive. Lowell's eyes bulged and the color drained from his face.

"That's not possible."

"Not possible? Papa, I have been married over two months now. We've—"

Lowell threw up his hands. "No, no, you're imagining things. It's too soon. You're upset about the situation and you—"

"Papa, I'm going to be a mother. I'm sick to my stomach, I've missed my last two monthlies, and I faint at anything. Flo says I'm with child, and I'm scheduled to see the doctor next week."

Sinking back to the couch, Lowell mopped his brow.

"So you see, I can't leave." Not that she would if she could.

Lowell absently stuffed the handkerchief into his pocket. "Does Walker know?"

"Absolutely not."

"Then all is not lost. A baby makes it even more imperative that you leave. No daughter of mine is going to trap a man into marriage."

"Trap? But, Papa—"

"Is this what you want, Sarah? To offer McKay no way out? Do you for one moment think a marriage could survive if based on treachery and manipulation? Your marriage has already suffered these setbacks, and what have you gained but hurt and disrespect from the man? And rightly so!"

Sarah didn't know what she thought. She would never *trap* Walker. She wanted his whole and undivided love. Anything less would be an abomination, a festering sore incapable of healing. Turning soulful eyes on Papa, she started to cry. "I love him, Papa. I don't want to leave him."

"You cannot make a man love you, Sarah. And you cannot put Walker McKay in a position where he has no choice. My heart breaks for you and the child you're carrying, but we can't heap trouble on top of more trouble. Arm-twisting is never the answer, and if you bind Walker to you by obligation, you will forever regret it."

Silence fell over the room. Sarah paced yet again, praying for a miracle yet knowing one wasn't likely.

"I'll send Wadsy to see you through the pregnancy. When the child is born, you can come home and then I'll have the infant brought to us in a few months, saying it's a foundling and we have chosen to raise it. No one need ever know that it's your child."

"You would allow me to keep the baby?"

His shoulders slumped. "It's my grandchild—my flesh and blood. I'm not an ogre, Sarah. I grieve for the circumstances your reckless behavior has brought upon this family, but I love you dearly, and I'll love your child. We will get through this, and someday you will thank me for saving you from a loveless existence. A fate far worse, child, than admitting a wrong."

"But I love him, Papa." Sarah wept openly now. How could she leave Spring Grass, bear Walker's child, and live with a visual reminder of the man she loved day after day after day? Where would she find the strength to walk away from Walker McKay? Sobbing harder, she went to her father and buried her face in the front of his shirt. The familiar scent of tobacco reminded her that he was Papa, reminded her of crawling onto his lap as a child when some other hurt found her. As he was then, he remained her one source of security. He was right. She could not, would not, snare Walker. She had done enough already.

"I will always love him."

Awkwardly cradling her in his arms, Lowell said gently, "But love isn't selfish, Sarah."

No, love wasn't selfish. It was just dreadful.

Chapter Thirty-Five

It was close to suppertime when Walker finished up in the barn. Diamond's filly was a rare jewel; she was dark and tall like her mother, but had the markings and spirit of her father.

Mother nickered quietly to her baby, and the filly responded by starting to nurse. The sight calmed Walker. He was going to be a papa. Would the child have Sarah's features and be delicate and winsome? Or stubborn like his pa?

His thoughts skipped back to the day the mare gave birth. She had managed to wait until nearly full term, and Sarah had been like a young schoolgirl, hanging over the stall railing, urging Diamond to bring the filly into the world.

"Come on, girl. It's time. You can do it!"

Walker recalled grinning as Sarah panted, trying to help. Later, she collapsed on a bale of hay, exhausted as if she'd been the proud mother. He'd covered her with a blanket and let her doze as he cleaned up.

After tossing hay into the other stalls, Walker exited the barn, his gaze drawn to a buggy sitting in front of the house. Company? Who would be visiting at this hour?

When he came in the back door, Flo put a finger to her lips, her eyes motioning to the study. "Lowell Livingston is here."

He continued through the kitchen and into the hall, pausing in front of the study door. Then he turned the doorknob and entered the room.

Two pairs of eyes focused on him as he removed his hat. The older man extended his hand.

"You must be Walker McKay. Allow me to introduce myself. I am Lowell Livingston, Sarah's father." He shook Walker's hand. "Mr. McKay, I was wondering if I might have a word with you alone."

Walker's gaze traveled to Sarah. For a long moment their gazes locked. "Of course."

Sarah eased past him and Walker closed the door behind her. The setting sun threw the room into partial shadow, so he lit a lamp. Sitting down at his desk, he motioned for Livingston to take a chair opposite him.

"I must apologize for my daughter's behavior. I can only say that I deeply regret any inconvenience Sarah might have caused. I realize an apology is weak in view of the circumstances, but I can assure you, Mr. McKay, Sarah and I find the whole episode highly regrettable."

Walker removed his hat and laid it on the desk. "My name is Walker."

"Please call me Lowell." The older man smiled and Walker saw a strong resemblance between him and his daughter. The same eye shape, the dimple that flashed when they smiled. "By now you're aware that my daughter has a stubborn streak the likes of which few have ever witnessed. But she's a good girl, Walker. Forgive the blindness of a doting father, but she has a giving heart."

Lowell rubbed his hands together, forming his words carefully. "I'm afraid after her mother died I indulged Sarah more than I should have. I accept full responsibility for her behavior. We argued fiercely the night she ran away. I've wished a thousand times I had been more patient with her—tried to understand this need she has for a family of her own. But I wasn't, and the last two and a half months have been extremely difficult. I've been worried sick about her, and when Miss Mallory wired, informing us of Sarah's location, I can't tell you how relieved I was to know where she was. I came immediately."

"Lucy wired you?" Walker forced back a spurt of anger. Sarah had befriended her and this was the thanks she got.

"I've had Pinkerton's detectives looking for my daughter for weeks."

Walker leaned forward, opening the cigar humidor and offering Lowell one. The older man declined. Sarah's father looked as if he hadn't slept much lately. Walker sympathized with him. He hadn't been doing a whole lot of sleeping himself.

"I'm sorry, Lowell. If I had known, I would have sent word of her whereabouts."

"I don't hold you responsible, Walker. On the contrary, I'm deeply indebted to you for looking after her."

Walker struck a match, meeting his gaze. "It was not an imposition."

"Yes. She tells me that she's never been happier," Lowell paused, clearing his throat. "We will be leaving for Boston immediately."

Walker's heart skipped a beat as he touched the match to the tip of his cigar. "Leaving?"

"Yes. Sarah is packing as we speak. Again, I hope that in time you will be able to forgive her. She isn't mean-spirited, Walker, only misguided and impetuous. Wadsy, her nanny, says she'll outgrow it. I hope I live to see the day."

Walker rose from his desk. "Did she tell you she's expecting my child?"

Lowell paused. "Then you know about the baby. She thinks that you don't."

Walker moved to stare out the window. "I didn't, not until a few hours ago. My foreman let it slip in an unguarded moment."

Lowell leaned forward. "I'm a man of great means. The child will want for nothing. You needn't worry about its welfare. It will be raised in a Christian home, and nothing will be spared for its care."

"Its welfare?" Walker repeated, closing his eyes. The situation had come to this? His child was an "it"? Something to be discussed in whispered innuendos, with a sense of shame?

"Sarah's baby," Lowell corrected himself. "My grandchild."

Walker rubbed a hand across his face. "My son or daughter."

"Yes, but under the circumstances I don't hold you responsible for events beyond your control. I understand your hesitancy about letting the child go. Any man worth his salt would struggle with the dilemma, but let me assure you, we are open to an amicable agreement. Once the child is born, you will be allowed visitation rights, if you so desire."

"That's not acceptable."

Lowell shifted in the chair, his eyes focusing on Walker. "Do you have a better suggestion? If it's a matter of money, I have more than—"

"Money has nothing to do with it." Walker met his gaze. "The child is mine as much as Sarah's. My blood runs through his or her veins."

Lowell shook his head, uncertainty filling his eyes. "Then what do you propose?"

"Sarah stays here."

Color flushed the older man's cheeks.

"That is out of the question. I won't permit it. I will not have my daughter in a loveless marriage, McKay. Sarah worships you. If I were to agree to such a marriage, she would inevitably end up hurt, and I will not allow that."

"Shouldn't the good Lord and Sarah be the keeper of her future?"

"Sarah isn't thinking clearly. She would jump at the chance to stay. But once the child was born, she would be forced to live with a man who doesn't love her."

"You don't know that."

"Do you?"

Sarah burst through the doorway, her fists clenched. Startled, Walker and Lowell turned to face her.

"How *dare* you bargain over me like some…some…broodmare? It's my child and *I'll* make the decision of whether to stay or go!"

"Sarah," Lowell chided, "we're only trying to do what's best for you and the child—"

"You're not doing what's best for either of us, Father. I've made my decision."

She addressed Walker. "I'll have our child in Boston, and the boy or girl will be delivered to you within a month after the birth."

Their eyes met and held.

"And then what?"

"I'll remain in to Boston and resume life at my father's house."

Her sudden strength surprised him. "You'd be willing to relinquish all claim to the child?"

Sarah bit her lip. "The baby is your heir, Walker, as you wanted all along. I'll lay no claim to it. When he or she grows up, you can tell him or her that I didn't survive the birth."

Lowell interrupted. "Sarah, you're talking nonsense! This child is part Livingston and the heir to the railroad. I'll not hear of you giving our flesh and blood away."

Ignoring her father, Sarah held Walker's gaze. "Is that acceptable to you, Mr. McKay?"

"You are willing to abandon your child?"

"I am capable of keeping my word. Maybe I lied in the beginning, but I knew what I was agreeing to: to provide you with a child." Her hand moved to her stomach and his eyes followed. "This is your baby, Walker. I will carry it, nourish it with my body, and deliver it safely into your arms."

Lowell sprang to his feet. "You propose to carry that child beneath your heart for nine months and then walk away? You have no idea what you're saying, Sarah. That child is part of you—part of me."

"And part of me," Walker reminded him.

Sarah squared her shoulders. "Do you accept my proposal?"

"Don't be foolish, Sarah. I've told your father that I'm willing to let you stay."

She lifted her chin. "I heard. My heart nearly stopped, knowing that you're 'willing' to have me around." She met his gaze defiantly. "But I am unwilling to stay."

Their eyes clashed.

"That's nonsense. My child will not be born away from Spring Grass."

"If you want this child, it will be."

"Sarah—"

"Papa is right. I won't live in a loveless marriage." Her bottom lip quivered. "I'm fully aware of how difficult it will be to leave my baby, but the child is yours."

He shrugged. "You have a deal—with one exception. You remain here at Spring Grass until the child is born. I don't want you hightailing off somewhere where I can't find you or the baby."

"Fine. I'll stay, but not of my own accord."

"Then we have a deal." They shook hands.

Lowell shook his head. "I have never in my life witnessed anything this disgraceful."

"Well, now you have, Papa." Sarah gathered up her skirts. "May God forgive us both. If you'll excuse me, I'm going upstairs to lie down. I'm not feeling well."

"Walker, if you'll excuse us for a moment, I want to speak to my daughter in private." Lowell started to follow Sarah out.

Walker nodded.

"Sarah!" Lowell caught his daughter at the bottom of the stairs. "You can't mean this."

"I do, Papa. It's Walker's child. That was the bargain."

"But it's yours too. Where is your faith? God doesn't send innocent children into the world to be bartered over. You could never live with yourself if you determined your child's future in a moment of anger."

Her hand moved to cover her stomach. "This child is part of Walker, Papa. Don't you know how difficult this is for me? Of course I love this baby more than my own life, but God also expects us to be trustworthy, and when we give our word we are to honor it. Isn't that what you've always taught me?"

"I never thought honor would lead to so great a sacrifice."

A few moments later, Lowell returned to the study, drying his eyes.

"Sarah will remain here with you." He reached for Walker's hand.

"Take good care of her, son. She means the world to me. And if the child ever needs anything…"

Getting up from the desk, Walker ran a hand over his face. He couldn't send the man away thinking he was allowing Sarah to stay only out of a sense of obligation to his child. It went much deeper than that.

"Lowell?"

"Yes, son?"

The two men faced each other, both loving the same woman yet in a different way.

"I'll see that she'll want for nothing."

Lowell's shoulders slumped. "If you should need anything—if there's anything I can do…"

"I have money to buy her whatever she wants. What I don't have," he said quietly, "is the ability to change her mind."

Chapter Thirty-Six

Sarah sat on the porch swing, praying for strength and guidance. Oh how she needed guidance. *And this time I will listen, Lord.*

The sun rimmed the tops of the clouds, spreading reds and golds across the barnyard. Occasional lightning flashes raced through the building clouds forming in the west. Walker came out of the barn and strode toward the house. The wind picked up, whipping his clothes around his tall, rugged frame. Sarah shivered, images flashing through her mind: pictures of how lonely Papa had looked when the train pulled out earlier, how big and incredibly lonely her bed was without Walker.

She held her tongue as he walked toward her, unaware of her presence. *Give me the words to soften his icy reception,* she prayed. Sliding off the swing, she met him at the foot of the porch steps.

"I want to talk to you."

Ignoring her, he reached for the screen door handle. Desperate now, she threw herself between him and the doorway.

"Just *listen* to me, Walker. We cannot live under the same roof for the next six months without speaking."

The coldness in his eyes stopped her. Within the blue depths she saw the pain she had caused, and she longed to erase it. He stepped back as if debating whether to move her aside by force. Sarah swallowed against her dry throat, determined to stand her ground. The air crackled with the building storm both within and without. He was still attracted to her; she could see it in his indecision. "Don't do this. Don't shut me out. We have to talk about this, Walker. It won't go away."

Turning on his heel, he started back to the barn—his sanctuary, the one place he could wrap himself in his misery and refuse to face the problem.

She pursued him across the dusty barn lot, unwilling to let him walk away. Dark clouds swallowed up the sun as she picked up her skirts and called out after him.

"You've never once asked why I was driven to such desperation. You have to believe that I would never deliberately set out to hurt you." The first wet drops struck the dusty ground as she followed him into the barn.

"I don't care why you did it." He disappeared into the dim interior, and then a moment later a lantern blazed to life.

"Well, that's a horrible attitude." Shaking the rain off her blouse, she sat down on a bale of hay next to Diamond's stall. Walker might not care why she'd lied, but he *was* going to hear her side of the story. "All I ever wanted was a husband and my own family and children. Papa never understood that need. Truthfully, he's spoiled me shamefully since Mama died, and I do know how to wrap him around my little finger."

She probably shouldn't be telling Walker that, but she refused to tell another lie. Never again. "This whole fiasco began the day Papa said he was going to send me to live with my Uncle Brice in Georgia. He said a year with my uncle might get my head on straight, but a few months with him would have been the death of me. Believe me, every time I acted up, off to Uncle Brice's I would go. So I ran away—and not for the first time. I've run away more times than I care to admit this past year, but only because Papa refuses to understand my needs. All of my life I've wanted my own home, my own babies, and a loving husband."

Walker glanced at her over his shoulder. She met his eyes defiantly. "If our butler hadn't happened along, I would have married a dockworker the day before I ran away."

Clearing her throat, she continued, "Papa and I quarreled, and the next morning I left the house and boarded a train to New York. I intended to live with my friend Julie until I could find suitable employment."

He glanced over his shoulder again, and then away.

"Rodney Willbanks is a no-good gambler Lucy was in love with. Lucy had cried herself dry when I sat down on the train to eat breakfast with her that morning. One thing led to another, and Lucy made it plain she didn't intend to marry you, Walker. And since you were willing to marry a stranger anyway, I thought, well now, this could be the answer to my prayers. And it was—until Lucy had to spoil everything."

She could see his silhouette against the glow of the lamp. His face was hidden in the shadows.

"When were you going to tell me?"

She slid to the edge of the bale. "I've thought about it every day. At times, I had my mind made up to tell you the moment you got home, but then something always happened to stop me. Fear, mostly. I was terrified you wouldn't understand."

"When, then? In five years?"

"Of course not. I couldn't keep a secret that long. Ask anyone who knows me. I tell everything I know."

"Except this time."

She studied her hands. "Except this time. Oh, Walker, I'd never leave you. I wouldn't walk out on you like—" She caught herself.

"Like who?"

"Like...Trudy."

She didn't have to see his eyes to know they had turned to granite. "You knew about her. You knew and yet you still deceived me."

"I didn't deceive you—well, I did, but I was going to tell you the truth. Why can't you believe me?"

"Sarah, I trusted you. I was—" He stopped, turning back to the rigging.

What had he been about to say? That he thought he was falling as deeply in love with her as she had with him?

"I adore you," she whispered. "I love living at Spring Grass, and I love our home. I've wanted to tell you the truth so many times, but I was afraid. I knew the lie was between us and it tormented me day and night. Every Sunday I sat in our pew and asked God for forgiveness… and I walked out of the church and continued the ruse. I was afraid that when you knew, you'd react exactly the way you have. And the thought of losing you—" Tears welled in her eyes and her voice trembled. "I couldn't bear it. But I also can't stay here with you if you aren't in love with me."

Thunder pealed in the distance, but the weather was of little concern. Why didn't he comfort her? Why couldn't he accept that she loved him more than anything in this world?

Lightning flashed outside the barn. Sarah slipped off the bale and approached him. "Walker, I love you."

Walker turned and their eyes met. For a brief, euphoric moment she thought he was going to take her in his arms. Passion and anger warred on his features. Pain and desperation battled between them.

"We can start over. I promise I will never lie to you again. However painful or awful the matter might be, I *will not* lie to you again." When he still didn't answer, she pleaded softly, "Say something."

Tossing the bridle over the stall, he brushed past her. "You should have married that dockworker."

With that he walked away.

Chapter Thirty-Seven

Days went by; long hours of impasse. Sarah stood at the parlor window, admiring the glorious early autumn colors. Warm sunshine filtered through tree branches of bright yellow and gold; the scent of burning leaves was a pleasant reminder of nature's cycle.

She sighed. She had been so certain that it would be only a matter of time before she was back in Walker's good graces, yet her time at Spring Grass was waning. Nothing she said or did had made the least difference to him. At times she'd caught him looking at her, studying her rounding belly, his face an emotionless mask. Her love refused to die; his would not surface.

Sarah rose early to eat with Walker. At first he had refused to sit at the table with her. He'd stride straight through the kitchen, reaching for a biscuit on his way out the back door. Sometimes he acknowledged her; more often he didn't. Eventually, hunger got the best of him and he began eating supper in the dining room. She cherished those brief interludes because they represented one of the few times she was alone with him. Communication was limited with Flo acting as mediator. Walker wasn't rude; he just wasn't there. Somehow he'd removed himself from the situation, and she envied him. She wished she could do the same, but day in and day out, memories of their love haunted her.

This morning the crisp fall air and her rapidly expanding middle made it hard to get out of bed. She dressed in half darkness, and as she slipped into her boots she realized that before much longer Flo would have to help her lace them. Happiness bubbled inside her as she felt the growing roundness of her stomach and the tight skin covering the child being formed. Then the futility of the situation hit her, and she lay across the bed, Papa's parting stern warning in her ear. *You will never be able to walk away from that child, Sarah Elaine. Never.*

But she would. As much as she cherished the new life growing inside her, she was strong, capable of keeping her promise. It would be better for the child to think he or she didn't have a mother than for Sarah to remain and have her son or daughter witness a loveless marriage. The realization brought tears to her eyes, and the bed shook with the force of her sobs. By the time she could control herself to rise and leave the room, she was exhausted from her emotional burden.

Flo was scrambling eggs when Sarah rounded the kitchen corner. She was ravenously hungry these days, and as she walked into the kitchen she eyed the mound of sausage and biscuits. The aroma of eggs fried in butter captivated her.

"Everything smells so good! I'm famished." She plucked a biscuit from the pile and peeled apart a hot, flaky layer. Steam rose from the bread and she sniffed appreciatively. "Who would think that it took this much food to feed one little baby?"

Flo smiled and ladled eggs into a white bowl. Sarah downed the biscuit and reached for a second one.

"Yer eyes are red as a beet. Have you been crying?"

Biting into the biscuit, Sarah nodded. "I think something's wrong with me. One minute I'm happy, the next I'm crying. I can't seem to stop once I get started, and I never know what's going to set me off. Yesterday I was watching Potster carry eggs from the chicken house into his kitchen, and all I could think of was how those mother hens would never know their babies because they would be eaten even before they hatched. I couldn't stop crying about it. Don't you think that's strange?"

Flo chuckled. "All part of having a young'un. You cry and laugh at the same time. There's no particular reason for either."

"Does it get any better?"

"Eventually, though never soon enough."

Sarah tried to laugh, but she ended up bursting into tears. Flo laid the spoon aside and stepped around the table to embrace her. Sarah sank into her warmth, grateful for the kindness. It seemed years since she'd had any physical contact with another human being, and Flo's hug was like manna from heaven. The older woman stroked her hair lovingly.

"Flo, will he ever love me again?"

"I don't know, honey. I really don't know. I've never seen Walker this stubborn about anything but love. You've got to hold on to hope. If you lose that, you don't have anything."

After drying her eyes Sarah went to the dining table, where she prepared a plate heaped with eggs and sausage. She glanced up as the object of her misery strode in, yawning. She sank into her chair. Former concerns about baby chickens and their unfortunate demise forgotten, she used the edge of a biscuit to herd a few stray pieces of egg onto her fork.

Walker sat at the far end of the table, as distant from her as possible without eating in the foyer. She'd realized what he was doing a few days into the game and tried sitting at different places around the table. He would invariably take the seat farthest away. Once she had tried removing all of the chairs except the one next to hers, but he only picked up the chair and carried it to the farthest end. She had finally given up and let him sit wherever he pleased.

"Walker, don't forget Caleb is coming today," Flo called as she scoured a skillet at the kitchen sink. "You'll need to leave the study key."

Caleb. In all her misery, Sarah had forgotten the accountant.

Walker dug into his pocket and produced a long skeleton key, laying it before him on the table. He'd taken to locking the study.

The key sat there, taunting her. Her food suddenly tasted bitter.

Resentment bubbled in her throat and before she could check them, the words tumbled out of her mouth. "How well do you know Caleb?"

Walker's fork hovered halfway between his plate and his mouth. He studied the utensil as if it were a foreign object. Sarah heard Flo cease scrubbing for a moment and then resume. The silence at the table was deafening. Walker slowly lifted his head to look at her.

"Are you talking to me?"

"You're not going to like this, but I think Caleb might be taking advantage of you." She bit her lip, wondering if she'd lost her mind. She had no real proof of the accountant's dishonesty, and she certainly wasn't on the best of terms with Walker, but given a few hours alone with the ledger, she was certain she could point out some puzzling inconsistencies.

Walker calmly picked up a biscuit and spread butter on it. "Are you suggesting that my best friend is stealing from me?"

She was but not so candidly. "Have you looked at your books lately? Really looked?" She wasn't going to win points on this one, but if he was so blind that he couldn't see what the man was doing, he shouldn't accuse her of bad judgment.

Walker slid a forkful of eggs into his mouth. "Snooping again?"

"I have no reason to steal your money, Walker. You're in such an all-fired hurry to believe the worst of me, yet you turn a blind eye to others' manipulation."

"You're speaking of Caleb again?"

"Yes."

She knew she was out of bounds, but she didn't care. Frustration drove her. Leaning closer, she quietly asked down the long table length, "Why doesn't he return the receipts?"

Walker took a moment to answer. "For safety, I suppose. I don't need to reexamine the receipts."

"Is it possible he doesn't want you to know how much he's skimming off the top?"

Walker locked gazes with her. "You're wrong, Sarah."

"Scared you'll find out your best friend is cheating you?"

"Stop it!"

"You two knock it off in there!" Flo yelled from the kitchen.

Sarah ignored her. She lowered her tone. "Are you afraid you might discover that your friend isn't your friend?"

"It wouldn't be the first time someone I trusted betrayed me."

Flo stuck her head around the doorway. "Sarah, those are mighty strong words."

The warning only stiffened Sarah's resolve. "I know the books have been tampered with and I can prove it."

"You're talking nonsense," Walker said, his face now red.

"Prove me a fool."

Glaring at her, he grabbed the key and rose from the table, the chair scraping behind him. Sarah rose also and followed him out of the room.

Flo trailed behind, whispering, "You better be able to back this up, young lady."

"Or what? Risk losing his favor?" Sarah laughed, suddenly light-headed with power. She could prove it, but would Walker believe her if she did?

Walker strode through the hallway. Inserting the key in the lock, he gave her a dark look and then opened the study door.

Sarah's heart tried to escape her chest, and she was short of breath by the time she approached the desk. She didn't have much time to prove her theory. Caleb would be here by eleven, and there were pages and pages in the ledger. Pushing Walker aside, she sat down and opened Spring Grass's financial records. Her hand shook when she realized that she had just touched her husband for the first time in weeks. Her hand burned from the brief contact, and she fought the desire to touch him again.

Reaching for pencil and paper, she started adding and subtracting, examining the columns of numbers for discrepancies. Walker stood behind her, his eyes fixed on the paper.

"I don't know why you're doing this."

"I hate to see anyone cheated." She rebuked his impatient sigh with a warning look. She glanced up. "And don't remind me that I cheated— I didn't cheat. I just didn't tell the truth."

Caleb Vanhooser had honed the art of embezzlement. Proving that his numbers were off was going to be more difficult than she had anticipated. Were there two sets of books? The ledger looked surprisingly clean today, as if he had tidied up his dirty work.

"Has Caleb worked on the books recently?"

"He works on them twice a month. You know that."

She could feel him watching her, and she dared not look up for fear of losing her place in the columns of numbers. Walker edged around the desk as if trying to get a better look. He accidentally brushed the side of her chair. She glanced up, realizing that he was studying her, not the numbers. She blushed with heat, and for a mere second she considered dropping the pencil and reaching for him.

He turned toward the window, clearing his throat. Sarah dared not take time to breathe. She found a mistake, and she circled it with her pencil.

She had reached the last page when a soft rapping at the closed study door made her start. Caleb's knock. Her heart leapt to her throat. She was so close! Walker glanced at her as the knock came again, more persistently.

"Don't answer it. I'm nearly finished. Just a few more numbers…" She hurriedly tallied the last three columns, praying that Walker would allow her sufficient time to finish. From the corner of her eye she could see him walking toward the door.

A moment later the accountant's thin frame appeared in the doorway. His smile faded when he saw her, and his eyes moved to the open ledger.

"What's going on here?"

Closing the door, Walker returned to the desk. "Sarah thinks there's an error in the books. Is that possible, Caleb?"

Caleb met Sarah's eyes. His normally pallid features flushed and his gaze pinned her. "I don't believe so, but I'll be happy to go over the entries in question."

"Some of your entries don't make sense, Mr. Vanhooser."

His left brow arched. "Are you an accountant, Mrs. McKay?"

Sarah felt heat suffuse her cheeks. "Of course not, but I've always been good with numbers."

Caleb forced a smile, giving Walker a long-suffering look. "Of course. Perhaps your condition has you…imagining things? I know when a woman—"

Sarah sprang out of the chair. "My condition has nothing to do with it." She thrust her calculations at him. "Where's the ledger—and receipts that were here a few weeks ago?"

Caleb reached out to catch the fluttering sheets.

"Walker," Sarah pleaded, "this isn't the same ledger that was here last month. That accounting had dozens of discrepancies. This ledger is a book of fabrication."

Papers collected, Caleb glanced at Walker. "I don't know what she's talking about. Perhaps she detected a slight miscalculation. Regrettable as it is, these things happen. I'll be happy to go over the figures with you and explain anything in question."

For a moment Sarah was almost swayed by his sincerity. Had she mistaken this man? Was her condition making her utter these wild accusations? But she'd seen the mistakes! The receipts were the only way to prove her claim. She snatched the papers out of Caleb's hand and scanned the long rows of numbers again.

She glanced at Walker, who said nothing. His grave features chilled her.

Caleb smiled, reaching for the papers. "After dinner? We'll come in here and I'll explain whatever's bothering you."

He met her gaze and she wasn't sure what she saw. A warning? Fear? *He's a fraud,* Sarah realized. *He's deceiving Walker and he's desperate. And desperate men are dangerous men.* "That won't be necessary," she said.

Walker broke the silence. "Caleb and I will finish up in here."

"But, Walker—"

"Sarah, go cool off. You are out of order."

Sarah bit back resentment. He did not believe her. And why should he?

"Go rest, Sarah." Walker opened the door and gently ushered her through it.

Over Walker's shoulder she saw Caleb's cold, hard face. "Fool," he mouthed. Although he didn't make a sound, she knew exactly what his warning implied. He was cheating Walker blind—and she couldn't do a thing about it. He may have cleverly covered his tracks, but someone with more knowledge about numbers could catch him.

A moment later, she was out in the hall, the door closed behind her.

"Don't be so smug, Caleb," she told the closed door. "You haven't won yet."

Chapter Thirty-Eight

After supper Sarah avoided Walker, going instead to the front porch. The encounter with Caleb had left her numb.

Gazing at the stars, she wondered why she'd opened herself to more of Walker's disgust. He didn't believe a thing she said. Her eyes traveled to the darkened bunkhouse. The ranch was remarkably quiet tonight. During supper, Flo had mentioned a grange dance that she and S.H. planned to attend, if they could stay awake. Apparently the ranch hands had taken advantage of the monthly social as well and left the bunkhouse early.

Drawing her wrap closer, she leaned against the railing, imagining herself in Walker's arms, dancing to the music of banjos and fiddles.

Sighing, she opened her eyes, aware that her dreams were as hopeless as their relationship. She would give everything she had to start anew, but she couldn't. Tonight she had only heightened his anger by accusing his best friend of being a thief. Maybe the time had come for her to go home. There, Papa and Wadsy and Abe would love her. After the baby came, Abe could deliver the child to Walker and...

Her hand slipped to her stomach, where part of Walker McKay grew. She'd seen the doctor, and he confirmed that her pregnancy was going well. The baby kicked, a strong flutter, reminding her that if anyone had been wronged, it was this innocent child who was created in love—if one-sided.

Stepping off the porch, she meandered to the side of the house and entered the rose garden. Sitting down on a bench, she stared at the neglected bushes—painful reminders for both her and Walker. Did he keep them to bolster his belief that all women were schemers? Her gaze swept the light that burned in Walker's study and then returned to the roses. Fall was here, and the flowers were almost gone, the vines withered and drawn. What must Walker think when he looked at the shriveled tokens of his and Trudy's love?

Hopeless tears swelled to her eyes. One moment she was reasonably optimistic that Walker would forgive her; the next, she wallowed in a pit of despair. Both Doc and Flo had assured her that mood swings were normal, but tonight they didn't feel normal. They felt hateful and strange, as if someone else occupied her body.

Tears ran down her cheeks. Her breasts were sore to the touch, her ankles puffy and swollen. She must weigh ten pounds more than she did last week, even though she'd passed on Flo's chocolate cream pie tonight.

Her eyes roamed the garden and then switched back to the light that streamed from the study window.

Walker had no right to treat her this way. Shoving off the bench, she gathered her wrap and marched around the corner of the house.

He couldn't treat her like this—barely speaking to her, ignoring her when she walked into a room, locking himself away in that hateful study every night, refusing to go to town socials. He made them live like hermits.

❖

Walker dropped the journal he was reading when Sarah pushed through the study doorway. "You can't treat me this way."

Retrieving the magazine, he grunted. "Ever hear of knocking?"

Striding across the floor, she cleared the top of his desk with a defiant sweep of her hand. Papers, journals, and blotters fell to the floor in a heap.

Shoving back from the desk, Walker stared at the carnage. "Are you in another one of those moods?"

"I'm not in a 'mood' and you listen to me, Walker McKay. Trudy might have betrayed you, and you might think I'm just like her, but I'm not! Do you hear me?"

He tried to straighten the papers. "The whole ranch can hear you, Sarah."

She leveled a finger at him. "Don't patronize me."

"I'm not patronizing you. I'm telling you that everyone in a ten-mile radius can hear you."

"Good. Then maybe they'll listen to my side of the story."

Getting up, he fetched a ledger, but she stepped in front of him before he could open the book. They faced off, neither giving an inch.

"You're in my way."

"You are not going to fix this by ignoring me. You're going to talk about us whether you want to or not."

Grasping her by the shoulders, he set her aside. She dogged his attempts to reach his chair.

"Trudy ran off with another man. I didn't."

"At least I knew who Trudy was."

"Just because I'm not the bride you sent for—and you should be down on your knees thanking the good Lord that I'm not!—doesn't mean I'm bad. What I did was foolish, and for the hundredth time I'm sorry. But if you're so pigheaded that you can't see that you and I belong together, then I give up."

"I understand what you're saying." He opened the ledger. "And it still stinks."

Tears surfaced to her eyes. "You're never going to forgive me, are you?"

"It's late, Sarah. Go to bed." He stared at the garden, eyes fixed, jaw set.

"Oh, Walker." Her voice caught. "There comes a time when you have to forgive or be eaten alive by bitterness. You stare at those roses and you won't allow yourself to forget. Did you love her that deeply?"

The accusation in her voice surprised him. Love Trudy? He almost laughed. No. In time he might have grown to love her. His bitterness hadn't been built on losing her love, he realized, but on the humiliation of being made a fool. He wasn't about to let Sarah do it a second time.

"Did you *love* her, Walker?"

Sarah's voice drew him back, and he turned to face her. "I fail to see how that should concern you."

She picked the ledger up and hurled it at him. He ducked, barely avoiding being struck. "Sarah, if you throw one more—"

She reached for the humidor.

"Sarah McKay!"

He lunged for her as she threw the humidor at him and then darted away. Bolting into the foyer, she picked up a vase and threw it. He sidestepped it, chasing her. She was going to hurt herself—or worse, hurt the baby. "Sarah!"

She dashed outside and down the front steps. Racing around the corner of the house, she fled with surprising swiftness. He watched her skirt fade into the darkness.

Turning, he went back into the house, slamming the door behind him.

Chapter Thirty-Nine

"Good heavens! Did a cyclone go through here?" Flo, hands on her hips, stood at the study door surveying the aftermath the next morning.

Walker looked up from pouring a cup of coffee. "Sarah stopped by to visit."

Shaking her head, Flo looked at tobacco ground into the rug. Setting the humidor back into place, she said, "It's a shame you two fight all the time. You could both put the energy to better use."

"Talk to her, not me."

Flo scooped the remains of the ashtray into the trash. "A few more months of this and you won't have a lick of anything left. Anyone ever mention that yer hardheaded as a gourd? You ever think about getting down on yer knees and asking the Lord to intervene in this mess?"

"I've been on my knees. It's the Lord who's not speaking right now."

"Who'd think?" Shaking her head a second time, she added. "By the time that young'un gets here, I'll be a mass of nerves."

"Open the drapes, will you, Flo?"

Tsking, the housekeeper shuffled across the floor. Sunlight streamed into the study when she parted the heavy fabric. Walker glanced up at Flo's soft gasp.

"What?"

"Have you seen this?"

"What?" Walker got up from the desk and walked to the window. Stunned, he viewed the carnage. Not one rosebush had escaped the bloodbath. Uprooted plants and clods of dirt filled the fountain. The rose garden was no more.

"What in the...?"

Flo chuckled. "Looks like the cyclone was still on the ground when it left the study."

Whirling, Walker strode out of the room and took the stairs two at a time.

Flo, a hand over her heart, stood at the bottom and yelled, "You harm a hair on that young'un's head and you'll answer to me, Walker McKay! A body doesn't feel like herself when she's in the family way! She's done you a favor by destroying those plants!"

Sarah turned quickly when Walker burst into the bedroom, hiding her battle-scarred hands behind her. She started backing up when he advanced on her, his face a thundercloud.

"Walker, I'm sorry. I don't know what got into me. I saw those roses and something came over me—" She edged toward the door and he lunged for her, missing by a fraction. He stumbled and hit the floor hard. Racing down the stairway, Sarah shouted, "Flo! Help!"

Walker got up and boiled out of the room, taking the stairs three at a time. When he reached the bottom Sarah was behind Flo, who planted herself in the middle of the ruckus, arms crossed, daring Walker to come any closer.

"You leave this poor little darlin' alone, Walker McKay."

"That poor little darlin' just tore apart my rose garden, Flo!" He glared at Sarah. She glared back.

"Needed to be done ages ago," Flo said. "Now get on out of here. I've got work to do."

"I want to speak to Sarah."

Flo's face hardened. "Why? You haven't wanted to talk to her before now."

"Women!" Walker turned and walked into his study, slamming the door behind him.

Flo shook her head, wiping her hands on her apron. "Hard to believe he once entered and left rooms like a normal person."

With a trembling hand, Sarah smoothed her hair. "Thank you, Flo."

"Girl, you'd better watch your step." Flo eyed her. "What in the world possessed you to tear up those rosebushes?"

"I hate them, Flo. Every time Walker looks at them they remind him of a woman's betrayal." Brushing off her skirt, Sarah said softly, "I'm reminder enough."

"Sweet Matilda," Flo said. "I'm too old for this."

Later that afternoon, Sarah watched Walker come in from the barn. By the looks of his clothes, he'd been working cattle and she knew it wasn't the best time to approach him. Still, she felt compelled to apologize for her behavior. Tapping lightly at the study door, she entered without invitation. He glanced up, his face darkening when he saw her. "What have you torn up now? The north or south forty?"

"Top of my list tomorrow." She offered him a timid smile. To her surprise, he returned it.

"You're ornery when you're riled. Did anyone ever tell you that?"

"Papa tried. I'm sorry about your rosebushes."

Removing his gloves, he laid them on the desk. He sighed. "The eyesores needed to come out."

And he needed to let go of the past. Flo's prayer advice had paid off. After Sarah had run off into the darkness, he had read the Bible long into the night, and by early morning he had felt the bitterness lift. God's Word was a balm to his heart. Maybe if he had turned there earlier, he would have realized it weeks ago.

Sarah released a quick breath of relief. "I want to replace the plants, if you'll allow me. I'm thinking some nice perennials, maybe a few flowering bushes."

He nodded, absently sorting through a stack of papers. "Talk to S.H. He'll get you anything you need."

"Fine, but I want to purchase them."

"You bet your life you will." He grinned, and she was happy to see the plants didn't seem to matter much to him. "You didn't hurt yourself, did you?"

"No." She eased her hands behind her back so he couldn't see the cuts the roses had put there. "Well, not much."

"Sarah." He moved closer, gently taking her by the shoulders. "I'm sorry I acted the way I did this morning. I would never lay a hand on you."

"I knew you wouldn't."

"Then why did you hide behind Flo?"

"Because I was frightened. You burst into my room and I was startled." She rested her hand on his arm.

Drawing her to him, he looked at her as if he were baffled by her charm. "Truce?"

"Truce," she conceded with a soft, tentative smile. A soft sound slipped from her throat when his mouth lowered to cover hers.

Slowly backing away, she smoothed his lips with the tips of her fingers. "We can't do this."

His hand refused to release her, and she thought that his eyes held more of a promise than she'd seen before. "You can't tell me that you love me, and I will settle for nothing less."

He squeezed her hand, his eyes darkening with respect. "Give me a little time, Sarah."

Nodding, she backed away. When he was near she lost her ability to reason. Their fingertips strained, stretching the contact as long as possible. When distance forced them to separate, she felt miserable. "Will you be joining me for supper?"

"I'm buried with work, but I'll make a point to be there," he conceded, his eyes still locked with hers. He seemed to war with his emotions before he released her and turned back to the desk.

Chapter Forty

Sarah clung to the wagon side as S.H. maneuvered the buckboard around potholes.

"Sorry! I don't want to jar the baby too much, hon," he said, frowning with concentration.

"You can go faster. You don't have to worry about me. I'm fine." She was better than fine. For the past few weeks, she and Walker had actually carried on a conversation at the breakfast table.

"Best quit that squirming," Flo warned, winking at S.H. "You'll have the baby spittin' up."

"Spitting up?" Sarah glanced at her skeptically. "It can do that?"

Flo and S.H. laughed, and Sarah realized she'd fallen for a joke.

Twenty minutes later, S.H. wheeled the wagon to a stop in front of the mercantile. Doc's office was on the opposite side of the street.

S.H. tied the mare to the hitching post and then extended Sarah a helping hand. Climbing down was troublesome now that she had gained weight and girth. Flo said she already looked as though she were carrying a watermelon, even though she was not long into her pregnancy. There was a hint of snow this morning, and Sarah sucked in the crisp air, enjoying the smells of approaching winter.

"Careful, little mama," Flo warned as S.H. carefully lowered her to the ground.

S.H. groaned with effort while she found safe footing. "What're ya havin', a heifer?"

"Sizemore! You don't say that to a woman!" Flo snapped.

"Aw, she knows I'm jest teasin'." S.H. winked at Sarah before turning to help Flo out of the wagon. Flo's joints were giving her fits, and though she never complained, Sarah noticed that she winced in pain this morning. How long would Flo be able to help care for a child? She was nearly as old as Wadsy. Wadsy always said, "God shore knew what he was a-doin' when he gave little folk to the young. A body my age is too old to be running after young'uns."

"I'll be getting supplies," Flo said. "S.H. can help you across the street."

"I know how to cross a street," Sarah protested. "I can still do some things by myself, you know."

"I'm goin' with ya and that's that," S.H. said. "You might trip and fall."

"S.H., I'm not an invalid. I'm having a baby."

"Yes, ma'am, I know it. Walker's baby, and he'd expect me to look after ya."

"I'm not going to get hurt. You can stand right here and watch me. You'd think you were my papa, the way you fret over me."

Lifting her skirts, Sarah glanced both ways for S.H.'s benefit. A driverless wagon sat at the end of the street. No imminent dangers awaited her. "I'll be back in a few minutes."

"Watch yerself. Look both ways! Don't walk too fast!" S.H. hollered. Sarah turned and waved him off.

Flo disappeared into the mercantile and S.H. joined a group of friends farther up the sidewalk. If S.H. and Flo had their way, they'd keep her in a glass box for the remainder of the pregnancy. Rarely a day went by that Flo wasn't coddling her with blueberry muffins or hot tea or a pillow for her feet. When her back ached, S.H. was there with a hot compress. She accepted their pampering with a smile, grateful for the affection. If only Walker would show the same concern—

Sarah looked up when a shout broke through her thoughts.

Warnings sounded, and before she could gather her wits, someone grabbed her arm and jerked her clear of the buckboard, the wheels brushing the hems of her skirts. Someone seemingly appeared out of nowhere to sweep her up onto the porch and out of danger.

"Get the doctor!" The male voice sounded familiar, yet in her confusion Sarah couldn't place it. The street tilted lopsidedly, and from a distance she saw S.H. sprinting across the street. She looked up to identify her rescuer and saw Caleb.

Flo bolted out of the mercantile, yelling, "Sarah! Oh, land sakes, are you all right? I knew we should have stayed with you!" The housekeeper approached and reached for her hand.

The excitement drew a crowd. Men stepped to the door of the saloon; women pulled small children across the street. She could hear Caleb calmly assuring the onlookers that everything was fine and asking them to stand back. He turned to her. "Can you sit up?"

Nodding, she allowed the banker to lift her upright. Caleb felt her pulse with cold precision. Of all the men in town, why did *he* have to be her knight in shining armor?

Brushing his hands aside, she straightened her blouse, embarrassed by all the fuss. "I'm fine, really."

Caleb smiled, but the effort didn't quite reach his eyes. "That was a close call, my dear. You have to be more careful." The smile widened. "You could have been killed."

"I'm always careful, Caleb." She stood up, her legs wobbly beneath her.

Doc Linder rushed across the street, his long strides eating up the ground. After a cursory examination, he straightened.

"S.H., we'll need to get her over to the office. I want to check the baby and make sure she's suffered no ill effects from all the excitement."

"Shore thing, Doc."

Caleb and S.H. escorted the expectant mother across the street and into the doctor's office. Excusing himself, Caleb then left, saying he had a customer waiting for him.

Doc took Sarah into the exam room and put the stethoscope to her stomach. Drawing a deep breath, she closed her eyes, praying the baby was fine.

He listened, stepped back, frowned, and moved forward to listen again. Sarah shrank against the table. The doctor moved the stethoscope back and forth across her protruding stomach.

"Is something wrong with my baby?"

"No, no, the baby's fine." He listened again, frowning. "But there's a lot going on in there."

"What do you mean?" Sarah's head came off the table. "Something awful?"

The doctor picked up Sarah's chart, his eyes scanning the information. "Not awful. Hmm." He placed the stethoscope on her abdomen again.

Sarah waited, holding her breath.

"Well, with this weight gain, I'd say twins are a definite possibility."

Sarah's jaw dropped. Her heart hammered so loud the doctor drew his instrument back. Two babies? Papa and Wadsy would just spit! "Are you sure?"

The doctor lifted her to a sitting position. "No, I can't say for certain, but it seems to me I hear two heartbeats. Now, I wouldn't get excited about it yet. Sometimes stressful situations can make a baby's heartbeat irregular, and that's what I could be hearing. Everything else checks out okay. Still, you need to be careful for a few days and pamper yourself a little."

"Doc, may I tell Walker about the twins?"

"No need to count your chickens before they hatch." Doc Linder patted her on the back. "We wouldn't want to get his hopes up only to disappoint him, would we?"

Sarah felt deflated. "No, we wouldn't." But he hadn't bargained on two heirs.

Doc ushered her to the waiting room, where S.H. and Flo were sitting. Flo shot to her feet. "Is everything all right?"

"Everything's fine." The doctor winked at Sarah. "You'll need to take special care of this little lady for the next few days. Make sure she gets lots of rest."

"We'll do it," S.H. declared, reaching for Sarah's hand. "I told you that you ought to let me help you across the street."

"What difference would that have made?" Sarah said. "We both might have been killed."

The three left the doctor's office and returned to the wagon. Due to all the excitement, the wagon was only partially loaded with supplies.

"Aren't you going to finish your shopping?" Sarah asked Flo.

"Heavens, no! We're going to get you home. I'll ask Denzil to send the rest with Caleb when he comes to supper tomorrow night."

Sarah glanced toward the bank and saw Caleb leaning against a post, watching her. His earlier warning rang in her ears. *You might have been killed.*

Was he responsible for the near fatality? The thought seemed preposterous, yet the wagon had come out of nowhere. She thought of his icy smile the last time he'd been at the house and it chilled her, as if warning her not to cross him.

"Why is Caleb coming to supper tomorrow night? He eats dinner with Walker twice a month."

"I don't know. I mentioned I was fixing roast and he kinda invited himself."

Sarah met the accountant's eyes. "I think he just tried to kill me."

"Kill you!" Flo stared at her. "What a thing to say. Why, he saved your life, young'un. Why would he pull you out of the way if he were trying to kill you? That's ridiculous. Caleb wouldn't hurt a fly."

Maybe not, Sarah thought. Perhaps her imagination was working overtime, but the man disturbed her.

S.H. hoisted Sarah into the buckboard and Flo climbed up behind. They settled in for the drive home, and as the buckboard passed the bank, Sarah glanced at Flo. "I don't want him at the ranch tomorrow."

"Mercy! I think that little scare addled yer brain."

Sarah settled back on the seat, adjusting her skirts. "Caleb resents me, Flo. Why, I don't know, but he does and I'm afraid of him."

Shortly after arriving back at the ranch, Sarah excused herself. "I think I'll lie down for a while."

Relief crossed Flo's features. "You do that, young'un. I'll bring up a tray of tea in a bit."

Sarah went to her room and stretched out on the bed, but sleep eluded her. She didn't know how she would sit at the supper table tomorrow night with Caleb Vanhooser and not find fault with him.

Rolling onto her side, she cupped her stomach tightly. "It's true, babies. Caleb is not your father's friend. I may anger him so that Walker will never forgive me, but I'm going to prove my suspicions." When a soft knock sounded a few moments later, she called softly, "Come in, Flo."

She slipped out of bed as the door opened. Releasing her hairpins, she freed the long strands of fiery tresses.

"While you're here, could you help me with my—" She turned to see Walker standing at the foot of the bed holding a tray. His eyes clearly appreciated her.

"Flo thought you might need a cup of tea."

"Oh—thank you. That was thoughtful of her." Sarah watched him place the tray on the bedside table, his eyes drawn to her.

"Care to share a cup with me?" she ventured.

"Thanks." He pulled up a chair and sat down.

"I wasn't sure I'd join you for supper tonight," she said.

"Why not?" Their eyes met and held.

"I'm not hungry. It's been a big day."

Did he know about the accident? Had S.H. told him of her newest charge against Caleb?

Their eyes met again. Then, lifting her hand to his mouth, he kissed her fingertips. Sarah shivered, closing her eyes. He was slowly coming around to the old Walker.

"S.H. said there was an incident in town this morning?"

"A wagon almost ran me down—"

Concern lit his eyes. "But you're fine? No ill effects?"

"None. As a matter of fact..." She paused, tempted to mention Doc's suspicions. How would he feel about twins? Better to wait. "He or she is perfectly healthy."

As if to prove the declaration, one of the babies put a foot into her rib. "Oh." Sarah laughed, holding her breath. A baby lay against her diaphragm, making it difficult to breathe.

Walker frowned. "What's wrong?"

"Nothing. The baby just kicked, that's all." She sat down on the edge of the bed, cradling her stomach. "Do you want to feel?"

"Feel what?"

"Your son—or daughter." She was pleased by his interest. She often wondered if he had feelings for the child—or children. She'd caught him looking at her stomach sometimes as if he felt fatherly pride. Did he feel anything other than relief that she was carrying his heir?

She reached for his hand and placed it on her stomach. "Here."

He examined the rounded stomach much as he had Diamond's when she'd foaled. The baby responded to the gentle pressure. A slow smile spread across his face and warmth flooded Sarah. His hand tenderly explored the new life, the pressure of his touch comforting.

His eyes locked with hers. "Feels like a strong, healthy boy."

"Or a feisty, healthy daughter."

"Like her mother."

He kept his hand in place, smiling when the baby made its presence known. The moment was special. Mother, father, child. His touch held everything Sarah ever wanted, except for one missing ingredient. A man who loved and trusted her, a man with whom she could share these babies instead of relinquishing them to him in a few months. Would he allow her to see the children through the years? She longed to see them grow, experience their first tentative steps, first everything. Though she had said she would stay out of their lives, she knew she would be willing to travel day and night to reach them as often as Walker might allow.

"Sarah." Walker's features sobered.

"Yes?"

"Exactly what happened this morning in town? Flo said you thought Caleb was responsible for the accident."

She looked away. "I don't want to argue, Walker."

"I don't want to argue either. I want you to tell me what happened."

"I was crossing the street and a wagon started toward me. A moment earlier, it was driverless."

"Caleb was driving the wagon?"

"No, of course not. I didn't see who was driving it."

"But you think Caleb is responsible for the accident?"

"I...don't know, Walker. Yes, I think he is, but I have no proof. I know he's your close friend, but the way he speaks to me...the way he looks at me...I know he resents my presence here at Spring Grass."

Walker shook his head, sitting back and reaching for a cup.

"You don't believe me, do you?"

His gaze moved back to hers. "I want to."

"You...want to?" Her heart tripped.

"Give me the proof, Sarah. Produce the second set of books you accused Caleb of keeping. Show me the evidence that says he was driving the wagon this morning. Caleb has been a close and trusted friend all these years. It's hard to imagine otherwise. I'm not disputing your claim, but I cannot agree until you can show me positive proof that he's cheating me."

"I can't," she admitted.

"What would you have me do then? Throw away years of friendship on speculation? You're a fair woman, Sarah. You tell me. I don't profess to be good with numbers. I can only rely on people whom I trust, and without evidence, I'm left with conjecture."

He was right, of course, but she had no evidence, just a growing conviction. She would bet her life that the books she saw were not the ones she'd seen months ago. Caleb was too smart for her. He could look her in the eye and lie, and she was powerless to do anything about it.

"He's not your friend," she said, getting up from the bed. "He... threatened me, Walker."

"In what way?"

She could see she was only making it worse, heaping accusation upon accusation.

"Sarah, he saved your life."

"If it weren't for him, my life wouldn't have needed saving." Her

cheeks burned. They had made too much progress to allow this conversation to turn into a quarrel. Both had grown in the past weeks, and
Sarah wanted to continue the progress, but today had only proved she
was a dreamer. Walker would never trust her—not the way a man trusts
a woman that he loves. She bit back hot tears of defeat.

Sighing, he got up. "The tea's cold. Come downstairs and eat. You'll
feel better."

She reached for the hairbrush, and jerked it through her hair.

"Are you coming?"

"I'm leaving, Walker." The impasse was too difficult; she couldn't go
on. It was upsetting her and the babies.

"What?" His features darkened.

"I'm returning to Boston for a visit. I miss Papa and Wadsy and Abe.
I've been rethinking the matter, and I feel it's best that I have the baby
there. Wadsy will be there to help with the delivery. And Papa will be
there with me."

His features closed. "What about our bargain?"

"The bargain is sealed." Her eyes met his in the mirror. "If that's your
only concern."

"No, the bargain is that you stay and have the baby in this house."

"I will send the child to you, Walker."

"I want my child born in this house, Sarah."

She turned, meeting his gaze. "Do I get nothing in return?"

"That's what you agreed to."

"I was upset. I hadn't felt the child move inside me. I love this baby,
Walker."

"If you stay, I'll grant you visitation rights."

Her heart sprang to her throat. "You'll allow me to see the baby?"

He conceded. "Visitation rights. The child can see you once or
twice a year."

"How gracious of you. Twice."

"Agreed, if you have the baby here."

She laid the brush on the dresser.

"Well?"

"I hope Flo's fixed chicken and dumplings for supper."

He walked to the door and opened it. "And I will expect you to be at supper tomorrow night. Is that understood?"

She shrugged. "If you insist."

When the door closed a moment later, she muttered, "Not that you're going to like it."

Chapter Forty-One

The next morning Sarah dressed early, eager to begin the day. Caleb Vanhooser was lower than a snake, but she was smarter than he and she was going to prove it. After breakfast, she pulled out the good silver and began to polish it. Flo watched the activity with raised brows.

"All this work for Caleb's benefit?"

"I've been thinking, and I realize how foolish I've been acting toward Caleb. I should be thanking him instead of persecuting him." She glanced up, smiling. "It's my condition, you know. And I want supper tonight to be special, a celebration."

Flo eyed her skeptically. "Then don't forget the soup bowl—we're having Caleb's favorite cheese soup."

Naturally. Sarah polished a knife and then held it up to view her reflection. *What else do you feed a rat?*

"You been reading your Scripture lately?"

"Every night."

"Have you got to the part about wives being submissive to their husbands? You plan to behave?"

Sarah glanced up and smiled. "I've been reading the Song of Solomon."

Flo tsked. "Walker has his hands full now."

When Sarah came downstairs that evening, Walker's and Caleb's voices drifted from the study. S.H. and Flo were in the kitchen, banging pans. Sarah could hear S.H.'s teasing banter as the housekeeper dished up potatoes.

The study door opened and Sarah watched as Walker and Caleb appeared. "Caleb. So glad you could join us."

Caleb glanced at Walker before addressing her. "I hope you have no ill effects from yesterday's unfortunate incident? I've been worried sick that you wouldn't be able to eat with us."

She smiled. "I wouldn't miss it."

"Very good. I thought the near tragedy might have left you too shaken." There it was again. That cold smile.

"Goodness, no. Everyone's made too much of the whole incident. I see you aren't carrying your briefcase—that's encouraging. Tonight is social only, no thoughts of work?"

"No. The briefcase is in the buggy."

"Good. I hope you're hungry."

Caleb gave Walker an inquiring look when Sarah drew him into the dining room. Flo appeared from the kitchen with the silver soup tureen. When she saw Caleb, she smiled. "Perfect timing."

S.H. blessed the food. Then the men picked up their napkins as Flo spooned soup into Walker's bowl.

"Oh—before we start." Sarah cleared her throat. "Caleb I must apologize for my atrocious behavior of late. I've made unforgivable accusations recently, statements that I don't fully understand myself. But as you know, I'm not myself these days."

Caleb glanced again at Walker. "No apologies necessary. All is forgiven. As I've said, I will be only too happy to go over the books with you to ease your concerns—"

"That won't be necessary." She snapped her napkin open, smiling. "Walker has complete trust in you. And since you saved my life yesterday, how could I feel otherwise? Please forgive me if I have cast doubt on your character in any way."

Caleb nodded pleasantly to Flo as she filled his bowl. "Ah, cheese soup. Flo, you're the greatest."

Sarah reached for a roll and butter. "I don't even like myself. I have all these odd feelings that S.H. and Flo and even the doctor assure me are normal, but still, they're there, and sometimes I'm unpleasant. Isn't that true, Walker?"

She met Walker's guarded look with a warm and friendly smile.

Caleb seemed embarrassed by the subject. "Don't worry about it. Everyone has bad days." He accepted the basket of rolls from S.H. "Did you ever find that lost heifer, S.H.?"

As they ate their soup, conversation circled around issues at the ranch, but eventually returned to the puzzling near accident.

Sarah picked up the butter dish and offered it to the accountant. "You didn't happen to see who was driving that wagon, did you, Caleb? It was so strange—when I looked a moment earlier, the wagon was sitting in front of the blacksmith's with not a driver to be seen."

"No. I'm afraid I didn't."

"Why, you could have been killed yourself," Sarah said.

Caleb looked relieved when Flo served the roast.

"Isn't it strange that wagon was coming at such a fast clip the very moment I was trying to cross the street? Don't you find that just the oddest thing? Usually there are hardly any wagons—and if there are, they mainly belong to families coming to town for supplies. But lo and behold, here comes that wagon out of nowhere, clipping along so fast. Why, it was almost as if the driver had deliberately set out to run me over. Me—an expectant mother! You'd think the person responsible had no shame." Cutting a piece of roast, she met Caleb's eyes.

"Sarah." Walker frowned. "Caleb isn't able to eat his supper for all the chatter."

"Really strange." Sarah slipped a piece of meat into her mouth. "As you said, a person needs to be careful. Why, I could have been killed."

"Sarah." Walker laid his fork aside. "We're indeed grateful that you are still among us. Now, will you please let our guest enjoy his meal?"

"Oh, certainly." She took a bite of potatoes, her eyes going back to Caleb. "But don't you find it peculiar?"

Murmuring a vague agreement, Caleb struck up a conversation with Walker, and the diners made it through the remainder of the meal with idle talk.

Flo was serving dessert when S.H. turned in his seat as he cocked an ear toward the barn. "It's Diamond again. She's been restless all day."

Walker pushed back from the table. "I'll check on her before she hurts herself."

Caleb half rose from his chair. "Do you need my help?"

"No, S.H. and I can handle it. Enjoy your cake and coffee."

The two men left and Flo started gathering up dirty plates. When she disappeared through the kitchen doorway, Sarah looked at Caleb. "Really odd. Don't you think?"

His eyes met hers now with no attempt to conceal his animosity. "I've heard of more bizarre things."

"In this town? An expectant mother being nearly run down? It's almost as if someone wanted me out of the way. As though I might be getting too close to something—but what that is, I can't imagine. What could I possibly know?" She handed him the pitcher of cream for his coffee.

The anger in his face chilled her blood, yet the desire to reveal his ugly nature was stronger than common sense.

"Your condition, Sarah, not only has left you delusional, but you're in dire need of a straitjacket."

"Do you think so?" She took the last bite of cake, removing remnants of fudge frosting with the tip of her fork. Rising from the table, she picked up her plate and bent close to his ear on her way to the kitchen. "Don't suppose for one moment, Mr. Vanhooser, that you can mess with me," she said in a voice as sweet as honey. "I know what you're doing, and I will expose you." Patting his shoulder, she moved on.

When she heard Walker and S.H. come in from the barn a few minutes later, she lifted the pot of fresh coffee. "I'll refill the cups, Flo." She entered the dining room and, after serving the men, sat down and listened to Walker and S.H.'s discussion

Walker finished his cake and shoved the plate back. He looked at Sarah. "There's a full moon tonight. Why don't we get a breath of fresh air? S.H. and Caleb can enjoy a smoke while we're out."

She wanted nothing more than a walk in the moonlight with him, but she knew it was merely fresh air that he desired. Meeting his eyes, she declined softly. "Thank you, but I'm going to retire early." Her heart tripped a beat when she saw the disappointment on his face.

"Caleb?" She turned to smile at their guest. "Why don't you accompany Walker."

"It's warm in here, Flo. Can you open a window?" Caleb mopped his brow and then absently returned the hankie to his pocket.

Flo glanced over her shoulder. "It feels about right. Must be that hot coffee making you sweat."

Walker got up, glancing at Caleb. "If the lady prefers her bed to my company, I guess I'm stuck with you. My new plow came this week. Are you interested in seeing it?"

"I'd love to."

Sarah excused herself and slipped through the kitchen. Flo was busy at the sink and didn't notice her entry. Tiptoeing to the open window, she lifted the curtain and watched Walker and Caleb leave the house and walk toward the shed.

Flo glanced over her shoulder. "Why don't you go with them? S.H. will help me clean up."

"Thanks, Flo, but I think I'll sit on the porch for a few minutes and then go upstairs."

"Go right ahead, but take a wrap. It's a bit cool."

Sarah grabbed her cloak and went out to the swing. She sat until she heard Walker's and Caleb's voices in the shed. Slipping off the porch, she hurried around the corner of the house. Caleb's polished surrey glistened in the moonlight.

Running her hand under the interior seat, she found nothing. It *had* to be here. Caleb had said he'd left his briefcase in the buggy. She noticed he never went anywhere without it. She stepped into the carriage and groped around the pleated upholstery, searching for openings. The buggy must have cost a handsome price. Had Walker's money bought it?

Nothing. The briefcase wasn't here. She sat back on the seat, breathing hard and thinking. Papa hid things in secret compartments. Tapping her feet along the floorboard, Sarah noticed that the thud that her left foot made was hollower sounding than that of her right foot. She leaned down in the semidarkness and felt along the floorboard, her pulse thumping when her fingers encountered a leather latch. She lifted it up—and inside was the briefcase! Pulling it out of the hole, she eased from the carriage.

Walking swiftly to the bunkhouse, she knocked softly at Potster's kitchen door. It seemed an eternity before he let her in, taking the case from her immediately and holding it up to the candlelight.

"I haven't seen one of these in years," he whispered.

"You can pick its lock, right?"

"I'd remember how to do this in my sleep." The old cook chuckled. "Spent my share of time behind bars to prove it."

He located his tools, and Sarah held the briefcase steady as he went to work on the lock. Uneasy, she glanced out the window, praying that Walker wouldn't see the light and come to investigate. If Walker caught them breaking into Caleb's briefcase, she could forget about a truce. He would have her on the next train to Boston.

"What is it you're looking for?" Potster fiddled with the lock, and they finally heard it click and the latch opened.

Sarah unfastened the case and hurriedly shuffled through papers. "I'll know it when I see it," she said, opening a contract, scanning it, and folding it back exactly as it had been.

"You think Caleb's stealing from Walker?"

"I'm sure that he is, but if I can't find the evidence, I have no way to prove it." She picked up a small book wrapped in a leather band. When she untied the strap, the ledger fell open. In the flickering light she could see numbers written out. A depositor's book! The dates went back several years and the notations showed both deposits and with-drawals.

"This is it, Potster. If I can show that Caleb's deposits are different from Walker's ledger, then I can prove once and for all that Caleb keeps two sets of books."

"You better be sure about yer facts."

Sarah hugged the old man's neck. "Thank you for your trust. You're the best friend a person could have."

Sarah tucked the bankbook into the front of her dress, rearranged the papers, and latched the case. Potster put the lock back into place and fastened it.

"You're the one who's really saved my life," she whispered.

"You just git that case back into the buggy before Caleb knows what you've done."

Sarah opened the door and slipped out of the bunkhouse. She could hear the men coming back from the shed. Easing into the shadows, she waited for Walker and Caleb to pass. They passed so close she feared they might hear her breathing. After they went inside, she slid the brief-case back in the buggy and latched the trapdoor.

When she crept back into the house, Flo heard the screen door. "That you, Sarah?"

"Yes, Flo. I'm going to bed now. Would you please say good night to Walker and Caleb for me?"

"All right, dear. Good night."

"Sweet dreams."

Once inside her room, Sarah drew the lamp closer, her eyes scan-ning Caleb's entries. She was tempted to take the evidence directly to Walker the moment she heard Caleb's buggy leave the yard, but she didn't dare. She had to make doubly sure she had the proof needed to convict Caleb.

Footsteps sounded down the hall and then paused in front of her door. Scrambling under the blanket, she hid the book under her pillow.

Please don't let Walker come in.

But the door opened softly and he stood in the doorway, his tall frame illuminated by the hall lantern. She lay still, affecting a steady rise and fall of her chest. Finally he closed the door, and she released a whoosh of air when she heard his boots fading down the hallway.

Sleep wouldn't come. Her heart pounded, and she knew it would leap from her chest if she lay still any longer. When she was sure the coast was clear, she got up, slipping the bankbook into the front of her dress.

Leaving the bedroom, she crept downstairs and out the back door. Diamond's restless nickers sounded from the barn.

When she entered the stable, she saw the horse milling about in her stall.

She put the lantern on a barrel and reached to comfort the mare. "Can't sleep, girl?" She knew how the mare felt. Even if she proved her accusations, it wouldn't change her and Walker's situation. It would only be one more disappointment, one more betrayal when Walker learned that his best friend was cheating him.

"Oh, Diamond, I'm such a mess. When I told Papa and Walker that I could leave the baby here, I didn't know it would be so hard." She choked back the hard knot crowding her throat.

Diamond rested her head over the stall, her brown eyes shimmering. Her foal was close beside her. She snuffed at Sarah's dress, and Sarah realized that she was looking for sugar. Smiling, she let the horse nuzzle her belly.

"Do you want some sugar? I suppose I could sneak into the kitchen and get some. Wait here. I'll be right back."

She picked up the lantern and started toward the door, but then she remembered why she was here in the barn. Removing the deposit book from her bodice, she looked around for a protected hiding place. Her eyes lit on the tool bin and she slid the book behind it, lodging it between the bin and the rough wall. Turning to leave, she noticed that the barn door was closed.

When she pushed against the heavy planking, it wouldn't move. In the distance she could hear Caleb's buggy leave the farmyard. The conveyance had a bell on top.

Standing back, she tried to remember if she had closed the door. She hadn't. Had the wind blown it shut? She shoved, but the door refused to give.

And then she smelled smoke.

Whirling around, she beat against the door, peering over her shoulder to see the first flames lick through the rear wall.

She pounded harder as a gray haze filled the barn. Diamond whinnied, thrashing against her stall. The other horses nickered, shifting around nervously. Smoke billowed throughout the rafters, and flames jumped from the back wall into the hayloft, trailing a stream of red flames.

The heat intensified, and Sarah put the hem of her dress over her mouth. The fire roared through the dry hay stored overhead like an angry beast, picking up fury. She pounded, screaming now.

Beating her fists, she yelled, black smoke clogging her throat. Her eyes ran with tears and she couldn't catch her breath. Finally, she slumped to the floor, the sound of Diamond's frightened cries ringing in her ears.

Twice in two days, she thought as fire consumed the hayloft. *Caleb is trying to kill me.*

Chapter Forty-Two

Tossing his sheet aside, Walker rolled out of bed. Sleep was slow in coming tonight; his mind kept going over the dinner. Sarah had been unusually polite to Caleb. What had happened to change her mind about him? She'd been so adamant the day before that Caleb was cheating him, yet tonight she played the happy hostess. She had been overly friendly, which was not like her. She was a woman with clear convictions, and he knew she was convinced Caleb was embezzling from him.

The problem was easy enough to correct. He would take the books to Pete McKinley and let him go over them. Pete was discreet; Caleb would never know his work was in question. But Walker would know, and that was the sticking point. He didn't want to believe his friend would do such a thing to him. He ran his hand through his hair. Caleb had been a loyal friend through the years. He'd listened to Walker's problems and been a solid supporter during Pa's death. What was it about Caleb that put Sarah on edge? She might be given to theatrics on occasion, but this accusation was something more. The least he owed her was an impartial look at the books. First thing in the morning, he'd take them by Pete's and get his opinion. If Sarah was right, he owed her a debt of gratitude. If she was wrong, it would deepen their rift into a chasm.

He moved to the window to look out. Moonlight illuminated the barn. Inside, he could hear Diamond bumping her stall. His eyes traveled the deserted barnyard as a matter of habit. Everything was quiet, the bunkhouse dark. The men had been asleep for hours.

Cocking his ear, he realized that Diamond's whinnies were different from a moment ago. Nervousness tinged the animal's cries now. Lifting the window, he studied the barn, searching for a source of concern. There was no wind tonight. A full moon mantled the farmhouse in mellow rays. Then he smelled it. Smoke.

Swiftly reaching for his pants, he slipped them on. Had a careless hand dropped a lighted match in the hay?

By the time he reached the barn, flames were licking through the roof. Pounding on Potster's door, he yelled for the cook to wake the men and then grabbed a bucket and raced toward the rain barrel. Within minutes the barnyard teamed with bare-chested men, still half asleep, racing against time. Fire shot out of the barn roof and spread to the back of the building.

Fumbling for the latch, he discovered that the door was locked from the outside. What fool had done that? Walker threw the bolt and lunged inside to free the animals but stumbled, dropping to his knees when he encountered an obstacle blocking the doorway. Black smoke belched from the blazing interior, and he grabbed his handkerchief out of his back pocket to protect himself from the smoke. Coughing, he tried to shove the object aside, but he came into contact with a feminine hand. He strained to see whose it was. Flo's? What would she be doing out here at this time of night?

The draft shifted, sucking the flames to the rear of the barn. Lifting the inanimate form, he carried her outside, laying her on the ground. S.H. ran up, tucking his shirttails into his pants.

"Sarah!" the two men exclaimed in unison.

Walker placed the handkerchief over her mouth, trying to shield her from the rolling smoke. Her eyes opened briefly and he saw recognition before they closed again.

Flo darted toward them, her unpinned hair streaming down her back. The old woman knelt in the dirt, cradling Sarah to her ample bosom. "What's she doing out here? She was in her room when I went to bed."

Walker scanned the area. Chaos reigned as men shouted, racing back and forth with water buckets. What *was* Sarah doing out here at this time of night? Even worse, why was the barn door locked from the outside? Spring Grass didn't have any trouble with theft—nothing was ever locked up at night.

Lifting Sarah into his arms, Walker carried her to the house. When he placed her on their bed, her eyelids fluttered and she moaned, coughing. Reaching for him, she clung tightly.

"You're all right, you're safe now," he soothed her.

"Fire...the door was locked...oh, Walker!"

"It's all right," he murmured, gently stroking her back. He could feel her trembling beneath his hands.

"I called for you...but no one came."

What if he hadn't gotten out of bed and smelled the smoke? The ramifications chilled him more than the November air. He could have lost her. He had no way of knowing she was in the barn, caged like a wild animal. Holding her close, he absorbed her scent, tainted by smoke, but still very Sarah. "Why were you in the barn this time of night?"

"I couldn't sleep..." She coughed, still trying to catch her breath. Gently wiping her mouth, he eased her back onto the pillow. "I couldn't sleep," she whispered. "I heard Diamond and I went out to keep her company."

Another spasm of coughing hit her. When it passed, she lay back again, her eyes meeting his wearily. "I'm sorry to be so much trouble."

"Nonsense." He poured water into the basin and wet a rag. Wiping her face, he cleaned the soot away, his eyes locked with hers. "I suppose you think Caleb locked you in the barn and set the fire?"

"I heard his buggy drive off as I tried to get out." She moaned, closing her eyes. "I had the deposit book...but it's gone, burned up in the fire."

"A thief wouldn't leave evidence in a deposit book."

"A smart one wouldn't."

"But you were so charming to him tonight. I was starting to think he was your best friend."

"I am a very good actress." Maybe he didn't need to know that.

He placed the cloth on her forehead. "Where did you get this book?"

"From his briefcase. When you and Caleb visited the shed, I searched his buggy and found a trapdoor. That's where he keeps the records, Walker."

"You searched his buggy. My friends are subject to searching before they can leave the ranch?"

"If Caleb is the friend in question."

"Sarah." He stood up, shoving his hands through his hair. How did a man deal with this? If what she was saying were true, there'd be no point in taking the ledgers to Pete because apparently there was a second set—or so Sarah said.

"Honestly, Walker! You'll defend Caleb to the death, but what about me? What about your child? If Caleb had succeeded tonight—"

"You're talking crazy, Sarah. This pregnancy, our situation—it has us confused. Flo says your frustrations are normal and nothing to be concerned about. She says they'll pass after the baby's born."

He returned to the bed, taking her back into his arms. Smoothing her hair, he said quietly, "Don't put me in this situation, Sarah. The Caleb I know is a loyal friend. He has his faults, but show me a man who doesn't. What do you want me to do? Have the man arrested on the suspicion that he's cheating me? If you're wrong, I've betrayed him."

"Potster saw the deposit book."

"The ranch hand cook is in on this now?"

"Ask him about it if you don't believe me."

"I concede Potster saw some book, but neither you nor he knows what it was."

Sighing, Walker rose and left the room. He had lost a barn. At least that was something he knew how to handle.

Chapter Forty-Three

Sarah opened her eyes early the next morning, awakening slowly. Her hand automatically reached for Walker's body beside her. Filled with the usual sense of disappointment, she got out of bed and padded across the floor. She couldn't go on this way. Her stomach hurt, her eyes were swollen from the smoke, and the whole situation was impossible. She wanted to go home, home to Wadsy and Papa and Abraham.

By sunup she had dressed, drunk a cup of hot tea, and packed her valise. As she walked to the barn, dawn was barely breaking. Her eyes took in the site and stench of the burnt structure, the barn animals grazing in the corral. What a dreadful shame that someone like Caleb could do so much destruction without retribution. *God, please open Walker's eyes before Caleb harms him.*

Hitching the buggy wasn't easy, but she'd seen S.H. do it numerous times. She found extra tack in a small shed near the house, and the carriage rattled out of the courtyard before anyone in the main house stirred.

The deposit book was the key to the mystery, but it was gone. Maybe Walker was right. Maybe she should have stayed and written her novel and forgotten all about her suspicions. She loved the babies she was carrying. How would she ever relinquish them to a man who did not trust their mother?

The train station was deserted when she pulled up. Unloading her valise, she rested it on the platform and purchased a ticket. "What time does the train arrive?"

The clerk consulted his pocket watch. "You got about half an hour."

She walked back to the buggy, wondering what to do with it. She supposed she could tie the mare to the bank post. Caleb would notice it and see that it was returned to Walker.

Her gaze moved to the bank. Or she could tell Caleb that he'd won, that she was leaving. Wouldn't he be pleased?

The McKay buggy was waiting in front of the bank when Caleb arrived a few minutes later. The whistling banker turned the corner, his jaw dropping when he saw Sarah sitting on the seat. Color drained from his face. "You're not…?"

Sarah smiled. "Dead? Nope, sound as a dollar. Sorry."

A shutter closed over his features. "Hallucinating again, Sarah? Perhaps the doctor can give you something to ease your discomfort." A sly grin crept across his face. "Why don't you cross the street? Doc will be in his office at any time."

"You'd like that, wouldn't you?" Climbing out of the buggy with some difficulty, she followed him into the bank.

"The bank doesn't open until nine."

"My train leaves in twenty minutes. I can't wait for business hours."

A smug look registered on his face. "You're leaving?"

"I am." She followed him to his office and watched as he stripped out of his coat and loosened his tie.

Seating himself behind the desk, he glared at her. "Dare I hope you'll be gone for a long while?"

"Ooooh. The real Caleb surfaces." She perched on the edge of his desk. "Yes, I'm leaving, and I don't plan to return except for occasional visits to my child."

"Does Walker know you're leaving?"

"He wouldn't care if he did."

"How sad." The banker looked anything but remorseful. "What do you want, Sarah?"

"What do you think I want?" He knew that she knew; the guilt in his eyes was proof enough. Should she tell him how she knew or just let him wonder?

Perspiration beaded his upper lip, although the stove had not been started. "I'm a busy man." He checked his watch. "Didn't you say you had a train to catch?"

"You win, Caleb."

Leaning back in his chair, he smiled. "Of course. Did you ever doubt it?"

"Last night when you locked me in the barn. I thought I was going to die."

His smile never wavered.

"And I would have, if Walker hadn't heard Diamond's cries and come to investigate."

Caleb shrugged. "Walker's always been lucky. What is it that you want, Sarah? Surely you know by now that your efforts to convince Walker that I'm stealing from him aren't going to work. He doesn't believe you."

"No, he doesn't. You're right. He accepts your word over mine. It's hard to find friends like that. Loyal."

"Yes, it is." Caleb turned to the stack of papers on his desk.

"But when I show him the deposit book, I imagine he'll change his mind."

Caleb glanced up.

"You know, the one you keep in the secret compartment of your buggy?" When he paled, she smiled. "Oooh," she mocked. "That ol' book."

The banker's eyes hardened. "What do you want, Jezebel?"

"Ahhh, Jezebel." She pretended to ponder the request. "Correct me if I'm wrong. Just last night, wasn't I 'dearest girl' and 'my sweet'?"

Shoving away from the desk, Caleb got to his feet. His hand hovered near the middle desk drawer and for a fleeting moment she wondered if he had a gun. It was a little late to think of that, but she supposed it was possible. A banker would be prepared to defend his establishment.

Keeping an eye on his right hand, she said softly, "Last night, when you and Walker went to the shed, I searched your buggy and found the briefcase."

"So? My briefcase is always locked." He patted his vest pocket. "The key never leaves my person."

"True, but I have my ways of unlocking things without a key."

Eyes narrowing, he took a threatening step forward. She backed a step away. "I have the book, Caleb. You're stealing from Walker."

The book was burned cinders, but he would never know. She would simply let the knowledge of his sins eat away at him day by day, until he was driven mad with wondering when and if she would convince Walker of his crime. She, on the other hand, would be eating Wadsy's cherry pies and growing fat and lazy with Walker's children. She might not have the home she wanted, the babies she carried within her, or the man she loved, but she would have the satisfaction of knowing that Caleb would never have a moment's peace.

He lunged at her and she jumped back, fear rippling through her. He was stronger than she was; he could quickly overpower her and shoot her, if he dared, and then take her somewhere outside of town and bury her body. No one would ever know what had happened to her. "Tell me what you want," he gritted between clenched teeth.

"I want you to tell Walker the truth. That you're embezzling money from him—that you have been for years." If nothing else came of this madness, Walker would know that she hadn't lied to him. That she was in her right mind.

Turning back to the desk, he said, "I'll do nothing of the sort."

"Then you admit you have been stealing from him?"

"I admit nothing." Pulling the drawer open, he removed a small hand pistol.

Sarah swallowed. Should she run? Scream? It was early; no one was moving about yet. *You're foolish, Sarah. You shouldn't have come here alone to prove a point. You should have gotten on the train and gone home.*

Leveling the gun at her, Caleb motioned her out the doorway.

"Don't be a fool," she warned. "Don't add murder to theft."

Shoving her out of the room and into the bank foyer, he glanced out the front window, apparently gauging his next move. "Open the door."

Shielding her stomach, Sarah edged backward. "If anything happens to me, Walker will know that you're responsible. He might not care about me, but he does care about his child—"

"Shut up. You talk too much." He backed her through the door, pausing to look up and down the deserted street. Nothing stirred.

She had one choice, and that was to make a break for it before he could stop her. She was fast, able to outrun all the other girls in her boarding school. She had an array of blue ribbons from sporting events in her room in Boston. But now she was thirty pounds heavier and pregnant.

Still, she turned suddenly to run, but Caleb was faster. Pinning her squirming body against the wall, he pressed close, his breath hot on her cheek. "Don't mess with me, Sarah!" Jerking her arm behind her back, he hissed, "I'd just as soon shoot you right here, woman."

"You wouldn't dare." She moaned as he twisted her arm tighter.

"What do I have to lose?"

"You're still able to convince Walker that you're innocent. If you shoot me, there'll be witnesses. You won't be able to talk your way out of this one."

"Witnesses?" He pretended to assess the danger and then grinned. "Seems that the town is deserted this morning. Pity." Thrusting her away from the wall, he herded her out toward the waiting buggy. She struggled to break his hold, but he was stronger than she would have guessed.

"Why, Caleb? Why would you do this to Walker?" She panted, out of breath. "He's your best friend. He won't hear of your deceiving him. He's willing to risk his future happiness because of you."

"You're breaking my heart. If I had a violin, I'd play it."

"At least tell me why. What can that hurt? You're obviously a big, mean brute who's going to do me harm."

"It seems certain bank funds are missing, funds I am held accountable for. I intend to pay Walker back, so don't fret your pretty little head about that."

"When?" She grunted when he shoved her up into the buggy, tipping her cumbersome body onto the seat.

His face closed. "I've incurred a few gambling debts lately. But that will change—and soon. When it does, I'll return the money and Walker will never be the wiser."

"He's not stupid." She twisted to release his hold. "If anything happens to me, he'll have his books audited."

"My dear, when word of your demise reaches him, nothing will matter for a time. By then the money will be replaced with no one the wiser."

"Walker doesn't love me! He isn't going to mourn my death!"

"You little fool. You think you're so smart, but you know nothing. He loves you. It's as plain as day in his eyes." Caleb sprang aboard the buggy and reached for the reins.

"You're wrong. He only wants the baby," she said, fighting against the temptation to believe him. "You kill me and you're breaking a commandment, Caleb. Think of your eternity."

"I'll make my peace with God later." Caleb slid her a sideways glance. "You'd best make your peace now, Sarah. In another few minutes, you'll meet your Maker."

Chapter Forty-Four

Walker squinted against the bright sunlight, groaning when he realized the hour. The fire had kept him up most of the night. He had fallen into bed a little before sunup.

He lay there for a moment thinking about his dream. In it he was holding his son, standing beside Sarah and looking out over Spring Grass. It was summer and the grasses were blowing, the sun hot on his face. He held Sarah's hand, and she was cradling a child, laughing up at him, only the baby she held was a girl.

His hand absently felt Sarah's side of the bed. He thought about the opportunities that he'd had lately to end the dispute—when he felt the baby kicking against his hand…staring at Sarah's smoky cheeks, so thankful she was alive as he wiped the soot from her tearstained face. He imagined the feel of her dancing in his arms, could picture her quick and easy smiles, and remembered the smell of burned corn bread and their laughter over the drunken chickens. He smiled at her bulldog tenacity and how much she wanted to make the marriage work.

He thought about the two near-fatal accidents coming one on top of the other. He could have lost her. Would his anger have been worth it? She'd done wrong, but he'd also done wrong by not forgiving her. She wasn't anything like Trudy. Sarah had a heart of gold, and if he continued to hold her at bay, he would be a fool.

The hall clock struck eight when he came downstairs—midmorning for him. Flo was busy in the washhouse, her face flushed with exertion.

"Where's Sarah?"

The housekeeper doused a shirt in the rinse water. "Still asleep, I imagine. Yer gettin' a late start, ain't you?"

"Yes. I'm going to fix a tray and have breakfast with her."

"Suit yourself. Want me to fry bacon?"

"No, I'll find something."

A little while later, he rapped at their bedroom door, balancing a tray in one hand. When Sarah didn't call out, he rapped again. Still no answer.

Pushing the door open with his boot, he was surprised to see that the bed was made. His eyes scanned the empty room. Maybe she was with Potster—but he'd seen the ranch hand cleaning the bunkhouse windows earlier, alone. He stepped into the dressing room. It was in disarray, but she wasn't there.

Walker carried the tray back down to the kitchen, glancing up when Flo came in.

"She wasn't hungry, huh? That's not like her. Are you two quarreling again?"

Walker shook his head. "She wasn't there. You haven't seen her this morning?"

"No. I assumed she was plumb worn out from all the doin's last night. Are you sure she isn't in her room?"

"She's not there."

They searched the house, to no avail. Walker caught a glimpse of S.H. from around the corner of the house as he was heading for the charred remains of the barn. He opened the back screen door and called, "S.H., have you seen Sarah around anywhere?"

"No. Been inspecting the damage."

"What did we lose?"

"Everything that was in the barn is gone—the hay, the tack, and the buggy. At least the horses made it out safely. Barn's gonna hafta be rebuilt."

Walker frowned. How could they have lost the buggy? It wasn't in the barn last night. He'd taken it out to mend the top and hadn't put it back.

"Are you sure about the buggy, S.H.? It shouldn't have been in the barn."

S.H. shrugged. "Well, it's not here."

"What do you mean it's not here?"

"If you didn't put it in the barn, I don't know where it is."

Flo came out on the porch, wiping her hands on her apron.

Walker glanced at her, and then turned back to S.H. "Check the shed and see if the extra tack is missing."

"Why?" the foreman asked.

"Maybe Sarah decided to use the buggy this morning." That seemed unlikely; she had never ventured anywhere on her own. Unless she had decided to run away. Walker's stomach churned at the thought.

Flo frowned. "Where would she have gone?"

"Check on that tack, S.H."

S.H. returned in a few moments, shaking his head. "You're right. The tack is gone. She must have took the buggy."

Walker closed his eyes and shook his head. Then he said, "I need a saddle, S.H."

"I'll scare one up—where are ya goin'?"

"To town. I'm afraid she might have decided to go back to Boston."

"Land sakes!" Flo exclaimed. "Why would she do that?"

"Because I'm a blind fool, Flo, and I just realized it."

S.H. disappeared and returned with a saddle, a blanket, and tack. Walker saddled Diamond and swung aboard, allowing the animal free rein. Dread washed over him as he rode out. The fall wind cut through his light jacket when he tethered the horse at the train station. Eldon Snides looked up, grinning when he saw him.

"Walker. What can I do for you today?"

"Did my wife board a train this morning?"

"Mrs. McKay?" Eldon scratched his head. "I just came on duty." He peered over the passenger list. "Ah, here it is: Sarah McKay."

"Was the ticket to Boston?"

"Yes, sir—'pears it was. Train left a couple hours ago."

Walker turned away from the window. "Why would she leave without telling me? She wouldn't walk away from the chance to have a place in her child's life."

"Pardon?"

"Nothing. Thanks, Eldon."

When Walker reached the Logans' store, he realized he was walking the horse instead of riding her. He secured the animal to the hitching post and then sat down on the bench outside the mercantile to gather his thoughts. Should he go after her?

Lowell Livingston would fight tooth and nail before he let Sarah return after all that Walker had put her through. He heard the door open and hoped Denzil would leave him alone with his pain. "Mornin', Walker."

"Morning, Denzil." He started to get up, but Denzil motioned him back down.

"Sit a spell." The storekeeper sat down beside him, taking out cigarette papers.

"I'm not good company right now, Denzil."

Denzil eyed him knowingly. "Female problems, huh?"

"What makes you think that?"

"Well…" Denzil rolled a cigarette, licked the paper, and sealed it shut. "You know I'm not one to pry." He struck a match, letting it burn. "It's just a downright shame that it had ta happen to ya twice."

Bad news spread quicker than poison ivy. Before long, the whole town would know about Sarah's sudden departure. Folks laughing behind his back, snickering. *That McKay can't keep a woman,* they'd say. *Wonder what's wrong with him?* Worse yet, he'd lost the only woman he'd ever loved.

"If a man cain't trust his best friend, what's the world comin' to?"

Walker frowned. "My best friend? What's Caleb got to do with this?"

Denzil shifted on the bench, fanning the match out as it seared his fingers. "Now, you know I don't want to get into your matters, but when I saw your buggy with Caleb and your missus leaving town this morning, I couldn't help but take notice." He leaned closer, whispering. "Martha and I had a little squabble ourselves and—"

"Caleb?" Walker interrupted. "Caleb was taking Sarah to the train station?"

Denzil pulled the cigarette from his mouth and studied the cold tip. "Train station? No, they left town in your buggy."

"Are you sure it was Sarah?"

Another match flared. "Yeah, it was your buggy, all right, and Caleb was in it with your wife."

Caleb and Sarah? Impossible.

"You can never tell about women. One minute a man's minding his own business, the next he's sleeping on the floor of his store."

Walker rose from the bench and began striding toward the bank.

"Good luck," Denzil yelled, flinging the flaming match to the ground. "Don't let a filly get ya down!"

Walker walked into Caleb's office without knocking. The banker glanced up, surprise registering on his face.

"Denzil said he saw you with Sarah early this morning. What's going on, Caleb?"

Caleb swallowed, his eyes darting past the open door. "Your wife asked me to drive her to the train station—"

Walker faced him coldly. "I know my wife better than that. You're the last person on earth she'd ask, and the station is across the street."

"She had a change of heart. She stopped by early to ask my forgiveness, and, of course, I gave it. Then she asked me to walk her to the train station."

The answer didn't surprise him. Why shouldn't she leave? He'd all but shoved her out of the house.

"Calm down, Walker." Caleb's features softened. "I know Sarah's departure comes as a shock, but it is the best for all. She's a wise woman."

Turning around, Walker strode out of the office. He walked out of the bank, determined to act as if the world went on. But deep down he knew Sarah was different. He'd known it from the day he married her. *Let her go,* a voice in his mind demanded. *She's been nothing but trouble since she got here.* Yet he rebelled at the thought. He didn't want to let her go. Mounting Diamond, he picked up the reins.

Then it hit him.

If Sarah had taken the train, where was his buggy?

Swinging off the horse, he strode back into the bank. When he reached Caleb's office, he asked, "Where's my buggy?"

"Buggy? Er…well, I…I suppose it's…maybe you should ask Tom Howell—"

"The blacksmith? Why would he have my rig?"

"He could have…I wasn't sure what Sarah wanted to do with—" The banker fidgeted with a stack of folders. "Sometimes, Walker, things happen…things we don't want—"

Walker's brow furrowed as suspicion crept up his spine. He'd never seen Caleb so defensive or so confused.

A large hand slammed over Caleb's, pinning the banker in place. "Where's my wife, Caleb?" It wasn't a question; it was a demand.

"I…" Caleb glanced away. "I resent the accusation in your tone. I don't know where your wife is. The last I seen her, she was boarding the train."

"What happened to my buggy? You were driving it, weren't you?"

"Yes. I left it over at the livery and asked that someone see that you got it. Perhaps I didn't secure the reins tightly—the horse must have wandered away."

"The horse wandered away?" Leaning over the desk, Walker grasped him by the collar. For the first time in his life, he wanted to hurt Caleb— badly. Fear constricted his throat. "Denzil saw you with Sarah, in my buggy, heading out of town early this morning. Now, what have you done with my wife?"

Caleb features crumbled. "Now, calm down, Walker. She's not hurt. She's…" his voice broke. "I didn't know what to do with her, so I locked her in a bedroom at my house." Breaking into tears, the accountant clutched Walker's shirtsleeve. "I've tried to stop her every way I knew how, but she persisted. I've agonized over what to do with her from the moment I took her this morning—I snapped. I planned to do away with her, but you're my best friend. I couldn't do it. If she'd only left things alone! She snuck into my buggy last night and found the deposit book. I planned to pay you back, Walker, every cent. I've borrowed money from you before—when have I ever failed to pay you back?"

Walker took off his hat, running his hand through his hair. "Why go behind my back, Caleb? You know I would give you anything you asked."

"I'm in deep, Walker. Deeper than I've ever been in my life. I haven't known where to turn—but my luck's changing! I'm playing in a high-stakes game Saturday night. You'll see, I'll win it all back and more. Then I was going to return Sarah and the money, and we could go on from there—"

Coming to tower over the miserable man, Walker grabbed his collar. "If you've hurt her..."

"I haven't," Caleb said, weeping. "I wouldn't do that, Walker. I know you love her."

The realization hit Walker like a ton of bricks. He didn't just need Sarah to produce an heir; he *loved* her. And he had done everything within his power to drive her away. The baby was important, but without Sarah they would be only half a family. His existence would be empty without her.

"Walker—"

"I'll deal with you later. Right now I'm going after my wife."

Squinting, Sarah leaned down, closing one eye as she jiggled a hairpin in the keyhole. Potster had made it look so easy, but she'd worked for an hour and hadn't cracked the rigid lock. If she didn't get out of here soon, she was going to burst. Hours had gone by without the use of a necessary, and she was desperate.

Rattling the handle, she gritted her teeth with frustration.

How long would Caleb leave her in here? And then what? Would he actually do away with her? Questions flashed through her mind. Would Walker figure out what had happened to her? Would he be so angry because she'd left without telling him that he'd think it was good riddance? Giving the handle one last vicious shake, she slid down the length of the door, sobbing.

When she heard a horse pounding along the rutted drive a few minutes later she felt faint. Caleb was coming back!

Getting to her feet, she yanked so hard that the door actually flew open, surprising her and causing her to land backward on the wool rug with a jolt. Grabbing her belly, she lay there for a moment, assuring herself that she wasn't hurt. Then, crawling on her hands and knees, she closed the door, her eyes searching for a weapon. The bedpost. It was long, angular, and loosely attached to the bedstead. When she heard the banker's footsteps coming down the hallway, she was waiting by the door, club extended over her head.

The door flew open, and Sarah swung the makeshift weapon with all her might. Her abductor caught sight of her from the corner of his eye and quickly sidestepped the blow. She shot out of the room, bouncing off the opposite wall and knocking vases and knickknacks off a polished table.

Hands shot out to support her. Strong, familiar hands. Wonderfully familiar hands. Turning, she met a man's blue, blue gaze.

"Walker! How did you know—?"

He latched onto her tightly, holding her close. After a moment, his mouth captured hers in a hungry, urgent kiss that sent her head reeling. It was many moments before she could break the embrace long enough to gasp, "How did you know where to find me?"

"Caleb told me."

"Caleb? But he—" A second, more urgent kiss prevented her from asking the myriad questions swirling in her mind.

"Sarah," Walker murmured, holding her close as he stroked her hair. "I should have listened—"

She stopped him, her fingertips tracing his mouth. Oh, how she loved him, more than she thought she could ever love anyone. But she didn't want him if her word would always be in doubt.

Straightening, she set the club aside.

"Sarah—"

"I'm going home, Walker. To Boston." He'd reacted and kissed her out of fear. He wasn't thinking straight.

"I know you're angry, but you can't leave me now."

"I'm not angry. For the first time in my life, I'm finally thinking straight. I can't make you love me, though I have tried. Until the day you do, I won't beg for your crumbs any longer."

His eyes softened. "What would I have to say in order to make you stay?"

"If you don't know, you're in worse shape than I thought." She brushed past him before she started crying. Not so long ago she would have accepted any terms he offered, but the stakes had changed. Now she wanted more.

He trailed her down the hallway. "What if I told you that you're going to break Flo's and S.H.'s hearts if you leave? They're real attached to you."

"Wouldn't work."

"What if I told you Potster thinks of you as the daughter he never had? You're not going to leave the old man without saying goodbye, are you?"

"Potster's my friend. He knows the situation." She hurried down the stairway.

"What about Caleb?"

"What about him?"

"If there's a trial, you'll need to testify."

"Are you pressing charges?" She stepped off the porch and headed straight for the necessary. Walker's long-legged strides kept up with her.

"Well?" she asked.

"Well, what?"

"Are you pressing charges against Caleb?" She'd bet her last dollar he wouldn't. Walker would be angry with him, but he would never send Caleb to jail.

"Sarah—"

"That's what I thought. You weren't willing to forgive me, but you will forgive Caleb." She disappeared into the privy and slammed the door.

Leaning against the outhouse, he said softly, "What if I say I forgive you? We can start over, Sarah. We've both made mistakes—"

"No."

She emerged shortly afterward and walked toward the buggy, which was in the yard where Caleb had left it.

"This isn't all my fault," he accused. "You could have told the truth and this wouldn't have happened."

"Could have, should have, might have, needed to. What difference does it make? I didn't, so here we are." She swatted his hand as he tried to help her into the buggy. She lurched aboard and picked up the reins, meeting his eyes for the first time. "None of these reasons you have stated are good enough to make me stay."

"Sarah, I'm begging you—"

Snapping the reins, she drove off, leaving him standing in a swirl of dust.

Chapter Forty-Five

Sarah Elaine Livingston McKay cried all the way back to Boston. Thirty pounds heavier and a whole lot smarter, she knew the remaining months of her pregnancy would be a picnic compared with what she faced once the babies came. She chided herself for her inability to accept Walker's roundabout apology. Wasn't that what she'd wanted? Yet he hadn't stated one good reason to make her stay. Oh, how she wished he had. She wouldn't be crying her eyes out over a man who didn't give a whit about her.

Stepping down from the train, she shaded her eyes, wondering how she would get home. She'd thought about wiring ahead but decided against it. How could she possibly explain in a few short sentences why she was returning? Her eyes traveled the terminal, pausing on Walker and then moving on. They switched back.

"Walker?" she murmured. Her heart sprang to her throat.

Pushing away from the post, the tall, good-looking rancher walked toward her. Stopping a few feet from her, he continued the argument as if they were still at Caleb's. "Flo needs you in the kitchen."

She raised her chin. "She does not. She hates me being underfoot."

"Doc says it's not safe to travel. You could hurt the babies."

She put her hands on her hips—or where her hips used to be. "You haven't talked to the doctor."

"Have so. We had a long talk while you were waiting to board the train."

"How did you get here before me?"

"I was on the same train—rear coach."

"That's not possible. You weren't on it when I left town."

"That's true, but I can ride cross-country and Diamond's one fast runner. We caught the train two towns later."

She shook her head.

"What if I said I'd rethought this, and I now concede that a child needs both parents?"

"A fool would know that." She picked up her valise and hailed a driver-for-hire. Walker trailed her out to the wagon and helped her onto the front seat. He stored the valise and then climbed into the rear of the conveyance.

She pivoted in her seat to glare at him. He said, "There isn't a train back until tomorrow."

After that the couple rode in silence. Sarah searched her mind for an explanation of her sudden appearance. What would she tell Papa? That he'd been right all along? That she should have accompanied him back to Boston months ago?

When the wagon rolled into the courtyard, Abraham came to greet the newcomers, a smile breaking out when he recognized Sarah. "Sarah girl!"

"Hi, Abe." Sarah smiled as the old servant lifted her out of the wagon and set her on the ground.

Holding her away from him, he examined her. "My, oh, my. Baby girl is surely fillin' out."

Patting her burgeoning load, she sighed. "Aren't I, though?"

Walker jumped down from the wagon and paid the driver. Then he turned to Sarah and the servant. "Abe, I'm Walker McKay."

Grinning, the white-haired servant gazed up and down at the rancher. "So this is Mr. McKay. Well, now."

Sarah reached for her valise and started off toward the house. Walker caught up, taking the bag out of her hand despite her protests. "I am capable of carrying my own luggage."

"No wife of mine is carrying her luggage."

"I am *not* your wife. Not anymore."

Wadsy's rotund bulk appeared in the doorway. "Oh, praise the Lord! Is that you, baby girl?"

"It's me, Wadsy!" Sarah gave the nanny a big hug before hurrying into the house.

Walker tipped his hat. "Walker McKay, Wadsy. Nice to meet you."

Wadsy turned to watch his swift passage after Sarah. "Pleasure to meet ya, sir."

"Papa? I'm home!" Sarah announced as she breezed past the study.

"Sarah Elaine? Is that you? What are you doing home?" He appeared in the study door as she climbed the stairs.

"I live here, don't I?" She walked down the hallway to her bedroom, with Walker in close pursuit.

"Is that Mr. McKay with you?"

"It is, sir," Walker said. "We'll be down in a minute. I'm trying to talk sense into your daughter."

"Well, good luck!" Lowell said, retreating back into the study.

Sarah reached her bedroom and turned the doorknob. Walker's hand blocked her. His breath was warm on her neck. "What if I said that I need you more than I've ever needed anything in my life? That life won't be worth living if you're not the first thing I see in the morning and the last thing I see every night? That I didn't know what love was until you stepped into my life, and that I thank God that he knew better than I what I needed or wanted. You are my life, Sarah. And I love you more than words can say. If you walk out on me now, you'll leave a hole in my heart I will never be able to fill."

She shook her head.

"I'll take you to Ireland."

She turned to him, suddenly feeling helpless. He'd never once ever said that he needed her. Her eyes gave away her indecision, and he took full advantage.

"I don't just need you, I love you. I've been a fool." He tilted her chin, kissing her lightly on the mouth. "I want what we first had, Sarah. I want it worse than I've ever wanted anything in my life. And so much more. Please say you'll forgive me so we can get married again and start over. I've got sick cows, a bull down, a heifer in heat, fence to mend, a barn to rebuild, and planting before spring, sweetheart. I can't be traipsing all over the country courting you."

"This is your idea of courting me?"

"It's my way of telling my woman that I love her." His mouth closed over hers a second time as his arms went around her.

Closing her eyes, she tasted him, so warm, so Walker. Other than the kisses at finding her unharmed at Caleb's, it had been ages since his lips had sought hers. Even longer since she'd felt this sense of hope. Their mouths brushed and lingered.

It was long minutes before she could bring herself to ask, "If I marry you again—*if*," she emphasized. "Will the reverend officiate at a barbecue?"

He grinned. "This time we're doing it right." His lips left hers to toy with the nape of her neck. "Your papa will be there to give you away, and Flo and Wadsy will both help you dress." Their lips drifted back together. "I love you. Please say you'll repeat our vows, Sarah McKay, and let's put the past behind us."

He'd finally found the right words.

"Of course I'll marry you, Walker McKay. What took you so long to ask?"

On the landing below, Wadsy, Lowell, and Abraham breathed a sigh of relief.

Abe smiled. "Looks like you finally got yourself a son-in-law, sir."

Lowell nodded, grinning from ear to ear. "It does, Abe. A fine son-in-law. Maybe now we can all rest."

Epilogue

On was a glorious Wyoming morning, Sarah silently thanked God for her bountiful blessings—far too many to list. Beside her, Walker handled the buggy reins as he drove home from church services. Reverend Baird's sermon this morning had been on forgiveness.

Now, that was a subject she and Walker knew a lot about.

Not much had changed in the past two years, yet everything had. Abe had gone to be with the Lord and Papa and Wadsy had moved to Wyoming to help care for the children and be cared for themselves. Sarah turned to watch them in the backseat, trying to keep the twins out of trouble. S.H. and Flo still ran the ranch.

"Lawsy me, I never heard such chatterin' in all my born days," the old nanny chided.

"Just like their mama," Papa added, drawing one of the two identical redhaired girls to his chest for a big Grandpa hug.

"Land sakes, you're sweet as honey," Wadsy said to the child on her lap, "though I would appreciate a decent night's sleep. Do these young'uns ever intend to sleep a full night through?"

Sarah grinned at Walker. "We were hoping you could tell us, Wadsy."

"Maybe I could watch them for a few nights," Papa suggested. "Take them off your hands for you."

"Mr. Livingston, these girls would run you to bits. You gotta remember your health!"

"Wadsy, don't start with me—"

Sarah grinned at Walker. Leaning closer, she whispered, "I haven't had the nerve to tell them we're expecting again."

Winking, he grinned at her. "I don't think they'll mind."

"What you two a-whisperin' 'bout up there?" Wadsy asked as Millie scrambled from her lap to the floor of the buggy. Molly extended her arms to the nanny, so Wadsy and Papa traded children.

"Nothing much," Sarah said over her shoulder. She turned to her husband and squeezed his arm. "Have I told you how much I love you today?"

"I don't mind hearing it again."

"I do—with all my heart."

His affectionate squeeze back told her all she needed to know. He was reserved around Wadsy and Papa, but he made up for it when they were alone.

Sarah Elaine Livingston McKay's dreams had all come true. She'd married the man of her dreams. The second wedding had been before God, in church, with baskets of flowers and family and friends in attendance. No barbecue permitted.

Today, she was the mother of two perfect little redheaded girls who, as their father had feared, had indeed inherited their mother's stubborn tendencies. S.H. and Flo were happy there were heirs to the Walker fortune, so there was little to fuss about at Spring Grass these days.

Only Caleb concerned her now. She had long ago forgiven him, but Walker was still working on it. He had pressed charges against the banker, who was now serving a prison sentence for embezzlement and attempted murder. Sarah hoped he had learned his lesson and would be released early for good behavior. Everyone needed forgiveness.

All in all, Sarah was happier than she'd ever dreamed possible. If anyone were to ask, she'd still say it was best to seek God's will for your life, though the road might not always be easy.

That Sarah McKay knew from personal experience.

Discussion Questions

1. Which character in the book appealed to you the most? Why?

2. How successfully does the author portray spiritual themes in this story? Did you find it thought-provoking, or was it just an entertaining read for you?

3. When Sarah ran away from home, did you sympathize with her, or did you feel she should have tried to work things out with her father?

4. On the train, what did you think of Lucy's plight? What was your reaction to the girls' decision to let Sarah pose as Walker's mail-order bride?

5. While not common in our modern American society, arranged marriages are still prevalent in some cultures. What do you think about such a custom? Was Walker wrong to have decided to go that route after Trudy's betrayal?

6. After learning the truth, Walker felt that Sarah had betrayed him as badly as Trudy had. Do you agree or disagree?

7. After the initial shock of finding out that Sarah lied to him, do you think Walker should have forgiven her sooner, or was his anger and mistrust justified? How do you think you would have responded?

8. Walker is fortunate to have friends in his life (Flo and S.H., especially) who love him enough to speak the truth to him and still support him in his pain. Are there people like that in your life? If not, is that something you would ask God for? Why or why not?

9. Sarah realizes after the fire in the barn that Walker may never forgive her for her poor decision. Do you think God can make all things work to good for those who repent and try to follow Him?

10. Caleb ends up in prison for his wrong decisions. Do you agree with Sarah that everyone deserves forgiveness, or are there some things between friends that cannot or should not be overlooked? Do you think your thoughts about this question influence how you give and receive forgiveness?

About the Author

Lori Copeland is the author of more than 90 titles, both historical and contemporary fiction. With more than 3 million copies of her books in print, she has developed a loyal following among her rapidly growing fans in the inspirational market. She has been honored with the Romantic Times Reviewer's Choice Award, The Holt Medallion, and Walden Books' Best Seller Award. In 2000, Lori was inducted into the Missouri Writers Hall of Fame.

Lori lives in the beautiful Ozarks with her husband, Lance, their three children, and five grandchildren.

Outlaw's Bride

LORI COPELAND

What are you going to do, McAllister? Put your life on hold forever and let a woman like Ragan slip through your fingers so you can pursue scum like Bledso?

Johnny knew Bledso wasn't worth a hair on Ragan's head. Why couldn't he let it go and just get on with his life?

❖

Convicted of a bank robbery he didn't commit, drifter Johnny McAllister is sentenced to do time in a rehabilitation program in the home of Judge Proctor McMann, a gentle, wise soul who believes in second chances.

Johnny's aim is to be a model prisoner. He hopes to be released early to return to his life's mission: to find and kill Dirk Bledso, the man who wiped out his family 16 years before. Johnny has planned for everything... except his encounter with Ragan Ramsey, the judge's beautiful and kind housekeeper, and his involvement with the generous folks of Barren Flats.

Can this would-be outlaw let go of his hate and anger and embrace something better—something he can't yet see?

❖

A tender romance that shows how even the hard law of the West doesn't stand a chance when God's mercy, warm friendship, and true love come to reside in a lonely man's heart.

A Kiss for Cade

LORI COPELAND

The corner of Cade's eye caught a glimpse of a redheaded woman entering the drugstore. His quickening heartbeat caught him off guard. For a moment he thought it was Zoe. It wasn't. He settled back in the saddle, grinning. Zoe Bradshaw. Now there was a woman not easily forgotten.

Famous bounty hunter Cade Kolby is forced off the trail to decide the fate of his late sister's orphaned children. He's not only returning to his hometown and nieces and nephews but also to a fiery redhead he loved and left 15 years ago.

The *last* person Zoe Bradshaw wants to see is Cade, but she does want to raise her best friend's children as her own. So she tries to be polite, if cool, even as the attraction between them flares up again. Only this time, Zoe is determined not to let Cade get close to her heart.

But the townsfolk have other ideas. They want to see the little orphans with a mother *and* a father, and they form a plan that includes the possibility of a kiss…

A tender romance that shows how even the hard law of the West doesn't stand a chance when God's mercy, warm friendship, and true love come to reside in a lonely man's heart.

Other Good Harvest House Fiction
by Lori Wick

YELLOW ROSE TRILOGY

Every Little Thing About You

Former Texas Ranger Slater Rawlings is startled when he is arrested by Shotgun's acting deputy, Miss Liberty Drake. Sparks fly as the cowboy's and Liberty's lives and faith intertwine. Love's path is delightfully unpredictable in this heartwarming romance.

A Texas Sky

As Texas Ranger Dakota Rawlings escorts his boss' niece, Darvi Wingate, to another town, he soon finds out that Darvi seems to attract trouble. But they also discover that they're both believers...and falling for each other. When Darvi is kidnapped, she can't imagine how God will rescue her—until Dakota appears!

City Girl

Nothing has prepared city girl Reagan Sullivan for the land of armadillos and tall Texans. When rancher Cash Rawlings comes into her life, Reagan is intrigued—but love and commitment are adventures this city girl has vowed never to embark on. Can Reagan come to terms with her fragile past?

THE CALIFORNIANS

Whatever Tomorrow Brings

In the midst of grief and unfamiliar surroundings, Kaitlin, the Donovans' oldest daughter, faces life in rugged California. Will she recognize God's unexpected gift of love and accept His strength to face whatever tomorrow brings?

As Time Goes By

When Bobbie Bradford returns to Santa Rosa to consider a marriage proposal, Jeff Taylor regrets not apologizing to her years ago when he humiliated her. Can forgiveness and love grow as time goes by?